The BERMUDEZ TRIANGLE

A NOVEL BY MAUREEN JOHNSON

razOr
bill

The Bermudez Triangle

RAZORBILL

Published by the Penguin Group
Penguin Young Readers Group
345 Hudson Street, New York, New York 10014, U.S.A.
Penguin Group (USA) Inc., 375 Hudson Street, New York, New York 10014, U.S.A.
Penguin Group (Canada), 90 Eglinton Avenue East, Suite 700, Toronto, Ontario, Canada M4P 2Y3 (a
division of Pearson Penguin Canada Inc.)
Penguin Books Ltd, 80 Strand, London WC2R 0RL, England
Penguin Ireland, 25 St Stephen's Green, Dublin 2, Ireland (a division of Penguin Books Ltd)
Penguin Group (Australia), 250 Camberwell Road, Camberwell, Victoria 3124, Australia (a division of
Pearson Australia Group Pty Ltd)
Penguin Books India Pvt Ltd, 11 Community Centre, Panchsheel Park, New Delhi – 110 017, India
Penguin Group (NZ), Cnr Airborne and Rosedale Roads, Albany, Auckland 1310, New Zealand
(a division of Pearson New Zealand Ltd)
Penguin Books (South Africa) (Pty) Ltd, 24 Sturdee Avenue, Rosebank, Johannesburg 2196, South Africa

Penguin Books Ltd, Registered Offices: 80 Strand, London WC2R 0RL, England

10 9 8 7 6 5 4 3 2 1

Copyright 2004 © Maureen Johnson
All rights reserved

 Produced by Alloy Entertainment
151 West 26th Street, New York, NY 10001

THE LIBRARY OF CONGRESS HAS CATALOGED THE HARDCOVER EDITION AS FOLLOWS:
Johnson, Maureen, 1973–
The Bermudez Triangle / by Maureen Johnson.
        p. cm.
Summary: The friendship of three high school girls and their relationships with their friends and families
are tested when two of them fall in love with each other.
ISBN 1-59514-019-0 (hardcover)
[1. Lesbians—Fiction. 2. Friendship—Fiction. 3. Coming out (Sexual orientation)—Fiction.
4. Family life—Fiction. 5. High schools—Fiction. 6. Schools—Fiction.] I. Title.
PZ7.J634145Be 2004
[Fic]—dc22
                                                    2004005093

Razorbill Splashproof paperback ISBN 978-1-59514-155-2

Manufactured in China

For the other sides of the hexagon:
Shannon Skalski, Peggy Banaszek, Alexis Fisher,
Laurie Sharp, and Dr. Kirsten Rambo

Acknowledgments

Many thanks are due to Leslie Morgenstein, Ben Schrank, Josh Bank, Claudia Gabel, and Liesa Abrams. Special thanks to Eloise Flood, whose faith and enthusiasm made it all happen.

For their insight: Elizabeth Freidin, Megan Honig, and the always-gracious Alexander Newman. For Kate Schafer, who has an uncanny ability to solve every crisis.

And to Jack Phillips, for putting up with me. Someday I'm going to get you that pet monkey I've been promising for so long now.

The BERMUDEZ TRIANGLE

1

The host stood at his podium under the pink-and-yellow neon arch and surveyed the three girls who had just come through the door. Avery Dekker stepped forward and gave him a huge smile.

"Bermudez," she said. "Two o'clock birthday party."

He looked Avery over, taking in her fishing hat and her For Good Luck, Rub My Belly T-shirt. His eyes passed to the two girls standing behind her. First they settled on the petite, pale redhead in a denim skirt and a pink tank top. Then they fell on the tall, cocoa-colored girl in a red summer dress and matching flip-flops. This girl looked around in bafflement.

They were not the five-year-olds the host had been anticipating.

"Just the three of you?" He looked expectant, as if he was hoping that Avery was about to produce a small child from the pocket of her oversized cargo shorts.

"Just us."

"And who's the . . . birthday girl?"

"Right here." Avery reached behind and grabbed the girl in the red dress by the hand. "This is Nina Bermudez. She knows the drill. She had every single one of her birthday parties here from the time she was eight until she was eleven. Didn't you, Neen?"

Nina was still looking around her, staring into the huge room that was just beyond the archway—at the video games, the indoor playground, the stage, and the costumed characters that mingled with the hordes of children.

"Okay . . ." He sighed while grabbing a boxful of small party bags. "Come this way."

He led them through a sea of small running bodies to a booth, cheerfully decorated in red and blue streamers that were covered in pictures of a smiling cartoon mouse. At each place setting there was a festive party hat and a decorative plastic cup. Avery jumped into one of the seats happily.

"Here are your tokens," the host said, hesitantly giving them each a small yellow mesh bag. "You also get your picture taken in the ball pool. And you get a birthday show. Do you want that before your pizza or after?"

"We don't need to have the show," Nina said. "It's not even my birthday. My birthday's in March, on Saint Patrick's Day."

This was totally unnecessary information, but when Nina got nervous, she tended to give too many details.

"It's kind of the rule," the host said apologetically. "You got the party package."

"Oh." A rush of pink crept into Nina's cheeks. "After, I guess."

"After." He wrote this down on his pad. "Okay. Your pizza will be out in about half an hour. This is your . . . playtime."

"I'm going to kill you," Nina whispered across the table as soon as he was gone.

The mechanical mouse behind Avery's head started playing a song. Avery did a little seat dance.

"*Death*, Ave. And they will never find your body."

"It was Mel's idea too. We wanted to give you a proper send-off to camp."

"It's precollege, not camp," Nina said with a grin.

"Whatever," Avery replied, with a flip of her hand.

Mel took the small conical hat from the table and planted it on Nina's head, stringing the elastic over Nina's Princess Leia buns, her signature hairstyle.

"Oh, yeah." Avery snickered, taking in the effect. "That is sexy. *Sex-hay!*" Avery looked around with an expression of undiluted pleasure on her face. She pointed to the play area, with its tangle of bright cubes and tubes and plastic webbing. "Everything is as good as I remember it. There's the net where Mel got her hair caught and started crying. And up there in the crawl tube, where those little yellow peepholes are, that's where Sarah Nickles *accidentally* kicked me in the nose with her heel and I started to bleed. Good times. Why did we stop coming here?"

"Because we started wearing bras and going to high school?" Nina offered, adjusting the thin elastic string that was digging into her chin.

"Sarah gave us the name when we were here," Mel said. "That was good."

"That's right," Nina said. "Because she was jealous that we were only playing with one another."

"Yeah, she was comparing us to some kind of evil vortex."

"It was still a good name," Mel protested.

The host returned with what he called a "bottomless" pitcher of soda. Avery tapped the base and glanced at the host suspiciously as she accepted it.

"That's going to be you in about three hours," Nina said as he hurried away. "Just keep that in mind when one of your customers gives you attitude."

"Attitude?" Avery said, widening her eyes. *"Moi?"*

Mel started filling all their cups with soda, trying hard to make sure everyone got the same amount of ice.

"You're going to call me every night, screaming." Nina grinned. "I know it."

"We're going to be waitresses at a high-class restaurant for adults," Avery said with dignity as she tried to affix her party hat to her fishing hat. "P. J. Mortimer's Fine Food and Drinks Emporium. Conveniently located in the same shopping center as Wal-Mart and Home Depot. The best Saratoga has to offer."

"We have to wear tweed caps," Mel said, passing Nina the first cup. "And green shirts with shamrocks on them."

"And suspenders," Avery added. "We can't forget the suspenders."

A girl about their age with two long blond braids and a Polaroid camera came over to the table. She had a stiff, straight smile that must have come from endless hours of being around swarms of screaming children—the kind of smile that looked like it might require muscle relaxants to uncurl.

"Ready for your picture?" she asked cheerfully.

Avery bounced out of her seat and hurried toward the giant pen of colored balls. Mel gave Nina a gentle nudge out of the booth. Avery was already sitting on a plastic tree stump, pulling off her red Chuck Taylors. Mel untied her white-and-pink Pumas. They both stepped over the short wall into the balls. Nina went to follow, but the girl with the camera stopped her.

"You have to take your shoes off," she said.

"They're just flip-flops," Nina replied.

The girl pointed to a sign that read: BE COOL, NO SHOES IN THE POOL!

"I have to go in there with bare feet?" Nina asked.

"That's the rule!" The girl smiled brightly at this, as if she were telling Nina that she'd just won a pony.

Nina kicked off the flip-flops and stepped gingerly into the pit, feeling the cool tarp under her toes. The balls came to a spot halfway up her thigh. Since she was wearing a dress, it was very difficult for her to move and keep her balance. She had to lean forward, holding her arms out in front of her, mummy style. Mel was having similar problems in her skirt (though she did have the advantage of small socklettes). Avery was having no problems at all. She had gone in deep, almost to the far side. A few children glanced at her with baffled expressions, wondering why their zone had been invaded by this *older person*.

Nina waded a bit farther in toward her, cringing with every step.

"I feel something wet," she whined.

"Probably just soda or something," Avery said with an evil grin.

"Since I'm in here, we're doing Triangle Power!" Nina shouted.

"I am not doing Triangle Power."

"We're in a *ball pool,* and now you're worried about looking stupid? Triangle off!"

Avery sloshed her way over. They arranged themselves in a triangle pattern and took hands.

"Okay," Nina said, looking at each of them. "We need the power to get through ten weeks apart. I need the strength of mind to get through this program and kick ass. Mel, what do you need?"

"Well," Mel said, biting her lip, "I'm going to miss you, so I need some help with that. And this job requires a lot of talking to people, so I can't be shy."

"Good." Nina nodded. "Avery?"

"Let's see," Avery said. "It probably would be good if I didn't kill any customers, so I need some help with my people skills."

"All right," Nina said, "so we call on the power of the Triangle. Everybody say it with me."

Even though they hadn't chanted it in years, no one needed reminding of the words:

Look at us, we are the three
Nina, Mel, and there's Avery

Shout it loud, then shout it louder
Shout it out, Triangle Power!

"Okay!" the girl said. "Everyone ready?"

"Do it!" Avery called.

"Smile and look at my hand!" She had put on a mouse puppet and was holding it next to the camera.

"Beautiful," Avery whispered.

The Polaroid coughed out a picture. The girl quickly inserted it into a glossy card with four punched-out corners. Nina carefully made her way back out of the pit.

"You love us," Avery said, jogging over and throwing her arm over Nina's shoulders.

"Remember, Ave." Nina was getting caught up in all the nostalgia. "The last time we were here, we were playing Spice Girls. That was our girl-power mantra."

Avery narrowed her eyes. She prided herself on her taste in music and hated to be reminded of things like that.

"I was a juvenile then," she said. "My record has been cleared, and the spirit of Jack Black has purified my soul."

"Be good or I'll tell everyone how you used to do that dance to 'Spice Up Your Life.' I'll bet the guys at the vinyl store would love to know that."

"At least you got to switch," Nina said. "I always had to play Scary. Make the girl with the curly hair play Scary."

"Ave switched too."

Avery was still very consciously not acknowledging this conversation.

"She was better as Posh," Nina said to Mel. "It was embarrassing to have a Sporty Spice who couldn't do a cartwheel. But she could do that little Posh walk."

"I don't remember any of this," Avery said. "You must be thinking of someone else."

"If you wanna be my lover, you gotta get with my friends . . ." Nina sang.

"It's going to be *so sad* when you leave."

"You miss me already," Nina said, throwing her arms around Avery's neck. "Don't you?"

Even the joking about Nina's leaving was too much for Mel. She got out of the ball pool.

"See what you did?" Avery said, though she didn't really look so happy herself. "Don't you know she's going to be crying on my shoulder for the next ten weeks? You're going to have to stay."

"It'll be nothing," Nina said, continuing her careful walk across the frightening tarp. She couldn't let herself get upset. "You won't even notice I'm gone."

Two hours later Nina was back in her room at home, gazing at the suitcases sitting open on her bedroom floor. She double-checked the color-coded Post-it notes that lined the edge of her desk, each one detailing a certain type of item: exercise clothes, casual clothing, dress clothing, sleepwear, underwear, sheets, towels. Everything was accounted for and had been packed in space-saver bags in between layers of dryer sheets. All of her toiletries were sealed up in Ziploc bags.

She poked into her carry-on and examined her computer and cords, her phone, her charger, her MP3 player, Starbursts to chew on takeoff and landing, the photo from the ball pool that afternoon. Everything was exactly where it was supposed to be, just like the last four times she'd checked.

Nina sat on the edge of her neatly made bed and looked around her room. She didn't want to touch anything, as she'd spent several hours cleaning and arranging it so that everything would be in perfect order on her return. She had Endusted, vacuumed, and Windexed. Her bamboo shades were lowered, making the room dark. It was as if the place had been prepared for some stranger who was coming to stay.

There was a knock on her door. Her mother poked her head in.

"All right," she said. "You're confirmed. The flight's on time."

"Great."

"Nervous?"

"No," Nina lied.

"Ready to go to dinner?"

Nina nodded. It was all happening now. An early dinner. A flight from Albany to Newark, where she'd get on the connecting flight that would take her to San Francisco. Once there she would have to find her contact from the program at the airport. She'd planned for this moment for months, yet she felt like it was sneaking up on her now, tearing her away from her mother, her bedroom carpet, her bed, and her friends. She wouldn't have a kitchen to raid whenever she felt like it. She wouldn't have a private bathroom. She wasn't even going to know anyone.

She wished her dad could be here, but he was traveling on business. Her brother, Rob, was an intern at Boston Medical and never had time to sleep or eat, much less come all the way to Saratoga Springs to help his little sister get on a plane. And Avery and Mel were at orientation for their new job.

You're being such a baby, Nina told herself. *Everything's going to be fine. It's just until August.*

She stood up, pulled on her denim jacket, and grabbed the second suitcase.

2

The Emil Watts Summer Program for High School Leaders wasn't actually run by Stanford University, it was just attached to the school during the summer. The students lived in Stanford dorms and used Stanford classrooms and the Stanford library, but the program's organizers constantly made it clear that Stanford was merely the host—as if the EWSPFHSL (pronounced "Oohspuffhisill") was some kind of parasite living in the belly of this great center of learning.

There was an unceasing cycle of orientation activities— lectures, a library tour, a mass trip to the bookstore for textbooks, well-organized games of Twister in the dorm lounge. Every morning the students took statistics and microeconomics, the mandatory college-credit classes. Every afternoon was spent in a rotating series of seminars and discussions on government, multicultural issues, leadership techniques, current events, and effective writing skills.

In fact, Nina barely had time to get homesick. Soon the red-roofed, mission-style buildings, the palm trees, and the breezes off San Francisco Bay were all pleasantly familiar. The only thing she couldn't get used to was her roommate, Ashley. Ashley came from Georgia and supposedly ran six different organizations at her school. She spent her time in incredibly odd ways, like practicing back bends for half an hour at a stretch or nibbling at the corks that she kept in a bag on her desk. She'd down a few caffeine pills with a can of Red Bull and then spend strung-out hours talking on her cell phone, chomping away on a cork, wearing only the tiniest pair of lingerie shorts and a low-cut tank top. This was her minor concession to wearing some clothing while she was in the room—she always slept naked.

At this moment, late on a Tuesday night of the second week, Ashley was sitting on her bed, considering a large, deeply ripe avocado. Nina didn't know where she'd gotten it; it was just the kind of thing that Ashley turned up with when she had enough stimulants in her system. She focused her clip lamp on it and stared at it as if it contained the secrets of the universe. Her foot tapped furiously on the metal bed frame and she scratched compulsively at her neck. Nina was sure ribbons of skin were about to come streaming down on the mattress.

"Hey, Nina?"

Nina didn't look up from her microeconomics textbook.

"Yeah?"

"What are you?" *Tap, tap, tap, tap. Scratch, scratch, scratch.*

"What?" Nina asked.

"What's your . . . heritage?"

Since her mother was black and her father was Cuban (and white), no one ever knew where to place Nina on the spectrum.

"Swedish," Nina said.

"Really?"

"Yeah."

"On both sides?"

"Yeah."

Ashley thought this over for a moment, then jumped off her bed and took off running down the hall. Nina could hear her bare feet smacking the linoleum. Since she was sitting cross-legged, the backs of her knees were getting too warm and the heavy book was growing uncomfortable. Nina shoved it off her lap and stretched out her legs. Then she flopped down on her back and threw her legs up against the wall and stared at her toes. It took her a minute to realize that someone was standing in her doorway staring at her. She tilted her head back to get an upside-down view.

The guy in the doorway was Steve Carson, a hard-core environmentalist from Oregon. His room was down the hall from Nina's, and from a few glances through the open door, she saw that he lived with all the flamboyance of a monk. He'd brought only a bike, books and music, some special environmentally safe detergent and lightbulbs, and a small bag of clothes. He generally kept to himself and could usually be found sitting on his bed, reading, or working on his laptop. Even when the whole hall would go together for meals, he often sat at the end of a table and read the little laminated menu tents over and over.

"Sorry," he said.

"For what?" Nina slid her legs down and went back to her cross-legged position. "Come on in."

"Nina?" he said. "It's Nina, right?"

Nina nodded.

"My computer is going crazy," he said. "The battery or . . . I don't know. Can I use your computer to check my e-mail for a second? I'm waiting for a message. There's this thing we've been doing for the Savage Rapids Dam on the Rogue River and . . . It would take a long time to explain."

He spoke quickly, in an insistent mumble.

"Don't worry about it," Nina said, waving a hand in the direction of her computer. "It's no problem."

Nina pulled the book back onto her lap. Out of the corner of her eye, though, she watched him. Steve had a strong, slim build, probably from his constant biking. The red T-shirt he had on had bled out in the wash, and his dark blond hair looked like it had been cut at home. He typed away at full speed without looking at the keyboard. Then he began to scrutinize her bathroom basket, which sat on the bureau, filled with a full line of aromatherapeutic shampoo, conditioner, body wash, moisturizer, and facial scrub. As he turned back, he caught her watching him.

"I was just looking at your shampoo," he explained, as if that were the most normal thing in the world.

"Oh."

"You have a lot of the organic stuff, all the same brand."

Steve reached up and plucked out Nina's green tea facial wash and examined the label. He turned the bottle over and examined it, then replaced it.

"All these big companies are jumping on the organic bandwagon," he said, typing away again, still without looking at the keyboard. "And then they put soap in a plastic bottle. Then sometimes they put the bottle inside a box. The amount of packaging they're using is insane. You must like it, though. You've got the whole line there."

"I get it for free. My dad works for the company."

"Oh," he said. A curious "oh." An "Oh, your dad works for a major chemical conglomerate" kind of "oh."

"In product development," she added, rather deliberately. "He's really proud of the organics line. It took a while to get it made."

"I'm third-generation hippie," Steve said. "I notice these things. My parents grew up on a famous commune in New Mexico called the New Buffalo. They lived in teepees in the desert. Everyone in my family has always used natural remedies and organics. It's just strange to see them in Wal-Mart."

"I guess you can thank my dad for that."

"I'm not saying it's bad."

Nina went back to reading and he returned to typing for several minutes. She saw him pause again and stare thoughtfully at the screen.

"We live alongside a berry farm," he said suddenly. "Berries love our kind of weather. I'm used to eating them every day, so I'm kind of jonesing for them. Do you like blackberries?"

"I guess," Nina said, once again stunned by the strange turn of the conversation. "I can't remember if I've ever had them."

"Really?" Steve shook his head incredulously. "I'll send you some jam. We make it at home. It's incredible."

It was too much. He had just gone through her toiletries, subtly accused her dad of wrecking the environment, then launched into his life story. Now he was offering to send her some of the family jam? Maybe he had been too busy chowing down on tempeh and chaining himself to redwoods to have developed social skills.

Suddenly there was an enormous boom from down the hall. Before Nina and Steve could get up to see what happened, Ashley swung through the door and shut it behind her.

"Did you hear that?" she gushed.

"Everyone heard that," Nina said. "What was it?"

"I put it in the microwave." Ashley laughed. "It blew up."

"Your avocado?"

Steve looked at Nina in confusion.

"She had an avocado," Nina explained. "I guess she blew it up."

"I did." Ashley belly flopped onto her bed, which gave a threatening creak. Steve shot a glance at Nina before going back to his typing.

"You're Steve, right?" Ashley asked.

"Yep."

"You're like a nature boy, right? Are you with Greenpeace or something?"

"No. Smaller group. We work with them, though. What do you do?"

"Oh, you know." Ashley sprawled herself over the bed and started braiding her hair loosely. "Food drives, stuff like that. Sort of. I lied about half the stuff on my application. They don't care, anyway, as long as you pay. It's all bullshit. You want a Red Bull?"

"No thanks."

Ashley remembered her manners and reached down into her

mini-fridge and halfheartedly offered a Red Bull to Nina as well. Nina shook her head. She didn't really feel the need to increase the number of hours she was awake with her roommate.

Steve typed. Ashley braided. Nina watched her visitor out of the corner of her eye. He had a deep tan and just a bit of a shadow on his chin, and his face was becoming more and more intent on the screen. Then his fingers stopped moving on the keys and he turned around slowly.

"What's bullshit?" he asked.

"This. Schools. Admissions are all bullshit," Ashley said, clearly bored by the discussion already. "Schools just want money. Give them money, they let you come. Get some bullshit recommendations. Whatever."

Steve regarded Ashley with a curious cock of the head. Nina, however, had to step in. She *had* to.

"It's not bullshit," she said. "I do everything I put on my application, and I'm here to learn how to run things."

"Oh," Ashley replied. She seemed completely content with her own thoughts; the opinions of others didn't affect her at all. She dropped the braid and let it unravel, then she sprang up, tugged her tiny shorts into place, and flat-footed it out into the hall.

Nina jumped off of her own bed and firmly shut the door. She could feel her pulse racing.

"I'm not going to make it," she said. "I can't live with her for nine more weeks. Can we switch rooms?"

"Some people are like that," Steve replied.

"You mean assholes?"

"The thing is," he went on, "if you let it get to you, you can never get anything done. But you can come down anytime, if you want to escape."

"Thanks."

He turned back around to his e-mail. Nina settled herself back down to her reading.

Steve suddenly interested her a lot. Maybe it was because he had expressed a mutual dislike of Ashley (the enemy of your enemy is supposed to be your friend, after all). Maybe it was because he seemed real—from his conversation, right down to his worn-out clothes. And maybe it was just because he was flat-out muscle-bound and appealingly rugged.

He thanked her quietly when he was done, then gave another quick glance at Nina's bath basket before smiling and backing out the door.

Later on, as she walked down to the bathroom, she passed Steve in the small kitchen nook. He had the door to the microwave open and was using a piece of cardboard to scrape out the green slime that coated the already nasty interior. She stopped and watched him, but his head was actually in the microwave, so he didn't notice. There was a bottle of some kind of environmentally friendly orange cleaner on the counter, which Nina guessed was his.

She hadn't liked what Ashley had done, but it hadn't occurred to her to clean the mess up, either. In fact, in a whole hall full of leaders and activists, Weird Steve was the only one who appeared to care about the fate of the cleaning people.

Independence Day

June 29
TO: Mel; Nina
FROM: Avery

Our manager, Bob, gave me my first point today because some people complained that I ignored them. (Eight points and you're fired. Either that or you get Valuable Prizes.)

I AM THE VERY FIRST P. J. MORTIMER'S EMPLOYEE TO GET POINTS! I WIN!

Later on I caught Bob sitting out back by the Dumpster reading *PC Gamer* on his break. I had a cigarette, and he gave me one of those "ew, you smoke?" kind of looks. So I gave him one of those "sex with your Sims girlfriend doesn't count" kind of looks back.

June 30
TO: Avery; Mel
FROM: Nina

You know, on TV the people you fight with are always the people you end up dating. ☺

Speaking of, there's this guy on my hall who's either v. cute and cool or totally out of his mind. I can't decide which. I think living with Strange Ashley is affecting my idea of what "normal" means.

June 30
TO: Nina; Avery
FROM: Mel

Ooh! Explain. Who is this guy?

And Bob's not that bad.

July 1
TO: Avery; Mel
FROM: Nina

His name is Steve Carson. He's kind of very different from me, sort of an eco-warrior but really, really nice. We study together a lot now. He works really hard—harder than pretty much anyone else here. He doesn't hang out or watch TV or anything. When he's not doing work, I think he sits in his room and coordinates an environmental campaign.

I am getting used to the Birks and the hemp shorts and the kind of choppy haircut because under all that he is seriously smoking hot. He's way healthy and rides around on his bike all the time, so he's got the biker legs going on.

This is really weird to me. I never thought I would like a guy who is so crunchy—not that I like him. I'm just kind of . . . intrigued.

Okay. Go ahead, Ave. Insert comment here.

July 1
TO: Mel; Nina
FROM: Avery

I smell a sitcom!

July 2
TO: Mel; Avery
FROM: Nina

Today's SAB (Strange Ashley Behavior): SHE STOLE ONE OF MY BRAS (the tiger-printy one I got on clearance at Victoria's Secret last year) and then denied it. I found it sticking out of her bag. She said that she thought it was one of hers. I know I always find my underwear hanging over the back of other people's desk chairs and carry it around to class.

3

It took Avery about a week to conclude that her entire job at Mortimer's consisted of (1) lying and (2) selling. That was it. Lie and then sell. It was kind of fascinating to watch the whole process. She felt like she had the smoking gun on the whole conspiracy of life.

First of all, the P. J. Mortimer's ads stressed that people were supposed to come and sit and stay for a long time, enjoying the warm Irish hospitality. This was the first big lie that Avery uncovered. One of the main issues emphasized in training was that she was selling experience, not product, which was some weird way of saying that she was supposed to entertain people. She was supposed to be cheerful and friendly, as if she actually *lived* at P. J. Mortimer's and the people at her table were unexpected but welcome guests in her living room. At the same time, she was told she had to get people out the door the *minute* they stopped ordering. If someone turned down a dessert or another round of drinks—*bam!*—she was to drop that check.

Then there was the selling. The entire existence of P. J. Mortimer's seemed to depend on appetizers, desserts, and frozen drinks—and these were the things she had to push. When people first sat down, she was supposed to interest them in some pub fries or onion blossoms or Paddy's Frozen Peppermint Patties. And when they were done, after Avery cleared away the plates of bones from the baby back ribs and the remains of the half-pound hamburgers, it was time to put her hands on her hips and say, "Okay. I know somebody wants dessert!" She should have just passed out the phone number of a good cardiologist.

Just to make things a little more unpleasant, management kept a scoreboard in the staff changing room (a hallway with some boxes in it), charting exactly how much money every server made each shift. Most of the guys, she noticed, got really competitive about it, like selling piña coladas and Paddy's Frozen Peppermint Patties was some kind of *sport* that required skill and prowess. Avery saw it as badgering people to buy things she didn't feel like waiting for at the bar all night, so she didn't bother too much. She felt that her soft stance on the frozen drink issue allowed her to keep a little bit of her dignity, which was rapidly eroding because of the very worst part of her job: the birthday jig band.

There was no way Avery could have known that by answering "yes" to the bizarre question "Can you play the piano or accordion?" on her job application, she would commit herself to becoming one of the official—and few—members of P. J. Mortimer's Birthday Jig Band. She soon came to the conclusion that her thirteen years of piano lessons were probably the only reason she was hired in the first place, since she didn't exactly seem to have the personality that Mortimer's was looking for. She was called into action when she heard a whooping noise and then the heavy beat of a mechanical bass drum that was mounted on the wall by the front vestibule.

She was hearing it right now, as a matter of fact. This was the P. J. Mortimer's Birthday Jig Alert.

Avery swerved around a busboy carrying a heavy load of dirty dishes and ducked into the pantry. If she could just slip through and get out the fire door fast enough, she could claim she was taking her five-minute break and never heard the alert.

Mel was right on her heels. Avery stuck herself in the corner, next to the ice cream freezer, and jammed her hands into her apron pockets.

"I'm not doing it this time," she said under her breath.

"But this one's my table," Mel pleaded.

"I'll make you a deal."

"What?"

"Come with me to Gaz's tonight," Avery said.

The alert was still banging and whooping in the background. Mel glanced through the doorway nervously and looked at the group of other servers, who were clumping together and all looking a little pained at the thought of having to sing.

"Come on, come on, come on. . . ." Avery scrunched up her face. "You know you want to."

Big parties always freaked Mel out, and she tried to get out of them whenever she could. But now that Avery had Mel on her own, she'd found that she had a lot of leverage. It had gotten incredibly easy to convince Mel to do things in the last week or so, now that Nina wasn't around to protect her.

"I guess . . ." Mel said.

"Say you promise."

"I . . . promise."

"Okay," Avery said. "Let's go."

Mel borrowed Avery's lighter to light the candles on a small green-and-white cake that was waiting on the prep counter. Avery headed out onto the floor and took her seat in front of a keyboard on a small raised platform in a corner of the room. The jig was a very simple tune that just about anyone with the most basic piano skills could play. Avery banged out the chords automatically, keeping her eyes trained on Mel as she brought out the cake. The other servers fell in behind her, letting her lead them to the birthday table. You could always tell which one it was by looking for someone trying to slide down out of sight or covering his or her face with a pair of hands. Sure enough, there was a group of women in one of the booths, and one was slinking down, looking like her cover in the Witness Protection Program had just been blown.

All the servers locked arms and began to sing:

We heard it was your birthday, so we've come to make a fuss!
So happy, happy birthday, to you from all of us!
Hi-di-hi-di-hi-di-ho
On this fine day we wish the best to you and all of yours
The merriest of birthdays, from P. J. Mortimer's!

This was followed by a short jig (skipping in circles), with several more hi-di-hos, after which the singers skittered away as quickly as possible, like roaches when the lights come on.

Back in the safety of the pantry, Avery grabbed a dessert fork and pressed it into Mel's hand.

"If I have to do that again," Avery said, "I want you to kill me with this."

"You can do me too," said a voice behind them.

Mel and Avery turned. One of the other servers had come in and was slouching against the wall, demonstrating his utter contempt for the official birthday jig. He was tall but had a young-looking face, with a dash of golden freckles over his cheekbones. His very dark brown hair had overgrown a bit, sweeping down over his high forehead in a thick swag that he kept pushing back with his hand. What really stood out, though, were his eyes, which were the same deep brown as his hair and were very intense and bright. They actually glistened a little just at the thought of the jig.

"Kill me, I mean," he added, after a moment's thought on his remark. "I trained nights, and they were even worse. We did the song about a dozen times every shift. I'm not kidding."

He leaned forward and stared at the name tag pinned to Mel's green suspenders.

"Molly Guinness," he read.

"I'm Mel," Mel said. "This is Avery."

He glanced over and looked at Avery's name tag, which read: *Erin Murphy.*

"I like that we all have these fake Irish names that double as beer ads," he said with a smirk. "It's good to reinforce the idea that all Irish people are alcoholics. Keep the stereotype alive."

Avery leaned forward to read his tag.

"You're Shane O'Douls?"

"I know," he said. "The nonalcoholic one. I'm Parker."

Though he made occasional attempts to turn his head and look in Avery's direction, Parker's attention was really on Mel. This was nothing new to Avery. All guys looked at Mel. Mel was candylike, adorable. Guys hung out with Avery and talked about music and maybe hooked up once in a while. They were usually a little intimidated by Nina because she was tall and assertive and she ran everything. They took Nina as a challenge. With Mel, though, guys developed instantaneous, epic crushes—the kind that caused them to want to iron their clothes and listen to the lyrics of slow songs.

The kitchen bell rang.

"Thirty-nine up," yelled a voice from somewhere behind a small opening. Two plates of buffalo wings were thrown down under the heat lamps. Parker pried himself from the wall and got the two plates. He took them over to the prep counter and reached into a large jug of carrot and celery pieces floating in water, snagging a fistful and setting them on the side of the plates. He grabbed a tub from the refrigerated cabinet, unscrewed the lid, and poured some of the contents into two tiny condiment cups. It oozed out in thick milky chunks.

"Blue cheese dressing is so pretty," he said, grimacing. "Doesn't it make you hungry?"

"I like blue cheese dressing," Mel said.

Parker flushed a little over the fact that Mel had chosen to reveal this to him. He seemed to take a more charitable view toward the dressing, replacing the lid with care.

"She used to eat a lot of paste," Avery explained.

When Parker had taken his plates out to the floor, Avery reached over and retrieved her lighter from the front pocket of Mel's apron.

"Looks like you have a new one," she said.

"A new what?"

Avery did her best imitation of Parker leaning in and reading Mel's tag at very close range.

"Shut up," Mel said.

"What? He's cute. He kind of looks like he's one of those guys who keeps going in Boy Scouts until he's legal."

"He's fine. He seems nice."

"Oh, you're not interested."

"In . . . what?"

"What kind of sign do you need?" Avery said, laughing. She grabbed Mel and wrapped her arms around her, coming in close to her face. "I love you, Melanie Forrest. Can't you see I love you?"

One of the cooks peered through the narrow kitchen window.

"Nice!" he said. "You guys dating?"

"You wish," Avery said over her shoulder. Mel still hung limply in her arms.

"I *do* wish."

"Tell you what, we'll kiss for ten bucks."

"Ten bucks?"

Avery nodded. She glanced at Mel, who was looking at Avery with amazing calmness. Usually everything embarrassed her. Waitressing was obviously toughening her up.

The cook was going through his pockets.

"I have . . . six," he said.

"Sorry."

"Hold on, hold on," he said, laughing. "I think I can get four more."

"Onetime offer," Avery said sternly.

"Damn." He slid over a large club sandwich and a burger. "Forty-six."

Avery released Mel, who stood there, seeming a little baffled.

"I'd better feed my people." Avery grabbed the two plates. "But you promised, remember?"

"I remember."

"No take backs."

Avery winked to the cook, who was still peering through the window, his face glowing an eerie red under the heat lamp.

"Stay back," she said, nodding at Mel. "She's mine, and I have claws."

4

That night they were in a yard behind an old house on some back road in Malta, just below Saratoga Lake. Mel had no idea whose house it was—it was one of those party places that just seem permanently empty and that no one claims to own. Angry Maxwell had set up on a patch of dead grass close to the house, right by the three coolers that constituted the bar. The party had only been going for an hour, and already the whole lawn smelled like old beer.

Angry Maxwell was basically Gaz and Hareth, Avery's musician friends, whom she always joked she met "this one time, at band camp." In reality, they all connected during freshman year in Music 101. Hareth was a self-proclaimed Persian rapper (his family was originally from Tehran) who always wore a knitted hat pulled low over his forehead. Gaz, the drummer, was extremely tall, with long, rubbery arms that flailed around behind the drum kit. He had shaggy golden brown hair and always wore the same pleasant half smile. He reminded Mel of a Muppet. There was also a girl with two long braids playing the bass. Mel didn't know who she was.

Mel didn't claim to know a lot about music, but even she knew that Angry Maxwell was not a good band. The girl seemed to be able to play the guitar, Gaz appeared to know what he was doing with his drums, and Hareth was kind of amusing and animated with his rapping—but they weren't doing any of this stuff together. It was like they were each playing with a totally different band that only existed in their heads. But nobody cared. The crowd was busy drinking up all the good alcohol before it was gone, and the noise that Angry Maxwell made somehow suited this activity.

Mel usually didn't drink, but tonight she felt like it. It seemed like the only thing to do here. Avery had enthusiastically gone off to the bar to get them something. Now Mel was just stuck in a loud place, backed up against a wall by a crowd of people and with a very drunk-looking guy heading right for her. Mel scanned the yard for Avery, but she was lost in the crowd somewhere.

"What's your name?"

The guy had made it across the yard and was leaning into Mel's face.

"Mel."

"Jill?"

Mel didn't bother to correct him.

"Want a drink?" the guy screamed.

"My friend is getting me one."

"What?"

At that moment there was a minor miracle. Avery pushed her

way back through the crowd with several small paper cups in her hands. Seeing Mel's plight, she shot her a "do you want to talk to this guy?" look. Mel widened her eyes to show that she didn't.

Avery came over and stood next to the guy, fixing him with a hard stare. People didn't mess with Avery when she had her eyes all smudged up with black liner. She looked very fierce. The guy threw Mel a puzzled look, but Mel was as unable as ever to express her wish to be left alone in actual words. Avery passed some of the cups she had collected over to Mel.

"Hey," Avery said, using her free hand to take the guy's empty cup and toss it over toward the bushes. "Go fetch."

The guy stared at Avery, looking like he was trying to gauge how much of a problem she might present, then walked away.

Mel would never be as cool as Avery. Ever.

"Brought you a lemon drop," Avery said. "You'll like it. It's sweet. And these are Jell-O shots." She showed Mel a few cups she had pinched between her fingers.

"They're really good," Mel said, nodding at the band.

"No, they aren't," Avery said, passing Mel one of the Jell-O shots. "It sounds like someone's screaming bad poetry over a lawn mower."

"Then why do you watch them play?"

"Sometimes you have to look the other way when it comes to your friends," Avery said with a shrug. "Even if it makes your ears bleed."

"You should play with them," Mel said. "They'd be great then."

"I would kill them."

"Yeah, but you're so good." Avery had natural talent—perfect pitch and an ability to play almost anything she heard. Years of piano lessons had only sharpened her ability.

Avery shrugged away Mel's comment. She didn't like talking about her musical skills, as if admitting her talent would cheapen it or make it go away.

As the crowd shifted past them, Avery and Mel were pressed flat against the outer wall of the basement.

"This is going to be fun," Avery said, trying to get her arm free enough to get her drink to her lips. "I don't even know who half of these people are."

"Hey," Mel said. "Can I ask you something?"

"Sure."

"This afternoon, would you have done it?"

"What? The thing in the pantry?"

Mel was glad Avery hadn't used the word *kiss*. It would sound way too weird to say out loud.

"Of course," Avery said. "Ten bucks? Why not? Guys are *ridiculous* that way."

Mel found herself sinking inside a bit at this response.

"Would that have freaked you out?" Avery asked.

"No," Mel said, trying to smile. "It would have been funny."

"Right," Avery said. She suddenly developed an intense curiosity about her Jell-O shot. She stared deeply into the tiny cup, wiggling it a bit.

"What do I do with this?" Mel asked, holding up her cup.

"Just toss it back, like this." Avery tilted back her cup. Mel did the same. The lump of gelatin was slow moving and seemed to take forever to reach her mouth. It burned with alcohol. She held it on her tongue, trying to absorb as much of the taste as possible.

"You never know," Avery said, looking over the crowd. "We could probably get more takers here. More cash, too."

Mel gulped down the Jell-O. It tickled as it slithered down her throat. She balled the tiny paper cup in her hand.

"You always have takers, though," Avery added.

"What?"

"That guy Parker is going to trail you all summer. I can tell."

"I don't think so."

"You're really not interested?" Avery asked. "Did you see the puppy dog look? What's not to like?"

"I don't know. I just don't."

Avery was looking at her curiously now, trying to figure out what that meant, because Avery always tried to figure out what everything *meant*.

Avery did another Jell-O shot and said, "Is it because he looks like Strange Mike?"

Strange Mike was a guy from their sophomore-year biology class who used to stick his fingernail in the electric socket of his lab station and watch his arm shake.

"No, he doesn't."

"So what is it? Why don't you like him?"

"I want to do another one of these," Mel said, holding up the crumpled remnants of her cup.

"Seriously?"

"Yeah," Mel said. "We're here. We might as well drink."

"See? I told Nina I'd take good care of you," Avery said, obviously pleased.

While Avery made another trip over to the bar, Mel sat down on the coiled hose that was attached to the wall. Avery's questions made her panic. It would have been nice, after all, if she could have explained why she never went out with guys more than once or why they never made much of an impression on her.

She knew the reason, though she'd never put words to it. It floated up in the back of her consciousness now, buoyed by Jell-O and vodka and the last of the warm evening sun. She found her attention completely focused on the small of Avery's back, just the little strip between the deep maroon of Ave's old T-shirt and the low sling of her jeans. The answer seemed to be written there, on that perfect piece of skin.

Avery had a great back—she'd actually won "best back" when they'd passed judgment when they were ten or eleven. Nina had the best hands. Mel had the best hair. Avery had the best back. Ave had balked at this, saying "best back" was a bogus consolation prize, but she was wrong. Her back was strong, not bony like Mel's. It was flawless. It was the perfect surface.

Stop thinking, Mel told herself, digging around in her crumpled cup for remnants of Jell-O. *Just stop.*

5

Later that night Avery leaned against a post of Mel's white canopy bed and watched as she drunkenly reached for the chest of drawers and missed by several inches.

"You want somethin' to sleep in?" Mel asked. "I got lots of pajamas."

After several attempts she finally hooked her fingers onto a drawer handle and pulled out a handful of clothing. She then grandly waved Avery toward the remaining heap of cotton and fleece sleepwear. While hardly hefty, Avery didn't have the pixie blood that seemed to run through Mel's veins; fortunately, Mel liked oversized pajamas. Avery pawed through the offerings for something suitable while Mel got herself tangled in her own tank top. She'd only removed it halfway before attempting to pull on the T-shirt she planned on sleeping in.

"You need help with that, Mel?" Avery asked.

"No. I got it."

"You sure?"

"Yeah, I got it."

Mel's confusion with her tank top was growing. She was

utterly baffled, with two shirts around her neck and one arm in each one.

"Take them both off and start over, Mel."

"Okay."

Mel carefully freed herself from the tank top, got the T-shirt on (backward, but who cared?), and squirmed out of her denim skirt. Then she tried to put both legs into a single leg space of a pair of pajama pants. It took a few tries, but she eventually managed to get them on correctly and then fall face-first onto the bed.

"See this, Ave?" she said conspiratorially, holding up a patchwork stuffed flounder that she drew from the folds. "This is the sleepy rainbow fish. He swims you to sleepland."

"Drink your water, Mel."

"You sleep here," Mel said, slapping at the empty spot next to her. "Okay?"

"I'm serious. Drink that water."

"Know what I *really* want right now?" Mel asked.

"What?"

"Fritos."

"Uh-huh." Looking back into the drawer, Avery decided against the pajama bottoms with the smiling M&M's and opted instead for a more subdued plain violet pair. "I'm not sure that's a good idea right now."

"We don't have to get a big bag," Mel said, pulling her hair into a lopsided orange geyser smack on the top of her head. "We could get one of those medium bags—the big single bags.

Or two of those. One or two, whatever you want. Or Doritos."

"The water, Mel."

"Oh my God—or Krispy Kremes!"

Having pulled on the pajama bottoms, Avery now found that the only shirt that looked like it would really fit was a white tank top with the word *Princess* written in gold sparkles across the chest. If her own shirt (a very fine T-shirt from Fat Ernie's Laundromat in Ann Arbor, Michigan) hadn't reeked so badly of smoke, she would have kept it on. Alas, the very fibers were carcinogenic now. Off it went and on went the embarrassing replacement.

"Wanna go to the grocery store and get a seedless watermelon?" Mel said, with wide, bloodshot eyes.

"No."

"Come on. It has water in it!"

Avery walked over and handed Mel the large red plastic cup and stood there until Mel took several large swigs. The hydration seemed to tap out Mel's energy completely, and she rested her head down against the pillow. Avery walked over to switch off the light. In the ambient light from the streetlamps and a few illegal firecrackers, Mel's white furniture took on an ethereal glow. The canopy over the bed seemed buoyant, as if it were floating on a gentle, steady current of air.

To make space for herself on the bed, Avery was forced to jettison an entire squad of stuffed animals that were hidden under the sheets. Along with some normal stuffed animals (bears, kittens, and a monkey) Mel had the rest of the ark in there. There were a lobster, an owl, an anteater, an elephant, a cobra (where do you even *get* a stuffed cobra?), a beanie stingray, and a bat. There were also nonanimals, like the stuffed happy face and the pink fur ball with eyes.

As Avery sank down under the fluff of the comforter, Mel flipped over, threw an arm over Avery's waist, and pressed her face into her friend's shoulder.

"Ave?" she mumbled. "The room is moving."

"That's normal."

"It is?"

"Yep."

"It's going in circles."

"I know."

"Ave? Why is it doing that?"

"It'll pass."

"You sure?"

"Yep," Avery said, patting Mel's head gently, "I'm sure."

A Roman candle whizzed and popped nearby.

"Ave?"

"Yeah?"

"Thanks for staying."

"No problem."

Thirty seconds later Mel was snoring lightly in the crook of Avery's arm. Avery stayed still, not wanting to disturb Mel. She liked this, just how things were at this exact moment. She caught a whiff of mingling odors of fabric softener, old smoke, and perfume. A cozy smell. She looked down at Mel's sleeping face. Her hair spread over the pillow so perfectly, you would have thought a stylist had arranged it, like for a conditioner commercial. It would still look good in the morning, Avery could tell. In contrast, when Avery woke up, she would look like she'd been spinning plates on her head all night.

With Mel, everything was just kind of delicate and perfect all the time, in a goofy kind of way. An endearing way. It was no wonder that you had to get in line to have a crush on her. Who *wouldn't* have a crush on Mel? She had universal appeal, like baby seals and koala bears. Avery should have gone ahead this afternoon and kissed her. It would probably have been great.

She'd kind of wanted to do it then. She kind of wanted to do it now.

What?

Avery took hold of herself. Never before had she even considered hooking up with another girl, except in the most purely theoretical sense. She wasn't biased. She'd given the issue its due consideration, and up until this moment, in the sexual preference category, her vote had been squarely for guys.

Besides, this was not just some random person she would only see once—this was *Mel*. Anything she did with Mel went on the Permanent Record. If this was a bad idea, then the results would be horrific because for the rest of her life she'd have to look at Mel and know that this *thing* had passed between them. Yet this also meant Mel was the very best person to try this experiment with. Here was someone she knew she loved, really and truly and totally. No surprises. No hidden agenda. This was someone she could trust. It would be secret.

And *was* it so weird, really? Somewhere in Avery's mind there was a thought that nothing truly awful could happen in a white canopy bed, one with a well-worn mattress that dipped in the middle and scooped the two of them together in a soft pocket of cotton sheets and comforter. This was womblike. . . .

Bad, bad, bad comparison. A comparison to be immediately forgotten.

Maybe she should sleep on the floor.

No. The floor was hard and cold. The bed was broken-down soft and perfect. Too good to leave.

She could sleep on the stuffed animals.

Too lumpy. She'd have noses and eyes and ears and beaks in her back all night, which was not recommended by the American Sleep Federation or whoever it was that came up with those ideal mattress guidelines. Neither were extremely soft mattresses, for that matter, but Avery liked them anyway. Especially this one.

She put her face next to Mel's on the pillow. Mel was gone, totally insensible. She could put her lips to Mel's and try this theory out and Mel would never, ever know.

No. That would be *very creepy*. Besides, it probably wouldn't even tell her much since Mel would respond with all the passion of a CPR dummy. There was no way Avery could get a true reading.

Avery forcefully shut her eyes, knowing that however awake she felt right now, the alcohol would put her under if she just stayed still. Eventually it worked, but not before Avery had opened her eyes a number of times, hoping to see Mel looking at her, suddenly awake and encouraging.

There was light now.

Mel opened her eyes and stared across the pillow at the tufts of brown-black hair that were inches from her face. She played with the tips of them. This gesture caused Avery to stir. She flipped over and faced Mel. Her mascara and eyeliner had smudged a bit, giving her vampy eyes.

"You're alive," Avery said, raising an eyebrow. "I'm shocked. How do you feel?"

"Fine. Why?"

"Fine?"

"Maybe a little thirsty."

"I don't believe it," Avery said, rubbing her temples. "It's actually kind of annoying."

"Sorry." Mel grinned. "Wanna get up?"

Avery groaned dramatically. "No. Need coffee. Will die. Please help."

"I think we have some downstairs," Mel said, thinking for a moment. "I'm not sure. I've never made it."

"Be really quiet for a few minutes. I'm going to communicate with Starbucks by telepathy."

"Ooh. Get me a chai."

"Chai?" Avery said, looking over in horror.

"I like chai," Mel said defensively.

"You also keep twelve hundred stuffed animals in your bed," Avery said, nodding at the heaped menagerie. "What does that say?"

"Well, I have to have something to keep me company at night. I don't like sleeping alone."

Avery smirked at Mel's explanation. "I guess you got lucky last night, then. A whole live person."

"Right," Mel said, tucking her head against Avery's on the pillow. "You're more interesting than they are. You talk and everything."

"I never shut up."

"Yes, you do."

"Not much."

"I could make you shut up."

"Oh, yeah?" Avery said, turning her face to Mel's. "How?"

In a way, Mel's answer was a surprise to both of them. She simply sealed Avery's lips with her own.

And she was right. That seemed to shut Avery up.

6

After Avery had gone home, Mel laid flat on her back on her bed in the exact spot where she had been when Avery was there. Avery's head dent in the pillow was gone, but Mel tried to preserve it.

She'd known for a long time that this was going to happen someday; she just hadn't realized that it would be today. And obviously it was going to be *with* someone, but she'd had no idea that someone was going to be Avery. She'd never mentioned it before because there was nothing to tell. It was all in her head. And now it had escaped. It was *on the loose.*

For years the signs had been there, but Mel had chosen not to interpret them. There were the pangs she felt when she saw Nicole Kidman floating above the crowd on her swing in *Moulin Rouge.* There was her weird obsession with the nurse with the long brown hair on *ER.* And while she loved Harry Potter, it was Hermione that she couldn't get off her mind.

When it came to people in her actual life whom she tended to think about a lot, Mel had plenty of excuses. Micky Jameson in seventh-grade band always covered for Mel when she messed up her flute parts. The girl with the shoulder-length blond hair and the slight lisp in her sophomore-year geometry class had always lent her a pencil or a piece of paper when she asked. And so what if she imagined going to Paris with her junior-year French teacher, Mademoiselle Hall, the woman with the dark curly hair and the sly smile? Who cared that in Mel's imaginings, they walked hand in hand through the market from page 76 of her French II book or that they went to dinner together in the romantic bistro pictured in chapter five, "Au restaurant"? She was just . . . thinking about French stuff.

But she'd known. She'd absolutely known. The only thing she'd never done was write the word in the caption of the self-portrait that she kept in her head. That kept it from being real—because if it was real, she would have to deal with *reality*—and who even knew what the reality of being a lesbian was? That meant coming out and all kinds of complicated things that she really didn't feel like thinking about before.

But now it also meant that she could have this morning happen again, over and over. With Avery. It was too good to be true. Avery, who she'd always liked and loved, had suddenly become Avery who she *liked* and probably *loved*. Avery who had slept over a hundred times before, but this time Mel could say that Avery had been in her bed and it meant something very different—so unbelievably strange and great that she wondered if she was still drunk or if she'd gone insane and hallucinated the whole thing.

She sat up and looked at herself in the mirror on her dresser.

"I'm gay," she told her reflection.

The girl she saw staring back at her looked puzzled.

"I'm a lesbian," she tried again. Somehow she drew out the word in such a way that it sounded French. She tried it more slowly. She put the emphasis on every syllable in turn—*LES-bi-an, les-BI-an, les-bi-AN.*

Nope. The girl in the mirror still wasn't buying it.

"You, Melanie Forrest," she said firmly. "You are a lesbian."

This caused her to involuntarily raise her eyebrows and move back. She'd actually *startled* herself. She dropped back onto the bed and held her hands out in front of her face. They were so tiny and pasty white—washed-out little twig hands. She grabbed a handful of her dry orange hair. Should she cut it? Get herself one of those cute little pixie cuts? She always liked those. Or was that too much of a statement cut? Did she want to make a statement?

If she got one of those cuts, she would look exactly like Peter Pan.

With her long orange locks, her petite frame, and her alabaster skin and gold freckles, Mel had long been an object of desire to some, envy to others. Mel, however, had always wished for a voice that was more than a high-pitched whisper, that her flaming locks weren't quite so Day-Glo, that her frame looked more like sleek muscle than spun glass. On top of it all, she had very, very slight points at the tops of her ears. Most people, when and if they noticed these, thought they were adorable. Mel didn't think so. She thought her pointy ears made her look just like something that lived in a magical glade under a giant toadstool.

She wasn't only gay, she was a gay elf.

She heard her father's car pull up in the driveway and pulled herself away from the mirror. Her legs felt shaky and light as she went down the stairs, and she had to hold on to the rail for support. She was amazed at how sunny it was—she could clearly see the dust motes floating around in the sunbeam that came in through the three glass panels on their front door.

"Doughnuts," her father said, coming in and holding up a white box that was already developing the telltale clear grease marks that really good doughnuts always left behind.

"Yum," she said automatically.

She followed him into the kitchen. One thing about living with her dad for the last nine years—they behaved like roommates in a lot of ways, and they ate like college kids. A dozen doughnuts was a perfectly acceptable breakfast. They'd be able to polish them off by the afternoon. It was a good thing that they were both naturally thin, and that he worked in construction and exercised off the fast food and pizza that constituted the majority of their meals.

"Did you guys have a good time last night?" he asked, setting his things down on the floor.

"It was good."

Mel kept her eyes trained on the box. She was sure that if she looked up, he would be able to see it all in her face, everything she'd done that morning. Some kind of mark had to be on her—

some physical sign. But he just grabbed a chocolate doughnut and glanced through the mail that was scattered on the table.

As close as she was to her dad (this was the man, after all, who'd had to give Mel the "something happens to girls every month" talk), she somehow didn't think that he would know what to make of this new information. Two subjects always made him a little upset: Mel dating and Mel going to college and leaving home. They usually got around these because Mel didn't ever date anyone for very long (for reasons that were now abundantly clear) and because she hadn't even started thinking about college yet.

It was possible, Mel realized, that he might be happy to know that this thing had happened with Avery. He knew Avery. He liked Avery. Avery was familiar. And Avery wasn't some guy who'd get her pregnant or something like that.

She brightened. Already she'd found one advantage to this whole situation—pregnancy would never be an issue. She would have to remember to use that when and if this subject ever came up.

"Was camping good?" she asked.

"Nice night. Yeah. Not too hot."

The phone rang. Mel's head jerked up, and she involuntarily sprang out of her seat.

"I'll get it," she said. She ran out to the hall and snatched the phone from the table.

"Hey." It was Avery. Mel couldn't hear her brothers screaming in the background—this meant that Avery had barricaded herself in the basement bathroom, her most private phone spot.

"Hi," Mel said, hurrying up the stairs. She could feel her heart beating in her ear. Every word Avery said had to be listened to carefully and interpreted. This was uncharted territory, to say the least.

"Are you . . . good?" Mel asked.

Very loud pounding in her ear now. It almost hurt. She got to her room and shut the door.

"Really good."

"Really?" Mel asked.

"Want to do something later? Watch a movie or something?"

"Or something" had never sounded so good. Mel sank down into the pile of animals that Avery had thrown to the floor and plunged her hand into them, squeezing them at random, trying to release the strange, wobbly feeling that was coming over her again.

Not too eager, she told herself. *Don't sound desperate. It's only Avery. Don't act like a freak.*

"Sure," she said. "If your brothers are bothering you, you can come over here and we could hang in my room."

Oh God. What was she saying?

She was saying what she'd said ten million times before, except in the last two hours the meaning had changed. She grasped a handful of hair in agony.

Like she could hide anything from Avery anyway. Avery had sixth and seventh and eighth senses and could tell more from the way someone stood or said "see you later" than Mel could if she stole the person's diary and read it cover to cover.

Avery didn't answer right away.

"Or something else," Mel said.

"No. That sounds good."

Avery's tone didn't give anything away, but Mel could tell. She was saying yes. Yes to coming back to Mel's room. Yes to everything. Yes, yes, yes . . .

Mel jumped up and got a head rush, and for a moment she couldn't tell if she was in the most bliss she'd ever experienced in her life or if it was just one of those things she got when she stood too fast. (Pale, redheaded, anemic—it all went together.)

"I have to practice for a few hours," Avery said. "How about six?"

"Okay," Mel said, sinking back onto the bed. "See you at six."

When she hung up, she listened to her father moving around downstairs, turning on the television. She tried to peel herself off the bed to join him, but it was impossible. She was stuck there, heavy, dizzy—and she didn't want to do anything that would make the feeling go away.

When Avery emerged from the bathroom with the phone, she found that two of her younger brothers were chasing their collie, Bandit, around the basement, banging into the piano bench in the process. No wonder the thing was starting to fall apart.

"Did you eat?" her mother shouted down from the kitchen. "I'm about to put this lunch meat away."

Avery dodged the chase scene and headed upstairs.

"Okay," her mom said, pointing at various square Tupperware

containers that were stacked on the table. "Turkey. Ham. Salami. Roast beef. Yellow cheese. Orange cheese."

Avery popped open these last two containers and examined the cheeses. "Provolone and American," she corrected. "Not yellow and orange."

"Rolls are in the bag on the counter," her mother went on. "There's white bread in the freezer. You want mustard? I got the kind you like."

Avery nodded, and her mother produced a jar of thick, grainy mustard from the refrigerator. Avery was a sucker for this mustard. She would eat it with anything.

"I'm taking these two to the mall for some sneakers," her mom said. "Have fun last night?"

"Yeah . . ."

"Good. I have a chicken defrosting in some water in the sink. Can you check on it every once in a while and see how it's coming? If it's not totally defrosted by four, stick it in the microwave?"

As her mother corralled her two brothers, Avery got herself a roll and made a sandwich. The events of that morning still weren't really sinking in. Making out with your best friend for an hour, making a turkey sandwich with provolone and mustard— these two concepts didn't belong in the same universe. Avery felt lightweight. Her legs were still shaking, and she was smiling involuntarily.

When Mel had kissed her, Avery had first felt a rush just knowing that she had guessed correctly. But then they didn't stop. Either of them. And though Avery had been curious the night before, she didn't expect for it to feel as comfortable or natural as it did. There were lots of little differences kissing a girl. Mel was smaller than she was, which felt kind of strange. Avery's arms went around her completely, with arm to spare. There was never a point where Avery felt like she had to be careful or that things might go too far. It was fun, and Mel giggled a lot, and Avery was soon experiencing a stupefying out-of-time feeling that she still hadn't recovered from.

She had, for instance, just used up about a fifth of the jar of mustard in quick, generous strokes. That was a lot, even for her. She put the lid back on the jar.

"I'm going now," her mom said, poking her head into the kitchen. "All right?"

"Yeah." Avery nodded. "It's all good."

7

Some facts.

Fact: It is difficult to commit microeconomic concepts to memory when your roommate's cell phone goes off once every two minutes and then she screams *very intimate information* to friends in a loud enough voice to be heard across the country without the aid of the phone.

Fact: It is *impossible* when said roommate also scratches constantly. Soon scratching is all you can hear. Scratching takes over your world.

Fact: At nine o'clock in the morning Nina would sit down to take her first microeconomics test of the term, and she was definitely going to fail if this ringing and talking and scratching kept up. And it *was* going to keep up.

If she wanted to get anything done, she would have to disappear, go bury herself somewhere. She packed up her books and her water and headed to the library.

Nina spent the next five hours in a lonely corner of the twenty-four-hour study room until the humming of the lights and the general desolation finally got to her. By the time she emerged, it was three in the morning. The path was empty, lit up brightly by the security lights. It was a gorgeous night, warm and fragrant. Nina took a deep breath, trying to revive herself a bit.

Behind her she heard a faint scraping noise. She turned around to see a bike turning around the corner of the path and coming right in her direction. Without thinking, Nina plunged her hand into her bag and grabbed for the pepper spray canister her mother had made her promise to buy on her arrival.

As it came closer, she saw it was just Steve. There was something weird about this—like déjà vu. Or maybe wish fulfillment.

"Hey, Nina. Where are you coming from?" he asked, coming up alongside her.

"I was at the library. Studying."

"By yourself?" He glanced around at the shadowy buildings. Nina felt a rush of indignation, but then she realized that she was still holding the pepper spray canister. She released it and drew her hand from her bag casually.

"What are you doing out?" she asked.

He dismounted and leaned the bike against his hip. "I needed to get out. Being inside in nice weather feels really weird to me. My brother and I sleep outside for about half the year."

"Outside where?"

"In hammocks, in the yard."

"You sleep in your *yard?*"

"Sleeping outside is great. You feel different—you feel really good."

"What if it rains during the night?" she asked.

"Then we go sleep on the porch. Sleeping in the rain is the best."

"You ready for the test?" she asked.

"Kind of," he said. "Not completely."

"Me either."

He rubbed his hair roughly, sending one chunk drooping over his eye. It was very cute. He seemed like an overgrown toddler. "Want to stay up? Only six hours to go."

"You want to pull an all-nighter?"

"I have flash cards." He pulled a stack of cards out of one of his cargo pockets.

"A man after my own heart," she said.

They circled the campus for an hour, each taking turns quizzing from the cards. They wound up at the quad, the grand arcade of ornately decorated arches that bordered a wide plaza. It looked like an old monastery. They each sank to the ground and leaned up against a pole, facing each other.

"My brain is starting to go," Nina said, closing her eyes.

"No!" Steve said. "You have to keep your eyes open. You're dead if you close them."

"Argh! I know." Nina forced her eyes open wider than normal, but her eyelids were heavy. The test seemed distant and unimportant.

"Talk to me," Steve said. "Tell me a story."

"About what?" Nina yawned.

"Tell me about your home. Come on. Keep your brain on."

"I live in a gingerbread house," Nina said. "One of those Victorian houses, with the little peaks and the wraparound porch. It's green. It's old. There's a new part off to the side where my mom's office is."

"What does your mom do?"

"She's a lawyer. My dad travels a lot. Pretty much all the time. My brother, Rob, is a doctor in Boston. He's an intern, anyway. I never get to talk to him. He lives at the hospital. So it's usually just me and my mom."

"We always have people staying with us," Steve said. "I don't think we've ever had dinner with just the four of us. We had this one guy who went to college with my dad who stayed with us for about two weeks. Right after he left, these two guys in suits came to our house and asked my parents a lot of questions. It turns out that he was under investigation for grand larceny and racketeering, and my parents were being watched by the FBI."

"You were harboring a fugitive? Sounds exciting."

"Not really," Steve said. "We didn't know he was a fugitive. He was really boring. He used to hog the TV every night."

"What do your parents do?" she asked.

"My mom runs a studio where people can come in and paint their own ceramics. My dad is an accountant, which is kind of weird, considering his background. I don't think he's really good at it, because he's always out of work. I'm here on scholarship because there's no way my parents could pay for this."

Nina was kind of amazed that he would just come out and admit something like that. Steve had a strange brand of confidence that Nina had never seen before.

"You know what's weird?" he said, looking over the archways

of the quad. "My parents always told me that people raised with a lot of money are obnoxious and spoiled and that they don't care about important things. But that's not true. I mean, you're staying up all night to study. And when you talk in class, it's obvious that you're serious about the work you do."

"I don't come from *money,*" she said quickly.

"Compared to me you do," he said plainly. "I don't mean it in a bad way."

Nina suddenly felt a bit odd about all the things she had at home. Her SUV, for a start. She quietly shuffled through her cards.

"I see sunlight," he said. "It's just starting."

Nina looked up beyond the palm trees in the courtyard and saw that the sky had gone from black to gray to a vibrant shade of lilac.

"We made it," she said, smiling.

"Yeah. See that? Feel awake now?"

"I'm getting there."

By seven they were sitting together in the nearly empty dining hall, drinking coffee and laughing uncontrollably at the term *marginal product.* By eight they'd run through the definitions so many times that their responses took on a singsong rhythm.

They were the first to show up in class for the test. It wasn't until she got there that Nina realized that both she and Steve were wearing the same clothes they'd worn the day before, but she didn't really care.

▲   ▼   ▲

It turned out that the test definitely didn't merit staying up all night. It was really just a fancy quiz, which probably explained why no one else seemed excited about it. Steve finished first, and Nina looked up and found that she was upset to see him leaving and actually sped up and handed in the test without double-checking. It didn't matter; he was waiting outside the door for her.

They looked at each other and laughed.

"That was ridiculous," he said. "Good thing we stayed up, huh?"

When they got to Nina's door, she wasn't quite sure what to do. She didn't really want him to go away, but they'd been together for hours and the whole point to their staying together had passed. Out of curiosity, though, she left her door hanging open to see what he would do. He stepped just inside of the doorway and leaned against the wall.

"You gave me the weirdest look when I was in your room that first time," he said.

Nina felt a flush of embarrassment. She tried to cover it up with an overly dramatic yawn, then she began rummaging through her closet.

"No, I didn't," she said.

"Yeah, you did. You were staring at me like I was a nut. Do you know how long it took me to come up with an excuse to come down to your room?"

"Excuse?"

"An excuse to come talk to you. I'd been trying to figure out how to do it since the day we moved in. And you just stared at me like I was a mutant."

Nina realized that her skin had broken out in goose pimples. Definitely not just the exhaustion kicking in.

"What do you mean?" she asked.

"So," he said, "I guess I have to ask."

"Ask what?"

But Steve didn't say anything. He seemed to be questioning her with his expression, asking if it was okay to come closer. Nina answered by staying right where she was and smiling. That's when Steve bent down and kissed her.

8

For the first few weeks it was like a game. Mel and Avery would "accidentally" find each other's feet under the table at shift meetings or bump into each other in the pantry. They'd lean over to whisper something, and they'd brush the other's earlobe with their lips. Everything was tiny and well disguised, but there were little electric moments everywhere.

At the end of the day, when they were alone, the next phase would begin. There was frequently an exchange of very fast test kisses, quick little brushes of the lips that, if a witness were pressed, might not hold up in court as *real* kisses. This seemed to be the way they asked each other if this was okay, if they should do it again. The answer was always yes, and then making out would commence.

For Avery the game was almost better than the kissing. She liked the slightly dangerous feeling that came from doing these things right under people's noses. No one knew, of course, because they weren't acting any different from the way they'd always acted.

One of the most amazing things was the fact that Mel had

kept this information hidden for so long. Mel was notoriously bad at hiding things. She was the great revealer of surprise parties, the one who turned three different shades of pink when she tried to tell even the smallest lie. Yet she had managed to go an entire lifetime without revealing the fact that she liked girls—a lot. And she definitely liked Avery—a lot. Avery could tell that it took every ounce of strength Mel had not to be the one who always initiated the kissing.

A month after the big event they were sitting at a back table at The Grind, a coffee shop on Broadway. The Grind was run and populated by the Skidmore College students who hadn't gone home for the summer. These were the intensely friendly people—the girls with the unwashed hair that they wrapped in colorful scarves or tied up in intricate knots that always looked like they were on the verge of coming undone, the guys with the beards or the out-of-control curls. They were also kind of unobservant and hopeless at giving the right change.

In Avery's mind it was the perfect place to hang out. Only a few people from their school came in during the summer, and the ones who did weren't the types who would be looking around and trying to spot the lesbians. The high-maintenance, gossipy, "I need my latte or I'll die" people went to Starbucks, where they had a blender and could make frozen drinks. The Grind served lower-tech iced coffees, which were kind of thick and just a little too strong. It was a trade-off Avery could live with.

She shifted in her chair, pulling up her leg to tuck it underneath her. As she moved, she ran her foot alongside Mel's calf.

"Okay," Avery said, her eyes gleaming once she noticed the effect her stealthy move had had on Mel. "Let's review. What's one way to tell that a band is really bad?"

"If it has five guys who do coordinated dance moves," Mel said, reciting the answer just as Avery had taught her.

"The exception to this rule is?"

"The Jackson Five."

"Who was in that?"

"Michael Jackson, before he was scary."

"Right! You get a prize!"

"What?" Mel asked.

"You'll get it later."

Mel smiled. "You know," she said, "it's a month today."

"A month what?"

"You know what I mean."

Avery poked around at the ice at the bottom of her glass. "Weird," she replied.

"So." Mel kept her eyes down. "What . . . are we?"

"Um, finished?" Avery grinned and held up her empty glass. "Want to walk?"

They continued down to the end of the stretch of shops, to Congress Park. Two busloads of elderly tourists had just been deposited there, and they were making their way around the Greek pavilion and the cupolas that housed the springs and the decorative ponds. They took pictures of one another and happily fumbled with their cameras and video recorders.

Mel walked along quietly. Avery could almost feel the question coming out of her pores, jumping over and invading Avery cell by cell.

"Mel," she said.

"It's okay. We don't have to talk about it."

This was a huge, obvious lie.

Alongside the path a woman in a flowing purple dress was sitting on a folding stool, stringing red and pink beads together and smiling to herself. At her feet were two flat, velvet-lined cases of beaded necklaces, earrings, and silver rings. Avery stopped and knelt to look them over.

"How much are these?" Avery asked, pointing to a selection of plain silver bands.

"Fifteen dollars."

"We should each get one," Avery said. "Friendship bands."

"You want two?" the woman said. "Two for twenty-five. It's a beautiful day. Why not two for twenty-five?"

The woman smiled at them, and Avery felt a wave of recognition. She *knew*. Avery was sure of it. The woman was giving her a coded message of affirmation.

Avery picked out a band for her left thumb. They had to find the tiniest band for Mel's index finger. It looked like it took a huge effort for Mel to keep her hands from shaking. She reached for her purse.

"It's okay," Avery said. "Early birthday gift."

Mel's birthday was in May.

"Know what?" Mel said when they were just out of the woman's earshot.

"What?"

"I have the best girlfriend in the world."

Avery squinted at one of the ponds, which was brightly reflecting the sun. She didn't reply for a minute.

"So do I," she finally said.

Labor Day

August 14

TO: Mel; Avery

FROM: Nina

ARGH! I wish, I wish, I wish that you could just come here for a day or something and meet Steve because it is almost impossible to explain how much I love him. Here is some evidence to show you just how great he is:

1. Makes me call him whenever I work late at the library so he can come over and walk me back to the building.

2. Rode his bike into town at 11 p.m. the other night to get me Pamprin(!).

3. Has never slept with anyone because he wanted to wait for the right person, and he says he thinks it is me, but only if I want—and he'll wait until whenever I'm ready, even if that means when we both get here for school next year (!!!!!).

4. Ave: He is a huge Elliott Smith fan. That's good, right?

5. Mel: He can't watch that part of "Finding Nemo" either.

August 15

TO: Nina; Avery

FROM: Mel

OMG. I thought about this all day at work. Keep him!

August 19

TO: Avery; Mel

FROM: Nina

RED ALERT!

MIR (mentally ill roommate) has been missing for two days. She left for class on Thursday morning and never came back. Our RA is freaking out because they are kind of extra responsible for us since we're the high school group. I am not freaking out so much. I sleep better knowing that a naked cork-eater is not sneaking around at night, stealing my underwear.

August 19
TO: Mel; Avery
FROM: Nina

UPDATE:

Sadly, MIR has returned. Not in M hospital, as hoped. She went to San Francisco. EWSPFHSL staff totally furious with her. She brought back a v. small turtle, about three inches big, which she keeps in a takeout container on the floor by her desk. She didn't feed it, so Steve rode down to Whole Foods on his bike and bought it organic lettuce. He says that he is going to take it from her if she doesn't start treating it right and will find an ecologically appropriate place to set it free, where it hopefully won't get eaten by something.

He is so good.

August 20
TO: Nina; Mel
FROM: Avery

I drove past school today. They finally took down the HAVE A GOOD UMMER sign and put up the WELCOME BACK STUDENTS one. I guess they bought a new S.

August 20
TO: Mel; Nina
FROM: Avery

Hey! Four hours later the *S* thief was back. Sign now says, WELCOME BACK TUDENTS. LONG LIVE THE *S* THIEF!

August 24
TO: Avery; Mel
FROM: Nina

36 hours until my flight. Going to be v. busy for the next day and a half. V. excited to come home, but leaving Steve is hard. So hard. I can't think about it or my head will explode. Need serious T. Power. At 9:15 tonight (your time) I will call you to take T position and say the chant. I need you!

9

"I like your hair," Mel's mom said, reaching out and feeling Avery's bobbed locks. "You've colored it. It looks good darker."

"Thanks." Avery nodded, not looking thrilled at being petted. She hunched up her shoulders.

Avery was just trying to make it a little more bearable for Mel by coming along for dinner at her mom's house, but Mel could see that she was already regretting her decision.

Mel was five when her mom met Jim Podd. Apparently her parents had been growing apart for some time, and this was the final push her mom needed to make the move out of the house. Jim already had two boys, so it was decided that Mel should remain with her father.

The oldest Podd, Brendan, was now about to start his freshman year at Cornell. He was also a known hacker and software pirate and had a padlock on his room. Richie, his brother, was a fifteen-year-old skater—friendly enough, but erratic and uncontrollable. Things tended to get broken around Richie. Lastly there was Lyla, the one child Mel's mom and Jim had on their own. The only thing Mel had ever seen Lyla do was watch television.

She had a TiVo in her room. She would only eat plain white rice, chicken nuggets, or hot dogs (boiled—not grilled), so she always had a special plate made up for her.

The Podds lived in one of the developments around Saratoga Lake, in a clump of absolutely identical houses bunched close together along the lakeside. Their house was much more expensive than the one Mel and her father lived in, as was everything in it. Whenever Mel got there, either Jim or her mom pointed out some new thing they'd just gotten, never once realizing that Mel not might want to know how much better they were doing.

"We drove Brendan out to Ithaca on Wednesday for move-in," Jim said, coming out of the kitchen with a plate of seafood and fennel sausage. "Freshmen aren't supposed to have cars, but he found someone to rent him a parking space at their house. For all I know, he won't even be in school that long. A lot of these companies, they hire people like Brendan. They show them the flaws in their systems. He'll probably get a great job out of it."

There was a thunk as Richie jumped down the stairs and leapt into the room.

"Hey, Mel. Hey, Avery," he yelped while stepping onto the recliner. "Guess what? I'm going sandboarding later this year. When are we eating?"

This last remark was yelled out to Jim.

"Soon."

"I'll be back," Richie said, springing off the chair and out of the room.

Avery silently mouthed the word *Ritalin* to Mel.

About ten minutes later Jim had arranged all of his platters on the table. Richie had been recalled, and Lyla had been coaxed downstairs with the promise of a boiled hot dog. Jim encouraged everyone to dig in. Dinners at the Podd house were always like something out of a magazine spread. Along with the seafood sausage, there was citrus shrimp, broccoli rabe with grilled cipollini onions, heirloom tomato salad, and some kind of purple Thai slaw. Mel and her dad tended to eat things like rotisserie chicken from the Price Chopper and hamburger mixed with mac and cheese, so even the Podd food was a little disturbing.

"So," Jim asked, "any summer love stories, Mel?"

Avery sighed. "She's got loads. Like, *hordes* of them."

Mel froze. Avery was staring at her from across the table with a "dare me?" smile twisting her lips. Mel rounded her eyes and tried to send Avery a telepathic message to cease and desist whatever it was she was planning.

"Really?" her mom said, not picking up on this battle of the Jedi mind tricks.

"Yeah." Avery nodded, spearing another piece of sausage. "It's weird. Guys seem to follow Mel wherever she goes. I try for her leftovers."

"So," Mel's mom said, leaning in eagerly. "Come on. Details."

"God," Avery answered, "there's been like, what, three or four? You know Mel, she's playing them off one another."

Mel's mother looked at her with an admiration Mel had never seen before. Dating was very critical to her mom. She really seemed to measure a person's entire worth in the world by whom they'd dated and what they'd gotten from that person. Mel's father, though handsome, was a contractor who didn't make nearly as much as Jim Podd. Mel hated seeing the big diamond that always flashed around on her mother's finger. She always had to make an effort not even to look at her mother's left hand.

"The last guy," Avery went on, now caught up in her own elaborate story, "was an actor who came up from New York to do one of the shows at the arts center. He was way too old. I think he thought Mel was in college or something. How old was he, Mel?"

"Um . . . I don't know." Mel stared down at her plate and twirled her fork on one prong, choreographing a delicate little ballet around the sausage. Sausage Lake.

"I think he was twenty-three," Avery said, nodding to herself. "Anyway, once he found out we were in high school, he was nice about it and backed off. But you could tell he was so into Mel."

As Mel sent her fork ballerina into a heroic leap over the pile of onions, she wondered what would happen if she slipped in a casual, "Actually, Avery's my girlfriend. She's incredibly hot, and I love her."

Avery just kept on going. "Then there was Patrick, this guy who kept coming into the restaurant to see Mel. He's a sophomore at Yale. I think he majors in microchemistry. So hot, but he just wasn't Mel's type."

Patrick was a mildly retarded dishwasher who spent his breaks playing games on an old PalmPilot. Even as she told this ridiculous lie, Avery's foot found Mel's under the table.

"Can I go to my room?" Lyla asked.

"Finish your hot dog, sweetie," her father admonished.

"I'm full."

"And what about you, Avery?" Mel's mom said. "Still playing piano?"

"Still playing piano," Avery replied.

"What are your plans for after graduation?"

"I'm thinking about applying to music school."

Mel raised her eyebrows. She hadn't known that.

"That's wonderful!" Mel's mother said.

"What would you do with that?" Jim asked in a clear "What? Don't you like money?" voice.

"I could play professionally," Avery said. "Or I could just become my parents' worst nightmare and live at home until I'm thirty-five."

Mel found this funny, but it ground conversation to a halt for a good minute or two.

"That's a new ring, Mel," her mother said, pointing to the silver band.

"Oh." Mel looked down at her index finger. A bolt of panic shot through her. "It's just from one of those people who sell stuff in the park in the summer. We just bought some when we were walking through."

Why was she explaining so much? All she had to do was say "yes." Instead she was giving the whole history of the ring. And why did she say "*we*?"

"I finished my hot dog," Lyla cut in, even though a good third of it was still on her plate.

"Why don't you try this seafood sausage that Dad made?" her mom offered. "It's like hot dog but seafood."

Lyla's expression indicated that this was not going to happen.

"Lyla's not a big seafood fan," Mel's mom explained to Avery.

"I guessed that," Avery said. Mel finally found the courage to glance over, just as Avery was sliding her hand under the table, where her ring couldn't be seen.

"I am so going to kill you," Mel said when they were safely out of the development and driving up the road.

"What?" Avery said, feigning offense.

"You gave me two boyfriends."

"*Potential interests.* Not boyfriends. I just gave you the greatest cover story in the history of the world."

"Maybe I don't want a cover story," Mel said. She smiled, trying to make the remark seem lighthearted, but she studied Avery's expression carefully. It didn't change at all.

"So, listen," Avery said. "Tomorrow . . ."

"Right." Mel nodded, moving back into her seat. "Tomorrow."

Tomorrow. When Nina returned.

"We have to decide, Mel," Avery said. "I don't think it's time to tell her."

"When will it be time?"

"Not when she steps off a plane. We haven't seen her since June."

"So why don't we get it out of the way?" Mel asked. "We can't lie to her."

"How do you think she's going to feel?"

"Fine," Mel said defensively. "Nina doesn't have a problem with this stuff."

"Nina doesn't have a problem *hypothetically.* Nina doesn't have a problem with *other people.*"

Mel bit down on her thumb for a minute.

They drove past school. The entire *tudents* part was gone and was replaced with a few hand-painted letters. It now read, WELCOME BACK ROBOTS.

"I have no idea who does that," Avery said. "But whoever it is is my hero."

Mel was still deep in thought. Avery glanced between her and the road.

"Mel?"

When she didn't answer, Avery turned the car unexpectedly and drove down to the wooded entrance to the Yaddo Gardens. Yaddo was a writers' colony—a big mansion surrounded by lots of ground that no one was allowed to go near unless they were invited. They let people come into a small part of the woods, though. It was a deeply secluded spot (when it wasn't loaded with amateur artists) with a creek and a tiny waterfall. Since it was early evening, the sun was deeply golden and rich, and it filtered through the trees and bounced off the surface of the water. No one was around.

Avery pulled off to the side of the thin gravel road. She got out, walked around to Mel's side, and opened Mel's door. She reached in and took Mel's legs, swinging them out, then sat on the ground. She put Mel's feet on her lap and kissed both of Mel's bare knees, going back and forth between them.

"It's not about us," Avery said. "It's completely about her. I mean, she has to leave this guy Steve, and then she'll have all the council stuff to deal with. I just think it's too much."

Mel was in a haze from the knee thing and could barely concentrate on what they were even talking about. It left her mind almost completely when Avery got on her knees and came right up to her face, pressing her forehead against Mel's.

"It'll be better this way. Trust me."

"I trust you."

Avery's lips were always slightly smoky, as was the upholstery of her car. It was a smell Mel reveled in as Avery leaned her back and they both stretched out across the front seat, their feet hanging free out of the open door. Somewhere in Mel's head, she knew these were the last moments of having Avery completely to herself. Even though she wanted Nina back, she was going to miss this time when it was just the two of them. This day, with the sound of the water and the sunlight and the breeze blowing gently into the car—this wasn't going to happen again. She knew she'd remember how Avery was laughing as she repeatedly bumped her head into the steering wheel (but she still stayed on that side to keep Mel from hitting her head—Avery was that kind of good girlfriend).

Tomorrow was still a long way away.

10

In Nina's head it was still only four in the afternoon, not seven, not time for dinner. It was already getting slightly dark out, and the dining room of the old Victorian hotel on Broadway was dim anyway—all candlelight and yellow wicker with black trim. A far cry from the dining hall, with the salad bar lettuce that was always just slightly frozen and the low-fat ranch that was usually contaminated with raspberry vinaigrette or peas or hard-boiled egg or whatever was positioned close by the dressings.

Beside her, Nina's mom was delicately eating her very rare tuna. On the other side of the table Avery tore into her chicken and Mel pushed a large mushroom back and forth across her plate. Avery's hair had grown a little—it hung about an inch below her earlobes now. Avery and Mel had almost nothing to say. In fact, only Nina and her mother were doing much talking. Nina heard herself say the words "so amazing" for what had to be the twenty-fifth time, and she had just finished up an extremely long and detailed description of her so amazing leadership class and her final project—a nine-month plan, totally overhauling the current student council activity program for the year.

She was only talking now to fill the void, to chase away the terrible feeling that seized her whenever she remembered that she wasn't going back to her building to see Steve after this. She would see Steve again in a year, if they both managed to get into Stanford.

A *year*.

It might as well have been that she'd see Steve on Mars once they both got into that new NASA program.

When her mother excused herself, Nina leaned over the table.

"So, what didn't you tell me?" she asked.

Glassy stares.

"About what?" Avery asked.

"This summer."

"What about it?"

"Was there anything you didn't tell me about?" Nina pressed. "Meet anybody?"

"Nope," Avery said. "It was a long, dry season."

"Mel? What are you holding out on me here?" Nina probed again.

Mel had abandoned the mushroom and was absently playing with a drop of water that had beaded on the tablecloth. When Nina said her name, she suddenly stopped.

"It was pretty boring," she said with a shrug.

"Oh."

It was hard for Nina to figure out where to go from there. Her summer had been anything but boring.

As she gazed at them over the bread basket and the water glasses that the waiter was constantly refilling until they were impossible to pick up, Nina had a strange thought. Maybe Avery and Mel were resentful that she didn't have to work, that her parents had flown her all the way across the country to go to a college program for the summer. This would never have even occurred to her before she met Steve, but now it seemed obvious. It was unfair that she didn't have to spend every day waiting on tables—and it was even more unfair that she'd have an advantage getting into a good school just because her parents had money.

It just brought her back to Steve. Steve had managed. He'd gotten a scholarship. It almost choked her up to think of how hard he worked, or how hard her friends worked, how hard her parents worked. . . .

She twisted her napkin into a knot under the table and tried to figure out if this wave of emotion was exhaustion or hormones.

"I got to see Mel sing and dance," Avery added. "We had lots of quality time."

These emotions had to be hormonal because they were shifting at every second. Now Nina was jealous. There were experiences Mel and Avery had had that she would never really get. And why? Because she was the spoiled one.

"Sounds hilarious," she said. She couldn't think of anything else to add, so she passed out the dessert menus. They spent a few minutes trying to figure out if they were sharing two chocolate fondues, or if Nina and Mel were getting the lemon cake and Avery was getting the blondie sundae.

"My ass is getting so wide," Avery mumbled. "Two airplane tickets wide."

"No, it isn't," Mel said. She actually seemed distressed.

"Yes, it is. I have to smoke more. Keep my appetite down."

Before Mel could answer back, Nina's mom returned, and the subject of Avery's smoking was dropped. Nina could tell, though, that Mel had been working on Avery all summer about that. Both Nina and Mel hated this new habit of Avery's, and Avery knew that. She'd probably said that deliberately just to get a rise out of both of them.

They picked the separate desserts, and the conversation switched over to student council—to the meeting Nina had to be at in the morning, to the speech she had to give on the first day of school, to the multitude of projects she would have to run. None of these things could have interested Mel or Avery much. They weren't interesting things unless you were the one doing them. But these were the kinds of things she was expected to talk about, and everyone listened. At least, they were quiet and they pretended to listen until the desserts came.

"Did you have a good summer at the restaurant?" her mom asked.

"It was educational," Avery said, spearing the lemon slice in her iced tea with her straw and forcing it to the bottom of her glass. "I learned how they make those fried onion blossoms. If that shows up on the SAT, I'm totally ready. The math is going to be bad, but I'm going to *nail* the appetizer section."

"Good to see nothing's changed," Nina's mom said with a laugh. Her mom always laughed at Avery's little comments. Avery had always been Avery—a little cranky, observant, wry. Avery was like that when she was *eight*, giving running monologues, entertaining the grown-ups. Mel had always been the sweet, shy one everyone said was cute. And Nina was the laugher, the talker, the planner. The loudest voice.

So why didn't she feel like it was the same? Why did she feel like she wasn't even here, like this wasn't her life?

Because she had a *life* with Steve. They had lived together, and done routine things together. They saw each other first thing in the morning in the hallway. (Sometimes they had their first kiss before Nina even had a chance to brush her teeth.) They'd meet up after Nina had her run and Steve had his morning ride, and they'd go to breakfast and microeconomics together. They sat side by side in class, and when it was over, they figured out when they would meet for dinner, since they had different afternoon schedules.

In the evening, they'd spend way too long at the dining hall with the other people from their floor. Steve would always watch Nina's big plastic cup, jumping up to refill it with water or diet soda whenever it got low. Someone would point this out and make a remark about it. These ranged from the nice comments about being the perfect couple, to the not entirely joking remarks about Steve being whipped, usually from one of the guys. (But he *wasn't* whipped. He was just unbelievably attentive. He was the best kind of abnormal, and those guys just didn't know how to take that. She always blew these remarks off, but they bothered her. She didn't like the idea that anyone thought she was ordering Steve around.)

Her soda was low now. And as obsessed as their waiter was with refilling their water, he didn't take the same interest in the other glasses.

Right about now, just as it was starting to get dark, they'd usually be having their nightly discussion about whose room they were going to work in. This depended on whether Steve's roommate

Mike or Strange Ashley were around. Sometimes they'd walk into town, to the place that sold both the regular and the soy ice cream, or they'd end up out in the hall, playing textbook hockey (a sport that was developed early on). Then there were the few, amazing nights when Ashley was gone and Steve had stayed with her. . . .

It was too much to think about. Nina stared at the lemon cake that had just been stuck in front of her and tried to look interested in Avery's story of how she'd managed to convince a couple of her customers that nachos were a genuine Irish food developed during the potato famine.

Everything was the same for Mel and Avery. They'd stayed here. They'd keep working during school, just switching their hours around. Nina was not the same, and she didn't know how to explain that Steve affected every part of her day, and that now she was away from him, she wasn't actually sure if she could breathe.

She took a moment and forced a deep, even breath from her abdomen. It didn't help. She took another.

"You in labor?" Avery asked, cocking an eyebrow.

Nina's mom paused with a spoonful of sorbet halfway to her mouth, obviously trying to figure out if jokes about pregnancy were funny or not.

"I'm just so happy to see you," Nina said, steadying herself and forcing a wry smile. "I can barely breathe."

"Yeah," Avery replied. "I have that effect."

11

Stickboy,

Back twelve hours and already busy. Everything feels off.

I just did the math, and guess what? If we arrive at Stanford this time next year, then we will be back together in 8,736 hours. I know that sounds like a lot, but I always feel better when I have exact figures and know what I'm up against. Besides, we can watch the number go down every day and feel a real sense of progress.

Do you know how much I miss you? No. You have no idea.

Neen

It was eleven o'clock in the morning. Nina's body was still on California time and she'd slept three hours later than normal. This left her with very little time to get ready, since she had to go to school for the first council meeting of the year. She had just enough time to take a quick shower (ah . . . privacy at last—that was a perk), throw on a sundress, and grab her keys.

It was a little creepy going into the quiet school. The air was hot and still. The secretaries were casually dressed in shorts and playing music in their offices, and some of the teachers were in their classrooms, pulling things out of cabinets. No one seemed to notice that Nina was walking around the halls, which were freshly polished and as glossy as decade-old linoleum could be. The lockers had been repainted in the same range of brown, putty, and salmon. The bathroom doors were propped open, and Nina could see that all of last year's damage was gone. All was white and sterilized.

"Bermudez!"

Okay. Someone noticed her.

Nina spun around and saw Georgia, the council secretary, heading for her. Georgia Barksdale was a large girl, both tall and broad, with chestnut-colored hair. Her family lived in and operated a bed-and-breakfast, so she'd grown up eating huge country breakfasts every morning at a grand Victorian table and collecting dried wood from the yard for the farmhouse's seven fireplaces. There was just something solid and warm about Georgia. She had been on the council from her freshman year. She seemed to know everyone in the school and was a walking, talking database.

"Sucks to be back, huh?" Georgia said, wrapping Nina in a huge hug. "You look great. How was California?"

"It was amazing," Nina said.

"Come on. Wakeman's waiting for us in the office."

"Tie?"

"Of course."

Nina had never known what to make of Devon Wakeman, her VP. For a start, he had worn a tie every single day since mid–sophomore year. At first people just thought that this was sarcastic fashion. But Devon pushed it further, past joke, statement, and quirk, taking it all the way to trademark. He was wearing one today—a nice maroon one with a gold stripe— even though it was hot.

"So," he said.

"So" was Devon's traditional greeting.

"Hi," Nina replied. She tried not to notice that he'd gotten a little better looking over the summer. He was the renaissance man of AHH: the reigning king of the photography lab, track and field star, coffeehouse guitarist, peer counselor, and vice-president of the AHH's National Honor Society. He was also physically distinctive, with his thick, wavy blond hair and long eyelashes. (Those eyelashes were *enviably* long, real eyebrow-sweepers. There wasn't a mascara in the world that could produce the Wakeman effect.) He had always managed to sweep elections, and he'd dated an entire cross-section of the AHH female population, from cheerleaders to the library volunteers. (None of his relationships lasted for more than a few weeks, so he also had the tragic romantic thing going on.)

Perhaps to offset the Wonderful Factor of all of the above, he also wore a permanent scowl—he constantly looked like he'd just been told that his car had been towed. For some reason (even though she was not one of the Wakeman exes), Nina felt like she and Devon had never gotten along. They'd never had an argument. It was nothing specific. He was one of the few people who really put Nina on her guard. She'd always tried to avoid him. Now she was going to see him constantly.

"Chocolate cheesecake muffins," Georgia said, pushing a box of baked goods at Nina. "Jeff's late. Shock. Amazement. I guess we should wait."

"I guess," Nina said. She had wanted to start the first meeting of the year on time (which set a good precedent, according to her instructor over the summer). Still, Jeff Burg was the treasurer, and it didn't seem right to start the meeting with him missing. Jeff's claim to fame was that he made piles of cash selling stuff online—making him Alexander Hamilton High's resident entrepreneurial genius. He was so famous for doing this, he'd actually been banned from bringing his laptop to school, since he used to spend most of his time monitoring his auctions. (He had what Avery called "fetal motherboard syndrome": he had to be touching some kind of online device at all times or he became skittish.)

For the next twenty minutes Georgia talked nonstop about a torrid affair she'd had with a handyman that her parents had hired and how they'd spent most of the month of July making sweet handyman love in the back cottage. (The whole thing sounded unlikely; then again, you never knew with Georgia.) Devon read his e-mail, but Nina knew that he was listening. It had to be hard to tune out this conversation. Nina noticed a slight shift that might have been a stifled laugh as Georgia described one encounter where she had to work around her lover man's tool belt.

Jeff chose this moment to finally come running through the door. His hair had grown a lot over the summer—it was almost down to his shoulders. He'd also dyed it a particularly bad shade of blond, Nina noticed. This might have been to cover up the fact that he was pale as a ghost and probably hadn't been in the sun for the last three months.

"Am I late?" he asked.

"What do you think, Burg?" Georgia threw open the three notebooks that she had spread out on the table in front of her and clapped. "Okay! Rundown of the year. September is freshman welcome week. October is homecoming and the hayride. November is the Thanksgiving food drive, the sophomore dance, and freshman rep elections. December is the toy and clothes drive and the holiday dance. January is nothing major. February is black history month and the Valentine's Day dance. March is women's history month and the junior prom. April is the senior prom. May is Senior Day, which the juniors will handle."

She took a breath and moved over to another book of notes.

"We'll have time- and stress-management workshops, suicide prevention skits, and college application preparation sessions. Coffeehouse is every other week. Each one needs a current event or specific topic for a theme. That's it, along with some other stuff. Nina talks now."

"Okay," Nina said slowly, taking out her final project from the summer ("Good Council: A Strategic Plan for Alexander Hamilton

High"), which she'd chopped down into meeting-friendly notes. "We'll start with the September activities. Freshman welcome week."

"Haze week," Jeff said, keeping one eye on his phone. He had made no attempt to hide the fact that he was somehow monitoring an auction.

"Right," Nina said. "I was thinking, though, that we could plan some other stuff. Have workshops every afternoon about different aspects of high school. How to study. How to handle peer pressure. Things like that."

"People are going to haze anyway," Devon said.

"That may be true," Nina said. "But if we held events that freshmen could go to, they'd be less likely to be targets. Plus we could give them some good advice."

"Everyone loves haze week, Neen," Georgia said. "Nobody's going to go to five days' worth of *workshops.*"

Jeff had totally detached himself from the conversation. Devon shifted around in his seat and pulled on his earlobe.

"What?" Nina asked.

"Nothing."

"If you have something to say, say it, or we won't get anywhere."

"This is student council. We're not the guidance department. We're not running classes."

"So we shouldn't try anything new?" Nina asked.

"We're already busy," Devon said. "Can we just get through what we have to? Maybe talk about extra stuff later?"

Jeff seemed very pleased by what he was looking at.

"What are you selling?" Devon asked.

"*Donnie Darko* promotional sticker I got off some guy in England."

Nina sighed.

"I'm listening," he said, correctly interpreting the noise.

"Okay," Nina said, "let's move on. . . ."

Despite what she'd been taught over the summer—that you could never judge a project by the tone of one meeting—Nina had the distinct feeling that running council was not going to be quite as she'd imagined it.

Nina came home that afternoon and put herself to work. She emptied her bags, finished the last load of wash, moved her fall clothes to a more prominent place in the closet. She cleaned her already-immaculate desk and restocked it with new school supplies for the year. These were normally some of her favorite activities, but they felt hollow.

She went downstairs and turned on the TiVo, flipping through all of the shows that it had saved for her in her absence. Days' worth of *Trading Spaces, Clean Sweep,* and *What Not to Wear* were waiting for her. These shows were Nina's way of rewarding herself—watching people rip down bad decorations, dump out contents of closets, cast aside bad clothes—these things soothed her. She never tired of them.

Except for today. She didn't feel the slightest twinge when the paint cans were dramatically opened and the room's new colors were revealed.

Maybe she was sick. She felt her head. It was cool.

Only 8,728 hours left until she saw Steve. She wondered if she should adjust that amount for the time difference. Maybe it was only 8,725 hours. It made no sense, but it was a small improvement, anyway.

She would never live that long. She might be able to make it to the end of the week, and then she'd be on her knees, begging for some of her dad's frequent-flyer miles.

"You've got that look," her mother said, glancing into the room. Today her mother had on a crisp yellow blouse, a white skirt, and a delicate pearl necklace. Since her home was her office, Nina's mom was always dressed up—this was a big part of the reason that Nina always dressed carefully, too. Her home wasn't like Avery's or Mel's, someplace where you could just do whatever you liked. Nina always had the lingering feeling that she was somehow on display. Like now. Apparently, she had *a look*.

"What look?" Nina asked.

"The 'I'm back from college' look. It's always a little strange at first."

"I felt like Mel and Avery were . . ." Nina searched her brain. ". . . mad or something. It doesn't make any sense."

"They're not mad," her mom said. "You've been away from your friends. They've been doing things here that you weren't a part of. You three have never been apart for that long. I went through it with my friends when I came back from school the first time. You need a girls' night. To catch up."

"They're at work," Nina said dully. "Besides, I have to finish getting my speech ready."

"You went right back to work this morning. You need to give yourself a break every once in a while, Nina. Trust me. I know. I've made that mistake before. I'm giving you the AmEx, and I'm telling you to go have some fun."

Her mom was probably right. Maybe she just needed to get up and put herself back in circulation.

12

Nina had never been to P. J. Mortimer's before. It sprang up in the middle of a shopping center parking lot, and it had opened while she was away. She sat in her SUV with the engine off and stared at it. The building was dark brick and had green awnings and seemed kind of sunless and prisonlike. Her own summer had been so academic and Californian, with the bay and palm trees and beautiful buildings—she'd never thought about the fact that her friends had spent most of their time cooped up. No wonder they had so little exciting news to report. It wasn't exactly a romantic hot spot. She would have hated to spend the summer at a place like this.

It was very dark inside. She approached a guy in a green shirt who was standing at the host stand. He didn't notice her at first because he was trying to assemble a little tower out of matchbooks and had already gotten up to the fifth level.

"Welcome to P. J. Mortimer's, where our Irish eyes are always smiling!" he said, his head jerking up as Nina approached. He was a tall guy with a young, smooth face—he looked like he only had to shave once or twice a week. Though his eyes were small and dark brown, they shone brightly.

"Can I talk with Mel and Avery?" she asked.

"Um . . . sure." He looked around, as if checking to see if he could leave his post.

"I don't want to bother you. . . ."

"No," he said, holding up his hand. "Hold on."

He opened up a cabinet behind him, hit a button, then quickly closed it and spun around. There was a strange winding noise, like the cranking of an oversized jack-in-the-box, then a heavy, pounding drumbeat. After a minute, somewhere in the depths of the restaurant, a piano started playing some kind of Irish tune. Then there was a ripple of sound, like someone running their finger down the keys, and the music stopped.

"I know who you are," he said, yelling slightly over the noise. "You're on the council, right? You're Nina."

Nina didn't want to yell, so she nodded back.

After a moment Avery came striding over. She wore a similar outfit, except her suspenders were laden with small pins, which Nina guessed were for various bands.

"What the hell?" Avery said angrily. "Nobody has a birthday."

He smiled innocently and knotted his hands together in a prayerlike fashion, setting them primly on the host stand.

"I hit it by accident," he said, straight-faced. "I was trying to get to the CD player. I thought it was skipping."

"Liar. I *will* get you, Park."

He nodded toward Nina. Avery turned around in surprise.

"Hey," Avery said, "we were going to call. . . ."

"We're going out," Nina said with enthusiasm. "My treat. You still off at nine?"

Normally the words *going out* and *my treat* practically caused Avery to break out in applause. Now she just pulled on her suspenders and gave a half smile.

"Yep. Only twenty minutes left," she said.

"Can you tell Mel?" Nina asked. "I can wait here until you're done."

"Sure."

Avery disappeared into the back, and the guy leaned over the stand.

"You've got very cool friends," he said.

Nina couldn't help but smile at that. It was true.

Mel came around a moment later and greeted Nina with a huge hug.

"This is Parker," Mel said, indicating the guy at the stand. Parker nodded and waved, then seemed to notice something going on back where the tables were. He disappeared into the restaurant.

"Can we bring him?" Mel asked quietly.

"Who? That guy?"

"He's off in a few minutes too," Mel said, nodding.

Nina was about to say that this was their night and that she wanted to spend time with her best friends, but there was an eagerness in Mel's eyes that told her there had to be a good reason for her to ask.

"Sure," she replied. "Great. Bring him."

Nina decided to wait outside for Mel, Avery, and Parker. Avery escaped first. She yanked off her green shirt to reveal a Ramones T-shirt underneath and pulled a pack of cigarettes from her apron pocket.

"I was hoping you'd quit," Nina said, stepping back. "I thought smoking was just an experiment."

"Those public service announcements don't lie," Avery said, lighting up. "It really is addictive. Don't start."

Nina looked through the front door to make sure the coast was clear, then she stepped a bit closer to Avery, trying to stay downwind of the smoke.

"What's going on?" she asked.

"With what?"

"With Mel and that guy? Or is it you? I thought you said there was nothing."

"Who, Parker?"

"Why did she ask him to come?"

"Oh . . ." Avery turned around and stared at the front door. "I didn't know she asked him."

"He's cute."

"Park? Park's great."

Avery was sucking so hard on her cigarette that Nina could actually hear it burning down with a little sizzling sound. She seemed a little edgy now. Before Nina could ask anything else, Mel and Parker joined them. Avery threw her cigarette to the ground and hurried over to her old blue Volvo.

"Meet you at the theater," she said, waving Mel in. Parker and Nina were left staring at each other.

"I guess I'll follow you," he said. "Unless you want to ride in the Roach."

"The Roach?"

Parker pointed to a corroded red VW Bug with a taped-up back window.

"Why do you call your car the Roach?"

"She will outlive us all," he explained, swinging his key ring around his finger. "In the end, it'll just be some rocks, Styrofoam, and my car."

"Right," Nina said. "I'll just take my car."

By the time Nina got to the theater, Avery had already chosen a movie for them and she and Mel were in line for snacks. Once they got these, they handed them over and she and Mel headed off for the bathroom. Nina and Parker were left behind again. This felt very odd to Nina, but Parker didn't seem to notice a thing. He simply suggested that they go into the theater to stake out their seats.

"You go to AHH?" Nina asked as they claimed part of a row. "I'm not sure if I've seen you around."

"I just moved here a year ago," he explained.

"From where?"

"Buffalo. My grandmother invented the wings."

"She did?" Nina asked.

"I wish. No. My grandma is the only grandma in the world

who can't cook. We eat at Arby's when we go to her house for Thanksgiving. We go to the nice Arby's, though."

"The nice Arby's?"

"There's this Arby's in her town that has a fireplace, and a waiter, and tablecloths, and real plates and silverware. But it doesn't cost more. It's just the really nice Arby's."

He seemed genuinely excited just thinking about it.

"So you were at Stanford, right?" he asked, picking through his tub of popcorn and plucking out the butter-soaked pieces. "That sounds like major advance planning."

"It was just a summer program."

"Still. It's, like, college. Which is, like, impressive. See. I didn't go. This is, like, what you sound like after a summer at Mortimer's."

He pushed his popcorn in Nina's direction, but she declined. She was a strictly Junior Mints kind of woman.

"So, what did you have to do there?" he asked. "Describe it. What's college like?"

"I guess the weird thing is, since you're not in class as much, I thought there'd be more time. You know—you think three hours of class is nothing. But it's *so much,* and it takes so much time afterward."

"Well," he said, plunging his hand deep into the popcorn, "I have this plan. I want to major in graphic art, to make cartoons and stuff. That way I can screw around and surf the Web and watch Cartoon Network for research. And it'll be totally legit."

"Do you draw?"

"I do computer animation," he said. "And other experimental art."

He cocked an eyebrow dramatically.

The room darkened, and the green screen for the first preview came up. Parker craned his neck back over his seat, then turned back around to Nina.

"Girls' bathrooms scare me," he said.

"Yeah," Nina agreed. "Where are they?"

She was pretty sure that Mel and Avery were powwowing over this whole Parker thing in the bathroom. She wished she'd been included in it somehow—or at least told what was going on.

They sat through four previews. The last one was for a movie about a renegade cop who thwarts a terrorist plot. Parker leaned over to Nina's ear.

"That looks *so good,*" he whispered. "A cop? Who breaks rules? And still gets the job done? And has an angry boss who yells at him? That's groundbreaking. No one's *ever* made a movie like that."

Nina giggled and shushed him.

"I mean, a cop!" Parker continued, dropping his voice lower. "Cops are the people who hold up the rules. So, if you have a *cop* who doesn't follow the *rules,* that's irony, right?"

The trailer ended with a huge explosion. Parker touched his heart and then rolled his eyes to the ceiling in ecstasy.

"*Irony* is the word that I forget the meaning of the minute after I look it up," he said as the green screen announcing the next preview came up. "But I kind of think I live in a constant state of it."

Mel and Avery finally rejoined them just as the theater intro rolled before the movie. They took the two seats at the end of the row. Parker accidentally formed a barrier between Nina and them. She thought about switching seats, but the movie started at that moment.

Nina spent most of the movie trying to figure out whether it was Mel or Avery who was interested in Parker. He acted a lot like Avery, but Avery didn't necessarily like guys who were like her. Mel, however, seemed to like people who acted like Avery—kind of snarky, lots of commentary. And there was something about the way that Parker had flashed glances at Mel as they'd been waiting in line for tickets that seemed to confirm the theory. It also made sense, now that Nina thought of it. Mel was shy and wouldn't mention any interest in Parker if there was preliminary flirtation going on.

By the time Nina had completed her analysis, the movie was a third of the way over and she really had no idea what was going on. It was a very Avery kind of movie anyway, so she just zoned out and waited for any kissing or good outfits. When it was over, Nina had every intention of heading out for some late-night ice cream, but Mel and Avery were very conspicuously yawning. Since she didn't work (and since she'd gotten up so late), Nina didn't feel like she could complain about cutting off their big reunion night at eleven-thirty.

"Shopping day tomorrow," Nina said. "Pick you up at ten?"

"Ten." Avery nodded.

"Shopping day?" Parker asked. "Do you guys do *everything* together?"

"Pretty much." Nina smiled. She noticed, however, that Mel and Avery didn't.

13

"Nocurnmufel."

"What?" Nina looked at the doughnut man.

"No corn muffins," he repeated, staring off into the middle distance.

"No corn muffins?" Nina stepped back and looked over the glass-domed case for visual proof. The corn muffin basket was empty. No corn muffin crumbs. They hadn't even baked any that day.

"Is there anything else that's fat-free?" She sighed.

"Apple, um . . . apple cinnamon?"

He sounded unsure.

"Never mind," she said. "I'll have the banana nut and an orange juice."

She took her juice and muffin over to a table and waited for Mel and Avery, who were on the other side of the food court. Nina pulled out her shopping list, the mall map, and a pen. There. At least Avery would be able to make her usual "Nina is an obsessive-compulsive" jokes. Finally they both came over with their cups.

"So," Nina said to Mel with a smile, "did Avery convert you to her evil caffeinated ways this summer?"

"No," Mel said. "It's tea."

"Tea?"

"Yeah. Tea," Mel replied, looking bashful. "I like tea."

"Botswana Blossom Red Tea," Avery said seriously. Mel elbowed her, and they both started to laugh. Nina smiled along, but she had no idea why that was funny. She was starting to wonder if she had that brain disorder that slowly scrambles the meaning of everyday words, so you start making crazy substitutions (like calling for your "telephone" when you want your "soup"), until you finally end up with your very own language that no one else can speak.

"Okay," Nina said, spreading the mall map on the table, "I think that I want to start at the Burberry store. Thoughts?"

"Plaid hats," Avery said, staring up at an enormous plastic pretzel that hung from the ceiling.

"They have more than just plaid hats," Nina replied.

"We could go to J. Crew," Mel suggested.

"Chino land," Avery mumbled.

"I like that store," Mel said. "I got that little blue tank top there."

"Which one? You're the *princess* of tank tops."

"The J. Crew store here doesn't do it for me," Nina said, taking a piece of the banana muffin. It tasted *wrong*. She had been so ready for the corn. "I really would like to go to Burberry, and it's just around the corner."

"I don't really want to go to Burberry." Avery sighed. "But I'll go to J. Crew with Mel."

"You guys want to . . . split up?"

"Just for the first store," Avery said. "Then we can meet up."

That was another first. They always shopped together.

"Sure . . ." Nina pushed the muffin aside and cracked open her orange juice. "So, do you guys want to get back together and look for shoes after that?"

"Sounds good," Avery said.

Once inside Burberry, the first thing Nina discovered was that Avery was right—the Burberry outlet seemed to be a wide vista of plaid hats and rack after rack of raincoats and trench coats. It looked like a secret-agent supply store. Mixed in with these were a few funky shirts that must not have thrilled the customers at the retail stores. The things she did like came in the usual outlet size range (sizes 0, 2, and 18) or were way too expensive, even by outlet standards.

Nina wandered in the direction of the J. Crew store to catch up with Mel and Avery a little early. She circled the tables and racks, making her way around a few clumps of unmoving, slack-jawed people who were contemplating the harvest of reject summer tank tops. She walked all the way around the shelves that lined the perimeter of the store, the Great Wall of Slightly Irregular Chinos. She poked her head back in the dressing room area but saw that only one was taken. She stepped back out to the sales floor and swiveled her head around again, searching one last time for the dark shock of Avery's hair or the orangey burst of Mel's.

Nothing. They were nowhere in sight.

A twinge of panic ran through Nina—an odd one that seemed weirdly reminiscent of the feeling she experienced when she was just a little girl and she lost sight of her mother in a crowded store.

"Can I help you?" A blond salesgirl in superlow khakis was at Nina's elbow.

"No." Nina shook her head distractedly. "No thanks."

"Do you need help with a size?"

A size? Nina stared at the girl.

"No," she replied steadily.

"Have you seen our sale on summer dresses?"

Maybe Nina really did have that word-substitution disease. She thought she was saying "no" but maybe what she was saying was, "I'd really like to troll through the dregs of your leftover summer crap. Would you be my guide?"

"I'm fine, thanks."

"Okay," the girl said uncertainly, "but I'd be happy to help you find anything you're looking for."

The salesgirl drifted away to adjust a pile of straw hats. Nina turned back to the dressing rooms to have one final look. As she did so, she heard a tiny peal of laughter from the one dressing room in the back. She moved closer and saw four feet at the bottom of the curtain. Two of the feet were in red Chucks, the other two were in Pumas. Definitely Avery and Mel. As she got closer, she could hear them moving around inside. They weren't talking, just mumbling some kind of approval.

Kind of weird, no doubt. Why they had chosen to share the room was beyond her; no one else was using any of the other compartments. She reached up and took a handful of the curtain. Gingerly she drew it back and peered inside.

In the first moment Nina thought Avery was helping Mel with a necklace. Then she realized that Mel wasn't wearing one. Also, putting on or removing a necklace doesn't usually involve putting your lips on someone else's. That's called kissing—and that's what Mel and Avery were doing.

They were kissing.

Kissing. As in kissing.

The real deal. Mel had Avery pressed into the corner. Her hands were on Avery's waist. Avery's hands were lost somewhere in Mel's hair. Full-on, serious making out. Nina got enough of a look to know that what she was seeing was real.

Nina froze, holding the curtain to the side. One of her atomic laughs almost bubbled up, but then it stopped somewhere in her throat and sank back down. Nowhere in Nina's arsenal of responses, replies, and reactions did she have anything for this. So she just stood there for a moment, trying to think of something neutral. Something you could say on any occasion at all.

"What's going on?" she asked. That was the best she could do. She meant it to sound cool, normal—but she heard a slight tremble in her tone.

Mel squealed just a bit, and Avery wheeled around to face Nina.

No one said anything for about a minute.

"Nothing," Avery finally said, stuffing her hands into her pockets. Mel just looked at Nina, met her square in the eye.

"Okay. I'll be out here when you're . . ."

She dropped the curtain and stepped back a few feet. Inside, Mel and Avery were mumbling and gathering up their things.

Nina sat down on a bench at the entrance of the dressing room, on a pile of discarded summer clearance dresses, the ones with the hideous patterns that no one will ever buy, even if they are marked down to $9.99.

Many things occurred to her at once.

One, this explained a lot of what she'd felt since she'd been back from California. The constant feeling of being out of the loop. The in-jokes she couldn't understand. Of course . . . Every bit of it made sense.

Two, *of course* they hadn't told her anything about the summer.

Three, they'd probably asked to go to another store *on purpose*. Now Nina was someone to be escaped from, like an annoying parent or a chaperone.

She could change that last one. She would show them, right now, in the first moments of discovery, just how fine she was with it. Because she was. She wasn't homophobic. Homophobic—did that term apply only to lesbians and gay men? No, it had to apply to bisexuals as well. Were they bisexual, or were they lesbians? Should she ask? Did it matter? It wasn't supposed to matter. Better not to ask.

Had they been joking?

Maybe this was a long setup for a prank. It didn't look like a joke. But then, wasn't that the sign of a well-executed joke? It looked so real. . . .

No. That *was* real. And they still hadn't come out.

Come out. Very funny.

"Um," a voice said, "you can't sit *there*."

Nina looked up. It was the salesgirl again.

"Why not?" Nina asked.

"You can't sit there," the girl repeated.

"Why?"

"Um, that's the clothes bench?"

Nina saw an empty rack not four feet away.

"What about that? That's a *rack*. It's for clothes."

"You can't sit here, *okay?*" the girl said, adjusting her pants on her nonexistent hips. "You're going to have to move, *okay?*"

With a sigh, Nina gave up the bench and slid down in front of the trifold mirror, the dressing room's one luxury item. The salesgirl flounced away with a snort.

To Nina's horror, she found that her eyes were tearing up and there was a heaving sigh building deep in her solar plexus—all part of a prelude to a sob, which she couldn't release here or now. Not in front of Mel, or Avery, and certainly not in front of that thing that had just tossed her off the clearance bench. Not under the fluorescent lights of the dressing room. Not sitting on the floor of an outlet mall, with all the discarded numbers and tags and crap.

She clamped it down and closed her eyes.

"We'll be right out," Mel called through the curtain.

"Okay!" Nina called back cheerfully. "I'm just going to wait outside."

Nina stepped back into the store. Everything had a strange pallor—the pinks and oranges and yellows were so garish they seemed to vibrate. The bins of excess flip-flops and sun hats had a sad significance that she couldn't quite pinpoint, and she was sure people were deliberately choking up the aisles so that she couldn't get back out into the main concourse.

She forced her way out and sat on a bench in front of the store. She looked up at the fronds of a huge potted plant. Celine Dion screeched about love over the sound system.

It took Mel and Avery almost five minutes to emerge. Mel came right to Nina. Avery hung a few steps back.

"I'm sorry," Mel said softly. "We were going to tell you. We were just trying to find a good time."

Nina knew this was the moment she was supposed to say something wonderful. This was when she lived up to her beliefs in equality, her conviction that homosexuality was completely normal and wonderful. Except—she couldn't seem to speak. "I need to get some air," she managed to say.

Nina was in a trance now. She got up and went back the way she had come, past Burberry, back through the maze of tables and people buying food in the food court, to the set of doors that led to the parking lot where they'd left her car just forty-five minutes before. It felt like her head was plugged up with something cottony that muffled the noises of the other conversations, the music, the mall. She stepped outside into the muggy afternoon.

The first thing she did was stretch a smile across her face. It took a great deal of effort.

Of course it was okay. She had no problems with this stuff. She was planning on having the council do stuff with the gay-straight alliance. She had no issues with this at all. So, she'd been surprised. That was okay. They'd understand that. The surprise would wear off. She just needed to turn around and show them it was all going to be fine.

Her knees were a little wobbly. She laughed at nothing in particular and turned to go back inside.

Nina guessed correctly that Mel and Avery would be waiting for her in the food court near the Orange Julius. She had a kind of natural GPS when it came to the Triangle. She fixed a smile on her face and sat down with them. They'd both gotten drinks and had one sitting and waiting for her.

"I was surprised," she said. "Sorry."

Possibly the understatement of a lifetime.

They sucked on Orange Juliuses for a minute. No one seemed to know where to start.

"So," Nina said, "how long have you . . . ?"

She left the definition open.

"Since July," Mel replied. "July Fourth."

"July Fourth?"

Nina slowly counted back in her mind, even though she knew that July Fourth was almost two months ago. She needed this time to be shorter—a week, maybe two, something passing. But it was about the same amount of time that she'd spent with Steve, and in her mind, that meant that the whole thing had been set in cement.

"How did this start?" Nina said.

"It just kind of happened," Avery said.

"But you never said—I mean, you've both dated guys. I know that doesn't matter. I mean, I know things can happen, but . . . you never said anything about girls."

"I knew," Mel said, shredding a napkin. "It was in my mind, but I didn't know if it was real. Then one day, I just knew it was."

Nina looked to Avery, but Avery just watched Mel destroy the napkin.

"Oh," Nina said. "Well, it's great that you've come out. . . ."

"We haven't told anyone," Avery said. There was something in her tone that told Nina that they didn't want her to say anything either.

"Or whatever," Nina added quickly. "That you know. I don't want you guys to act differently around me. Don't feel like you can't do things because I'm there."

This was a lie. Nina knew deep down that if she saw another one of those kisses right now, she was pretty sure she would have to be medicated.

"It won't change anything," Mel said. "It's really not that different."

Nina was pretty sure this wasn't true either, but she appreciated Mel's saying it anyway. She started talking quickly. She tried to spit out all the things she knew she believed—that it was wonderful, that it was all going to be fine, that they could be honest with her. It was like she was reading verbatim from a brochure called "My Friends Are Gay! Now What?"

Talking fast helped. It was just like swallowing cough syrup. Don't avoid it—just do it. Gulp it all. Mel was nodding away, agreeing with everything, but Avery seemed lost, her brow furrowed.

"So, should we keep shopping?" Nina said, as brightly as she could.

They made the rounds again, but it soon became obvious that no one was actually going to buy anything. They were just dragging themselves from store to store, sticking tightly together, as if trying to prevent anything bad from happening again. The only thing Nina could think about was that she was walking along with a couple. Mel and Avery were a *couple*. They gave up after a half hour, and Nina dropped them both at Mel's house.

Nina raced up to her room the second she got home. She needed Steve. She tried calling, but no one picked up. She turned on her computer and opened up an e-mail.

Steve,

Where to start?

I don't even know where to begin.

Okay. Inhale, then exhale.

I'm going to say a lot really fast because I'm still kind of shaking.

Since I've been home, Mel and Avery have been a little weird. I know why now. We went out shopping today, and they asked to split up. I found them in the dressing room of a store when they weren't expecting me, and they were kissing. Like really, really deeply kissing. We sat down and talked and Mel said she had kind of known for a long time that she was attracted to girls but didn't really know what to do about it. (I guess she figured it out.) Avery didn't really say anything except that no one else knows and that they want to keep it a secret.

What were the chances that both of my best friends would be gay?

This was a good point. After all, didn't that say something about her? And she was part of a *triangle*. Hello!

She was so gay.

No, she wasn't. She had a boyfriend. She was writing to him now to get advice about her gay friends.

A boyfriend who lived three thousand miles away. How convenient! Unconsciously she had been setting herself up for this all along because she must have known that deep down, she was *a total and complete lesbian,* part of a lifelong lesbian trio.

Focus.

She had to put her head down against the edge of her desk and count backward from twenty and then again from twenty-five before she could continue typing.

I know there's nothing to do, and I really am okay with it in the sense that I don't think there's anything wrong with it. But I'm totally in shock and I need help and please can you call me or IM me or something as soon as you get this because school starts tomorrow and I am pretty sure that I will burst some kind of v. important blood vessel in my head between now and then. I don't mean to sound selfish, but I am starting my job tomorrow as president of the council and I have to give a speech in front of the entire school. I was fine with that until about two hours ago, and now—

A speech she still had to polish. She still kept screwing up that one part.

I am a mess. Cannot Dr. Phil this one away. Need help. I'll be here, trying to learn this speech and probably just pacing around.

God, I wish you were here. I miss you so much I seriously can't stand it, and there is no way that I will actually survive until next September, or the summer, or whenever. I need to be there with you NOW, or you have to come here. We have to do something.

Anyway, please, please, please get in touch with me.

—Nina

Nina sent the note.

She had no idea what to do now. Normally when she was stressed, she called Mel and Avery. She would have to fall back on her secondary activity—organizing. She got up and tore into her closet, pulling down everything, emptying boxes, dumping out containers of papers and photos. She piled clothes by season, shoes by color. She fixed her attention on anything that could be sorted or filed or repacked. There were at least a dozen more important things she needed to do, but they would all have to wait. Everything was going to have to wait.

A few hours later, as Nina was creating labels for an expanding file of papers and notes she'd saved for the last three years, she heard the tiny *pong* she had been waiting for.

Neen,

Sorry it took me so long. I was camping with some people from school. It rained and about twelve of us ended up in the one tent that stayed up. It leaked. We all slept in about a half inch of water. I probably caught the flu. Or gangrene.

So, I wish I had been here instead when you wrote, for lots of reasons.

I don't want to say that I know exactly what you're going through, but I definitely know this feeling of surprise and confusion. I remember when I found out that my friend Paul (the guy in the picture who was on the tire swing—the one who looked kind of like he was going to crash into the tree and die) had kissed another guy. I remember having no idea what to think at first. Granted, I was fourteen at the time and didn't know what I thought about a lot of stuff. I even thought I had to be gay if I had gay friends. I thought he was going to want to kiss me too. So much stuff was running through my head.

I barely even notice it now. It seems like at least a quarter of my school is openly gay, and I kind of assume that another quarter is probably gay. Maybe more than that. In fact, I feel like one of the only really straight people I know. (Believe it or not, where I come from, I'm really conventional and even seem kind of Republican or something.)

But I know this has got to be hard. Call me later tonight, around eleven your time, and I promise I will be here waiting.

Love, Steve

Nina read those last two words over and over.

14

Mr. Zimm only had one lung. Everybody knew this. No one knew how they knew it, because obviously no one could check, and no one had ever gone up and asked, "Hey, Zimm? One lung or two?" But there was something in the way that he held on to the middle of sentences, turned just slightly purple, and leaned against his desk that screamed *one lung.*

The rest of this apocryphal tale was that he lost the lung after being stabbed in the chest with a broadsword during a medieval battle reenactment. There were confirmed sightings of him buying chain mail at the Renaissance Faire, which seemed to give this story some credence. It was probably bullshit, but most people wanted to believe it, so most people did. What else was there to think about a forty-year-old single guy with a snowy white beard who obsessed over the English library and displayed his own decorative dragon bookends on his desk? Since he was also a notorious droner, there were always bets going that one day he would just try to keep talking and would die right in the middle of some interminable explanation of "what Tolkien was *really* trying to accomplish."

Mel liked Mr. Zimm, mostly because he was familiar. He was the only teacher she'd had every single year. This was especially comforting on the first day of school since there was always something foreign and spooky about seeing everyone in their new clothes with their tans and their three-month backlog of stories. It was alarming to know that the rules for this year had yet to be established. Everything on those first days mattered a lot, like where you sat, and what you did over the summer, and how much weight you lost or gained, or who you saw.

It wasn't like Mel could tell anyone what she'd been doing (or really, who). So having one class where she could kick back and completely slip out of focus was a good thing. She got there early to make sure she got her favorite seat—right in the middle of the room. Not too far back (Zimm watched those people), not too close (Zimm was a spitter).

Doug and Jean, the school's gothic lovers, came in together and took two empty seats next to Mel. Jean was a tiny girl with a small head, which was crowned with several pounds of flowing ink black hair (obviously dyed) with a white skunk streak cutting through it. She wore a long burgundy-colored dress, black boots, and a spiked dog collar. Doug was a very tall, hulking guy with the same unnaturally black colored hair and a sharp widow's peak. He wore a black cowboy-style shirt and black pants.

Just as the bell rang, Parker came into the room. He took the very last seat, which was in the front row, dead center.

"This is English four," Zimm began. "I am Mr. Zimm. We're going to be covering British liter—oh no." He stopped short and pointed to Doug and Jean. "We've gone through this before. Doug, move over a seat. Melanie, you sit where Doug was."

Mel took her place between the couple. They gazed at her as if this was her fault. She shrank down a little.

"We'll primarily be covering English literature this year. We'll be reading two Shakespeare plays. . . ."

Someone dropped their bag in the back of the room and mumbled, "Oh, shit." A pen slid by Mel's foot.

". . . along with some Charles Dickens, Jane Austen, Wordsworth, a bit of *Beowulf,* a section of *The Lord of the Rings: The Fellowship of the Ring,* which we'll compare against a scene from the movie. . . ."

Parker turned and smiled at Mel.

"In the spring we'll be covering how to write a college term paper, so as you read throughout the year, you might want to think about which book you'll be writing on and maybe begin keeping a list of potential topics. Okay, first let me go over, once again, how to check books out of the English lab library. . . ."

Doug and Jean communed with each other by exchanging penetrating glances over Mel's head. Mel checked out of the room completely and started going back over the schedules. She already knew Avery's by heart. They had nothing together because Avery took Spanish and had two weird music classes that made her schedule very strange. If Mel was lucky and timed it just right, she would be able to catch a minute with Avery in the hall between sixth and seventh periods.

She flipped through her English textbook. Zimm had apparently purchased a whole crate full of copies of *The Hobbit* from England and proudly explained the cover art right up until the time the bell rang. Parker lingered.

"Gotta love Zimm," he said. "And now, assembly. Makes doing the jig seem a lot less painful, huh?"

Mel and Parker headed to the auditorium together, stopping at Mel's locker, where Nina was waiting.

"Ready for your big speech?" Mel asked with a smile, expecting a return grin from her ever-confident friend.

But Nina's anxiety-lined expression didn't change. She leaned into Mel and spoke quietly into her ear. "I think you can see through this blouse," she whispered. "I don't know what the hell I was thinking when I got dressed. With the lights it's going to be like, hey, check out my—" She cut herself off and leaned against Mel's locker, absently touching the buns on either side of her head. "I shouldn't have done the Leia buns today," she said lamely. "This isn't a freaking Star Wars convention. Oh my God . . ."

Mel was still back on the thing about the blouse. Nina's comments about her hair were totally ridiculous because she *always* wore her hair that way. Nina had changed topics because she didn't want to say that her blouse was see-through in front of Mel. What was even worse was that it *was* kind of see-through. Mel directed her eyes down at the floor. There was no way she wanted Nina to catch her staring deeply into her chest, even if it had been Nina's idea for Mel to look in the first place.

"The buns are good," Parker said. "It would have been even

cooler if you'd made a video recording of yourself and then projected it out of a little robot. You'd totally sew up the geek vote. But I guess you don't need a vote because . . . everybody voted. Which is why you're doing this. Feel free to jump in anytime. . . ."

"I have to go," Nina said. She pressed her bag into Mel's arms. "Keep this for me?"

Mel nodded and clutched the bag tight to her own chest, as if covering herself could somehow make up for this whole mess.

"I could have said that she should have done the Leia-in-the-bikini thing," Parker said with a smile as Nina hurried down the hall. "But I'm a sensitive guy. I hate it when girls beat me up in public."

Mel smiled weakly. She didn't want to talk any more about Nina's chest or bikinis or anything like that.

"Why do you look like you're going to puke?" he asked.

"I'm nervous for her," Mel lied.

They were pushed into the crowd by the door. No one was making any kind of an effort to stream the mass of people into a line. Mel and Parker just got caught in the crush. Parker leaned down to Mel.

"Want to know a big secret about me?" he said in a low voice.

"Okay," Mel said warily.

"Sometimes . . . when I'm all alone in the house . . . or when everyone's asleep . . . I drink Tabasco, right out of the bottle. I just open the fridge and I see that little red bottle and I just *get thirsty.*"

He flashed Mel a grin, and she loosened her grip on Nina's bag just a bit.

"Big secret," he said as the clog by the door gave way and they were jettisoned into the darkened auditorium. "Tell anyone and I'll have to . . . um, zero-tolerance threat omitted, but you know what I'm saying."

He gave her a light bump with his elbow. Parker just had a way—things were a little bit more bearable with him around.

She'd only been in school for three hours, and already Avery had noticed several things that seemed to indicate how the year was going to go.

Omen #1: She got a basement locker. Seniors were never supposed to get basement lockers. For some reason, though, everyone with a last name from *Cl* to *E* had a locker at the bottom of the fire stairs. Nina, a *B*, was up by the front lobby. The *F*'s, including Mel, were right outside their homeroom. Avery, of course, was the odd woman out—the one who would need a passport and a visa to get to her stuff.

Omen #2: Here she was at the first lunch of the year, and they were already serving the peas and carrots—with *tacos*. No one ate the peas and carrots to begin with, but to serve them with tacos was nothing short of a slap in the face.

It wasn't just the poor menu planning that bothered her; it was the ridges in the carrots. Was it supposed to be fancy? Was there a chef somewhere with a special knife and a pile of carrots mumbling under his breath, "For you, students, I will cut ridges . . ."? And if he cared so much, why did he allow them to be so ridiculously overcooked to the point of mush?

What made things worse was the fact that the tray she'd pulled from the stack (still hot, still moist) was one of those runt trays—the ones that popped up every twenty-fifth tray or so and weren't gray or orange like the others. They were red and noticeably smaller and thinner. Getting one of these was a bad sign.

She pushed along and accepted a soft-shell taco, declined the peas and carrots, discovered that her fork had a seriously bent prong, and considered omen #3—the fact that she had just returned from an assembly where one of her best friends was the main speaker. She couldn't just make fun of assembly now. Or the dances. Or the spirited bulletin boards, or the fund-raisers, or the idiotic coffeehouses where people sat around in the student lounge in their spare time, drinking donated Starbucks and discussing things like "fairness" and "diversity." Making fun of those would be making fun of Nina, so Avery was now tied to the establishment, forced to keep a straight face and pretend like all of this stuff was important—like the council was actually some serious organization that might someday end up commemorated with its very own library or dollar coin.

It couldn't be forgotten that life with Nina as she had always known it was over. Nina had been nice about what she'd seen—meaning that she hadn't actually started screaming and crying or tearing out her hair—but there was a nervousness in the way she spoke. Not that Avery could blame her. The fact that she and Mel were together changed things, whether they wanted things to change or not. Mel never seemed ready to accept that fact, but Avery had known it all along.

Omen #4 was that Gaz and Hareth were sitting in the back of the cafeteria, which was why she was walking in that direction. They would obviously be her lunch companions for the year, which meant she would hear all about the exploits of Angry Maxwell.

But all of the above were overridden by omen #5—the little piece of triangularly folded paper that she had slid carefully into the front pocket of her jeans. It was a note, folded in the classic Triangle style, left for her by Mel. (She was, of course, using Mel's locker as her own from now on. That went without saying. She wasn't going to set foot in the basement if she could help it.)

It just said: *You are beautiful.*

Avery tapped her thumb ring against the edge of her red tray. She passed a table that had a few of the school's deeply uncloseted students sitting around it, and it occurred to her that she could sit there now. She could sit with Jen Habett, the classic short hair, jeans, and pride chain girl. Or Felicia Clark, the outspoken "If you have a pulse, I'm interested" bisexual sex addict. Or Montgomery Allen, the geek-chic chick with the two male first names, who gave off an "everyone knows I'm a lesbian, but I'm not saying anything unless you ask me" vibe. They were part of a pretty tight group, which included a lot of guys whom Avery didn't even know. Still, she was pretty sure that they'd take her in. Felicia would, anyway.

But Avery wasn't looking for solidarity. In fact, she liked keeping her relationship with Mel a complete secret. She wanted to be the only one who knew what it was like to be with Mel—to be able to look at her and know that Mel was all hers, and she was all Mel's, and no one else with all their posturing had *any idea* what that meant.

Well, Nina knew. About the relationship, at least. That hadn't gone well. The whole event had replayed itself in Avery's mind endlessly the entire night. But at least it was done.

Avery suddenly became aware of the runt tray and the peas and carrots and the locker and the assembly all over again.

Nina knew.

15

Early decision.

These were the two words that Nina focused on now—the two words that would realign her life. Early decision would set her future in motion and get her closer to Steve. She'd have to take her SATs right away and have her applications out the door by the first of November. She'd be blindingly busy right until December, which she figured was just about the right amount of time to get her head around all the things that were going on. If she had her head in her laptop, she figured, she wouldn't even notice if Mel and Avery decided to make out in front of her.

Not that she'd really seen them. There'd been no time. Between school, homework, and council, the only other extracurricular activities Nina could fit into her schedule were eating and sleeping.

In fact, all of her classes turned out to be more work than she had anticipated, but one was killing her—AP U.S. history, which was a legendary class at AHH, mostly because Dr. Evangeline Frost was the instructor. Her reputation was so frightening that only eight people out of the eligible twenty opted to take the class.

Dr. Frost was a rogue, with a huge mass of tightly curled,

overly frosted hair that rose up high and wide and made her head look like a lightbulb. She had sharp, clear blue eyes and wore wool crepe suits with very short skirts. (Nina believed she was trying to showcase her runner's legs, which were thin and rock solid and, strangely, tanner than the rest of her body.) She came to AHH only to teach the AP history class and could be seen peeling in and out of the parking lot in her little blue Mini Cooper right before and right afterward. She seemed like someone who constantly lived her life as if she were in the middle of a divorce.

For the first few days she'd toyed with Michelle Path, the fragile, 4.2 GPA hyperglycemic. Michelle spilled her saline by the end of the first day of class, when Frost commented that Michelle's note-taking habits were "definitely good enough to get her into one of the better technical schools." Michelle had eventually cracked completely and had to excuse herself, never to return to the class.

Frost went right down the row from there. Susan Yee got it for three days straight and started digging scratch marks into her leg with her nails. Frost spent a few days working on Devon Wakeman, but she didn't make a lot of headway.

On Friday afternoon Nina was scribbling a weekend to-do list in the margin of her notebook.

"Nina." Frost said her name abruptly, kind of like a shriek: *NEE! nuh.*

Nina's head jolted up.

"You look busy," Frost said. "Taking notes. That's good."

Frost sat on the edge of her desk, exposing more runner's leg than Nina felt like seeing.

"Give me some of the highlights of the Great Awakening," Frost said.

Nina glanced down at what she'd been writing: *Sat. A.M.: w/Georgia to look at catering hall for prom. Sun. P.M.: help with coffeehouse. SAT vocab lists 20 through 35, first draft of personal statements, card to Steve.*

The rest was just some vines and squiggly lines she had drawn up and down the margins.

Busted. Two minutes out of her entire academic career. Busted.

"Better yet," Frost said, "why don't you do something for me this weekend? I'd like a rundown of all the biographies of Benjamin Franklin published since 1900. Just a list and a few comments on any that have come out since 1990. I'd like that on Monday."

It was so unfair—but there was no way she was going to show Frost that. Her recommendation requests would be going out within the week.

"Okay," Nina said, as if this was completely normal. "No problem."

She wrote it down, even as her hand shook a bit. Out of the corner of her eye she noticed that Devon was watching her reaction closely. She held it steady. She didn't smile or look defiant. She wrote, and then she looked Frost right in the eye with complete composure.

To Nina's amazement, Devon smiled, just a bit.

▲   ▼   ▲

Later that night Nina was staring at the wrinkled, half-smiling face of Benjamin Franklin. He looked back at her from a Web site called Our Ben. He seemed to be gently chastising her for the fact that all she'd really done all night was clamp a bunch of multicolored binder clips into her hair and then amuse herself with the noise they made when she shook her head.

She just wanted to talk to Steve. She knew by now that he never got home until six since he tutored after school and then took an hour-long bike ride. So the earliest she could call him was nine, and even then she usually had to try several times because his line was always busy. (Not only did Steve not have a cell phone, his family didn't even have call waiting. Because it wasn't enough that Steve had to live on the *other side of the continent.*)

She got lucky on the first try tonight. He sounded a little winded, as if he had just come through the door.

"I can't talk for long," he said apologetically. "I'm supposed to be somewhere in half an hour."

"Where are you going?"

"We're having this dance thing," he said. "It's a fund-raiser."

"Oh." She heard her voice lift just a bit.

She would never join the race of bad, clingy, evil girlfriends who didn't want their boyfriends to go places without them, especially places like dances. She was the trusting, mature kind of girlfriend who didn't mind at all if her boyfriend went to a dance. It was *fine,* because they were both active, committed people who had to go to all kinds of events.

"I have to go to it," he said, as if he had heard her thoughts.

"Oh, I know! I'm going out too." A lie, but necessary to make herself sound a little less dependent and pathetic. A lie that would *help their relationship.* "Mel and Avery and I are going out."

"How's that going?" he asked.

"I don't know." Nina rolled onto her back and sighed. "I've only gone out with them twice since then, and we didn't talk about it. At all."

Nina heard a loud noise in the background at Steve's house—the sound of many people arriving and talking all at once.

"Uh, hold on. . . ." Steve must have put his hand over the phone. Everything was muffled. She heard him saying that he'd be ready in a minute. It was hard to listen to. She would have given anything to be one of those people—to be in Steve's house. To be able to come in anytime she wanted and see the mold and the jam and the crazy hippies and in the middle of it all, Steve. Steve—who was responsible, who cleaned and took care of people and had zillions of friends and who understood everything.

"They're here," he said apologetically. "I kind of have to—"

"I know."

"Olive juice? Oh, wait. I can say it now. I love you."

Nina sat up so quickly that the binder clips in her hair clanked loudly against the phone, and she let out a little "yah!" sound in surprise.

"Okay . . ." he said.

"I love you too."

She could have happily spent the rest of the night saying that back and forth, but Steve took it as a goodbye. When he hung up the phone, Nina felt herself stop breathing for a minute and consciously had to tell herself to start up again. She stared at her bamboo blinds and the dark outside. She heard the quiet whir of her computer.

Benjamin Franklin or no Benjamin Franklin, she had to get out of here.

When Nina arrived at P. J. Mortimer's, Mel was standing near the front with Parker. He appeared to be doing some kind of puppet play for her, making little bunny gestures. Mel was laughing hysterically. Nina watched the two of them for a minute from the safety of the takeout order station. Her theory was holding up—at least on Parker's end. He was working hard. It was almost a shame. He clearly had no idea that this was going nowhere. It would be merciful if she interrupted them. And while she was at it, she should probably try to show Mel how comfortable she was around her.

Nina walked up quickly, startling both Mel and Parker. She put her keys down on the stand, then looped her arm through Mel's and pulled her off to the side.

"I had to get out," she said. "I was going nuts. Want to do a movie at my house tonight? I can run and get it now."

Mel threw a helpless glance at an antique print of a horse jumping over a fence.

"It can be Disney," Nina said. "We can beat Avery down."

"It's not that . . ." Mel said.

"What is it?"

"It's just, we were going to . . . spend time. You know."

Nina felt a huge pressure drop in her stomach. This was not a "we" that included her—this was a private "we." They needed time. *That* kind of time.

"How about tomorrow night?" Mel asked.

Nina had to talk herself through this one as well. It made perfect sense that they would need some time alone. Every couple needed that. It was fair, and Nina was going to be fair. She had promised them that much.

"Are you sure?" she heard herself asking.

Or not.

Suddenly having her friends with her tonight was the most important thing in the world to Nina. Tomorrow night, next weekend, the rest of her life—none of it mattered. Survival meant the next few hours with Mel and Avery.

"I guess," Mel said. Her face was twisting into all kinds of agonized spasms. "But tomorrow, you know, we could have the whole night. We could grab dinner and then get movies. . . ."

Mel was clearly trying to balance out some delicate equation that Nina wasn't even aware of. Someone called Mel's name from the direction of the dining room, and Mel signaled for Nina to stay put.

Nina was not going to cry here in the foyer of a family restaurant. She was *not*.

"I'll be right back," Mel said. "I just have to grab this check."

Mel went back into the restaurant. Parker looked down and

started playing with Nina's bright disco ball key ring on the stand.

"My inner raccoon likes the shiny thing," he said while looking apologetic, as if he hadn't meant to witness this awkward conversation—not that he could have understood its real meaning.

"I guess Mel's going out with her boyfriend?" he asked, nonchalantly passing the keys back to Nina.

"She doesn't have a boyfriend."

"Oh."

He couldn't quite disguise his relief or the fact that he clearly pitied Nina. After all, she had just been abandoned by her best friends on a Friday night.

"I was thinking about going to The Grind after work," he said. "Getting all wound up on caffeine. Playing me some board games. It makes everybody sad when I sit there and play Candyland by myself. Want to come?"

"I think I might just go home."

"They have Jenga! Everyone loves Jenga. Jenga, Jenga, Jenga."

Parker's friendliness only made Nina feel weirder. Now she just wanted to go home, put on her pajamas, and curl up in her bed. Cocoon. Watch TV. Block everything out. Besides, he probably just wanted to pump her for information about Mel—information she couldn't give.

"No," she said. "That's okay."

He was staring at her strangely now. She felt a burning in her eyes. They were probably getting red. She didn't feel like having part two of this conversation with Mel. The outcome was going to be the same: She wasn't invited tonight.

"Can you just tell them I had to go?" she asked.

"No problem."

Nina smiled at him and turned away quickly. She just managed to get out of Mortimer's before she lost the battle to the tears.

Homecoming

October 3
TO: Steve
FROM: Nina
Steve,

I wish I could say that things are improving and I'm taking this well and I'm learning and growing, because I'm not. That's crap. I hate this. I hate feeling like I'm always intruding on my friends. This is MEL AND AVERY! I am SUPPOSED to be with them. But they kind of shift around and look at each other with love eyes and I end up saying I have to go home, which I always do anyway since I have NO LIFE and NO TIME and my AP history teacher HATES ME and I'm not done with my applications and I have to raise my SAT verbal by at LEAST 30 more points.

This whole early decision thing is a lot more evil than I thought it would be.

I want my friends to be happy, but I also want my old life back.

I feel like some big homophobe for complaining about Mel and Avery. That makes it even worse. And I'm not. At least, I don't think I am.

You're the only person I can even tell about this.

Help,

Neen

October 4
TO: Nina
FROM: Steve
Neen,

I went to this thing at my friend's house after I got your note. It was just people sitting around smoking a lot of weed, and I don't smoke, so I just watched people get stoned and changed the CDs.

Anyway, a few lesbians that I know were there, so I went over and explained your situation. Most of them were pretty mad on your behalf because they thought Mel and Avery should have told you instead of making out at the mall. The girls here thought they were trying to get caught, which in their opinion was really lame. So, the lesbians of Portland are totally with you.

And, of course, I am with you. I talk about you all the time. It's kind of good to talk to the stoned people because they let me go on forever and they never notice that I've been talking for an hour. They just smile and say, "Awesome." The girls thought you sounded really hot, which you are. They all seemed jealous of me.

You should come out here. You have fans.

On another note, this may not be the time to tell you I am thinking about working with this program to save the tree kangaroo in Papua New Guinea.

October 5
TO: Steve
FROM: Nina
S,

OMFG! What are you talking about? Kangaroos in trees? Going where? For how long? V.v. freaked out . . .

I don't want to be the reason these kangaroos die off or anything, but life without Steve unthinkable. UNTHINKABLE. CERTAIN DEATH. V.v.v.v.v.v.v.v.v. bad for Nina.

October 5
TO: Nina
FROM: Steve
Nina,

Just something I was thinking about. I'd miss you too much, though. Don't worry.

Love from here to there.

16

There was a fenced-off area behind the cafeteria where delivery trucks came to unload food (or whatever it was that they made lunch out of). It was called the pen. It wasn't a very pretty spot—just an offshoot of the parking lot butting up against a concrete wall with a single door and vent. This was where Avery and Mel met every day after school. There were about a hundred better places to meet, but Avery liked the pen the best. Even though they weren't doing anything there that required privacy, Avery still liked the fact that it was their place.

The pen was also where the grounds crew piled the mountains of leaves they blew out of the administrators' parking spaces and the path. These piles were like the Alps of Saratoga. They were supported by the cyclone fence and completely obscured the view of the road. These were the perfect leaves—the ones that hadn't gotten wet or started to decay. Some were still fresh and soft, in gold and orange and red. There were enough dry ones to make the right crunching noise.

Mel was there, gazing up in awe at the trees. She almost blended into the pile, with her orange hair and brown hoodie.

As Avery approached, Mel tossed herself backward into the leaves.

"Congratulations," Avery said with a smirk. "You're eight years old."

Mel reached forward and grabbed Avery by the front of her jeans and tossed her lightly into the spot next to her, where she landed face-first and coughed unappreciatively.

"Smells nice, huh?" Mel grinned, grabbing a handful and throwing it at Avery.

"You are *so* going down."

Avery managed to get up and cover Mel with a blanket of leaves within about two seconds. Unable to shake them all free, Mel did the more appealing thing—she just grabbed Avery again and pulled her down on top of her. She felt Avery resist for just a second—they were outside the school, after all. For a minute Avery really didn't care. All that mattered was that she was sinking deeper into the pile with Mel under her.

"Okay . . ." Avery said, extracting herself. She glanced around to see if anyone could have spotted them, but there was no one in sight.

"Where are you going now?" Mel said, pulling herself out of the pile.

"Home. I have to practice."

"Can I come?"

This was a new thing of Mel's. Avery would normally drop Mel off, but now whenever Avery said she had to practice, Mel wanted to come and be her audience. The attention was nice, Avery supposed, even if it was a little weird to have someone staring at her back while she worked. Piano practice didn't exactly make for fun listening unless, of course, you *liked* hearing the same two or three bars of a piece of music played over and over again.

"Don't you get bored?" Avery asked.

"Nope." Mel grinned.

"Then you're weird."

"If you say so."

"Okay, weirdo," Avery said. "Come on."

The house was mysteriously quiet when Mel and Avery arrived. This was never a good sign.

As Avery went to sit down at the piano, she jumped back in alarm as a tinny version of "Take Me to the River" assaulted her from the suddenly animated mouth of a mechanical fish. Laughter from the direction of the stairs. Running feet.

"Your brothers are so cute." Mel laughed.

"Uh-huh," Avery growled. She reached up and popped the batteries out of the Big Mouth Billy Bass that sat on top of the piano and shoved them into her pocket. Billy Bass was her greatest enemy, but she couldn't convince her parents to part with it. They thought it was *hilarious.* Avery plucked out his batteries every time he came on and blamed the theft on her brothers.

She sat down on the bench and closed her eyes for a moment. That fish always put her in a mood.

"Did you get your application yet?" Mel asked.

"For?"

"Music school."

This was not a topic that Avery liked to discuss. There was nothing Avery wanted more in the world than to go to music school, but just the thought of applying terrified her.

"Which ones are you going to apply to?" Mel asked. "Have you decided?"

"Not yet."

"But you're applying to ones in New York, right?"

"I guess so," Avery said mindlessly, setting her fingers in position for her C scale. "I don't know yet."

"But you want to go to New York, right?"

"I'm going to get started, okay, Mel?"

No answer. Pages flipping.

Running through her scales took twenty minutes, and she wanted to keep her concentration. She liked to put some mental energy into them, even though they were automatic. Once she was finished, she set her task for the night on the music stand. The piece she was working on was Prokofiev's Piano Concerto no. 3. She'd been avoiding work on this for over a week. Two bars were tripping her up and driving her crazy—she couldn't seem to get through them, no matter how hard she tried. Today she had to crack them.

Behind her she could hear Mel gently clearing her throat.

Page one was fairly painless. She reached up and flipped to the second page, down the third. . . . The beginning, she had. It was coming, though. There they were, the dreaded two bars with her teacher's notes scrawled between them in tiny spider print.

And . . . she did it again.

Wrong. *Wrong, wrong, wrong.* She wanted to kick the piano right in the guts, stomp on the pedals until they snapped off. The fact that she had someone staring at her became unbearable.

"Mel," she said, turning around on the bench, "would you mind if I took you home?"

"What?" Mel said, looking up from her statistics book.

"Can I take you home?"

"Why?" Mel asked, while clearly trying to quell her quivering lower lip.

"Because I really need to work."

"I'll be quiet."

"You're already being quiet," Avery said gently. "I just need to be by myself and do some work on this."

"What's the matter?"

"There's nothing the *matter*," Avery said as a sudden edge came into her voice.

"Then why do you want to take me home?"

Avery groaned out loud and put her hands over her face. Mel got up and came toward her. Avery stiffened. She didn't want her shoulders rubbed, or her hand held, or her arm touched. She wanted to get these two bars right.

"Mel, please," Avery said.

"Are you mad at me?" Mel asked. She started blinking rapidly, and Avery could tell that she was on the verge of tears. "I can sit upstairs."

Now she really wanted Mel to go, and since this was her house, she could get stubborn about it and force the issue. But that would only cause a big argument, and her brothers would probably hear. It just wasn't worth it. And that annoyed Avery even more. She felt trapped.

"Fine," she said. "Sit upstairs."

Mel didn't say anything as she gathered her things, but Avery could tell from the way Mel avoided looking at her that she was hurt. She probably even wanted Avery to feel guilty about sending her away.

When Mel was gone, Avery sat for a moment with her eyes closed and tried to collect herself to start again. But she was anxious and annoyed now, and there was no way she'd get through the piece. She'd just have to go back and work on the material she already had down.

"How can I go to music school if you don't let me practice?" Avery muttered under her breath.

Instead of starting again, she kept her eyes closed and sat there, soaking up the quiet as if it were sunlight.

17

Essay #2: Write a note to your future roommate. Describe an experience or a person that has had a special influence on your life. Do not exceed 300 words.

Nina sat in her living room and looked over her list of possible candidates.

<u>*Mom and Dad.*</u> *Pros: Good to say that m&d inspire, very touching. Also, biracial relationship shows built-in diversity. Cons: Cheesy to say that m&d inspire. Seems like I have no one else to write about. Exploitation of parents' brave and romantic biracial relationship for essay purposes could seem cheap and obvious and make admissions people hate me.*

<u>*Steve.*</u> *Pros: Want to write about Steve. Cons: Admissions committee will think I am insane and boyfriend-obsessed and will do no work, spend entire time in school planning wedding and monitoring b-friend's every move.*

<u>*Mel and Avery.*</u> *Pros: Want to write about them. Also, probably truest answer. Cons: Admissions people may not be interested in the story of how we used to buy coordinated underwear and wear it on the same schedule as a*

*joke, which for some reason is the only thing I can think of
right now.*

*Gandhi. Pros: Who isn't inspired by Gandhi? Cons: Know
almost nothing about Gandhi except that he was a good man
who worked for peace but wore almost no clothes.*

Nina groaned out loud and put her hand over her eyes.
Everyone else applying for early decision was going to ace this
one. They would all have pithy, unbelievable experiences to
describe. "My six months in the rain forest made me who I am
today. . . ." "As a professional ballerina, I have always been accus-
tomed to discipline. . . ." "My friend Maggie is 106 years old, yet
she seems younger than me. . . ."

It was probably a good thing that Nina heard a car door shutting in her driveway and looked out her window to see Avery
heading for her front door.

She set her laptop down on the couch next to her and got up
to let Avery in. Avery dropped heavily onto the chair-and-a-half
and jutted her legs out straight in front of her. She examined her
red Chucks for a moment with a dissatisfied expression. Nina
waited for her to say something, but Avery had nothing to offer
but a view of the soles of her shoes.

"Something up?" Nina finally said.

"No."

Avery puckered her lips and exhaled deeply. Nina glanced
over at her computer and wondered if she should pick it up and
keep working. She poked at the keyboard to keep it awake and
looked at the hopeless fragments of her essays.

"I know Mel likes to cheer people on, but sometimes it's kind of too much," Avery managed to blurt. "She's always asking me about applying to music school."

"It just sounds like Mel is being Mel," Nina replied nonchalantly.

"It's different now," Avery argued.

"How?"

"Well, the reason she's asking me about music school in New York is because she wants to know where I'll be living."

"That's not weird," Nina said. "*I* want to know where you'll be living."

"Yeah, but you just want to know. I think Mel is making her plans based on where I'm going to be."

Nina felt a strange pang of jealousy at this.

"How do you know that?"

"I can just tell," Avery stated with a sense of authority that only a girlfriend would have. "It's the way she asks."

"How does she ask?"

"Remember how Spaz always used to message you to find out where you were going to be, and it was just kind of creepy?" Avery asked.

Spaz was Avery's nickname for Mark, a guy Nina dated for two weeks in sophomore year. He texted Nina all day long and used to freak out if she didn't reply right away.

"Mel's not like Spaz," Nina said.

"No, but she's kind of getting there. And the other thing is, when I practice, she always wants to be there. Which is kind of fine, but then she interrupts me."

"She talks?"

"No, I mean she wants to . . . do things."

The obvious fill-in was that Mel wanted Avery to stop for snuggle time, and as much as Nina wanted to be open and accepting, she didn't really like picturing Mel's attempts at seducing Avery away from the piano. She had her limits.

"What are you working on?" Avery whimpered, shyly playing with a thin, thready patch that was developing in the knee of her jeans.

"Admissions essays."

"Right." Avery exhaled deeply. "I forgot you have all this stuff going on."

The thought of admissions essays visibly depressed Avery.

"I should let you finish," she said.

"You should stay," Nina said. "I'm just working. We have ice cream. You want some?"

"I'm good."

Avery sat for a few more minutes, saying nothing. Nina put her computer back on her lap. It was scorching hot on the bottom, so she layered a few of her mother's law journals under it. Nina wanted to talk more, but she had no idea what to say. If she got any deeper in this, she wasn't sure she could really handle the details.

"You want to watch TV?" Nina offered.

"No." Avery fished around in her pockets. "I'm going to head out."

Nina didn't try to stop her this time.

She already had a very clear snapshot in her head of Mel and Avery making out, but now she saw a different angle of it. It wasn't like they just kissed and that was it. They had a relationship. They noticed things about each other. They probably even dressed up for each other, just like she would dress up to get Steve's attention. They read into each other's signals, and they probably marked little anniversaries. Their relationship was a hundred times more complicated than the plain old Triangle stuff.

She shook her head, blinked, and focused back on the screen.

Stanford. Early decision. That was her goal. She couldn't change what was happening with Mel and Avery, but she could make sure that she would spend the next four years with Steve. This was a long, shaky bridge, and she just had to cross it.

She sighed and highlighted the word *Gandhi.*

18

On Sunday afternoon Avery and Mel were walking through a cold early October rain. They'd wanted to get coffee at The Grind, but it was packed with people. So now they were stuck on the street without a destination, their clothes slowly growing heavy and wet in the mist.

Mel gently bumped her hand into Avery's. They'd come to this compromise early on—instead of hand-holding in public, they could hand-bump. It was their secret signal, and at first Avery had loved it. Now she stuck her hand in the pocket of her wine-colored leather jacket. Mel could see that she was playing with the hole in her pocket—the one that caused her to leave a trail of cigarettes, lighters, change, and balled-up pieces of gum behind her.

"It's too nasty to walk," Avery said, shivering.

"Want to go to Borders?"

"I guess."

When in doubt, wander the bookstore. Always the same pattern. Avery would go right to the music section, slap on some broken, flaking headphones, and start punching in album codes. Mel would drift around, look at the calendars, reread *Olivia*.

"Okay," Avery said, already looking bored. "Meet you in a few at the coffee bar."

Mel watched Avery hurry off. She stood by the front table and looked down at the shiny new releases without a great deal of interest. She never knew what to do once she got in here anymore. There were only so many times she could look at blank journals or racks of books she didn't really want to read. Rather than giving her music lessons, Avery seemed to want to spend her time checking out new records on her own.

Mel began her aimless wandering. Jazz was playing. This was music she knew she was supposed to like, but it always sounded so dull and annoying to her, the notes buzzing around in her head like trapped flies.

There was one section she'd never gone near: the gay and lesbian corner. It filled up two of the wall bookcases, and there was a huge green sign over the shelf. It was fairly public, as it was over by the wide cookbook nook. That was probably why she had stayed away before. Today, though, she was feeling a bit more courageous. The store wasn't very crowded. She should at least be able to go over and *stand* by the books.

Mel walked over and surveyed the offerings from a distance of a few feet.

It was like she had just discovered a candy store in her own basement.

Here was everything she ever hoped to know. Books on dating. There were a few books of correspondence between famous lesbians that looked like literature books. There was half a shelf of lesbian erotica. Though she wanted to look, she felt like if her hand came into contact with any of them, alarms would start going off, a huge spotlight would fix on her, and pink triangle confetti would be released from the ceiling.

She reached out anyway. She started randomly pulling things off the shelf and skimming the pages. It was strangely liberating, standing in the corner of the bookstore reading a gay and lesbian travel guide to Istanbul.

"Hey," came a voice behind her. She turned to see Avery, holding her ground on the edge of International Cooking and Dietary Concerns. Avery looked at Mel and then at the books. "Come listen to something," she said.

"What?" Mel said innocently. Normally she gave in when Avery got nervous that they were doing something too obvious. Today she was determined not to move. She was only reading, after all. It wasn't like they were making out against the *Harry Potter* display.

"Come on," Avery said, more insistently this time.

"I'm reading."

"Well, don't."

"Calm down, Ave."

"I *am* calm," Avery said in a low voice.

"Couples counseling works."

They turned to see Devon Wakeman, wearing his signature tie under a heavy hooded sweatshirt. He had just turned the corner of the aisle.

The remark probably didn't even mean anything, but neither Avery nor Mel replied. Avery, in fact, was staring at Devon with a look of horror, like he had just crawled out from under her bed wearing a hockey mask. Mel took refuge in her normal rabbitlike defense tactic: when confronted, stand still and believe that you blend into the surroundings.

Devon looked at each of their faces, then at the shelf, then at the book that Mel's hand was still resting on. A thought bubble practically appeared over his head, showing the equation that was quickly drawn, checked, and confirmed.

"So," he said, leaning back against the local interest shelf. "What are you guys doing?"

"What do you normally do in a bookstore?" Avery said.

Devon held up his hands, as if to say that he was only making conversation.

"Gay and lesbian studies," he said, nodding. "That's cool. What are you guys working on?"

"Something for English," Mel mumbled.

"Oh."

The conversation fell dead to the ground. Devon had no reason to stay, anyway. He had all the information he'd ever need about them.

"See you guys around," he said.

The moment he was gone, Avery turned and left the store. Mel shoved the book back on the shelf haphazardly and followed her. By the time Mel got out the door, Avery had cut across traffic and was on the other side of the road. Out of the corner of her eye Mel noticed Devon and two other guys conferring. They glanced over in her direction and watched Mel's pursuit.

Mel caught up with Avery on the opposite side, just as she was about to turn the corner and storm down Philadelphia Avenue, probably on her way home.

"Wait up!"

Avery stopped but didn't turn. She patted her pockets down nervously, searching for her cigarettes.

"Why did you have to do that?" Avery said as Mel caught up to her. Now that she'd found the cigarettes, she was struggling with her lighter in the misting rain. "Why couldn't you just leave it alone?"

"All I did was stand by some books," Mel said.

"You didn't stand by *some* books."

"I'm not allowed to read?" Mel's voice got embarrassingly high when she got angry.

"Well, now Devon thinks I'm gay," Avery shot back.

"It's fine. Who even cares?"

"Mel . . ." Avery's voice cracked, and she almost laughed. She managed to light her cigarette, and she held it tight between her teeth as she squeezed her face with both hands.

"It's hard," Mel said calmly. "I know. It's kind of weird when people know."

"Weird?" Avery said, a note of slight hysteria coming into her voice. "It's not weird. It's *beyond* weird."

"What do you mean?"

"I'm not gay," Avery said, sticking her free hand into her pocket.

"Ave—"

"I'm not gay." Avery said it again, very clearly and sternly.

"Okay," Mel said, trying to be conciliatory. "You're bi."

"Stop trying to tell me what I am!" Avery snapped.

Mel stepped back in shock. She could understand that Avery might not feel comfortable being labeled gay—Mel still had trouble with this sometimes—but being bi wasn't exactly something she could deny.

"This isn't the same as other people," Avery went on. "The bi girls, they go back and forth. We're just . . . together."

"So?"

"It's more serious with us. We act like lesbians. Real ones."

Avery was shaking her head as she spoke, as if the concept of "real lesbians" wasn't something she could quite comprehend.

"I am a real one," Mel said. "But you can be whatever you want. I don't care. It doesn't matter."

"Yes, it does."

"Why?" Mel's voice was high again, but this time out of a rising panic. "You're the one who always says that labels are stupid."

Avery took a long drag on her cigarette. She started running her hands over her face again, over her eyebrows, along her nose, up her cheekbones—like she was trying to rub her own face off.

"I'm just going to walk home," she finally said, putting her car keys in Mel's hand.

Mel watched Avery walk away. Her shoulders hunched against the rain as she walked down the sloping street and then around the corner. It wasn't until Avery was out of sight that Mel realized that she was cold, wet, and strangely alone, right in the middle of town.

19

On Monday morning Devon came into the council office and said, "So."

Except he didn't just say, "So." He said, "Soooooooooo." It lasted for about three minutes.

Nina looked up from the sheets of elaborate pumpkin-shaped tickets she'd designed for the hayride. (Oh, they had laughed when she was a kid, but years of watching Martha Stewart were finally paying off.) Devon sat down at the table across from her and looked down at her little pumpkin patch.

"I didn't know your friends were gay," he said. "How long have they been dating?"

Before Nina could even react, Georgia came into the room. She threw down a box of muffins, extras from the buffet her parents put out every morning.

"Who's gay?" she said. "What did I miss?"

Devon was playing it very close to the chest now. He took a muffin, tore off a chunk of the top, and popped it into his mouth, eyeing Nina all the while. Georgia looked to Nina for her explanation.

"Come on," she said. "I had a shitty morning. A big branch fell on my car. It dented the trunk. Tell me something good."

"I don't know," Nina said. It came out clumsily. "Devon was just talking. . . ."

"About who?"

"I think he's joking or something," Nina said, narrowing her focus to her pumpkins. Even as she spoke, though, she knew that this was a bad thing to say. The "think" and the "or something" implied uncertainty. Or worse yet, they seemed to confirm what he was saying. Unless she flat-out lied, everything out of her mouth was suspect.

From the look in his eye, though, Nina knew that Devon had already gotten the confirmation he wanted.

"What?" Georgia said. "Aren't you going to tell me?"

"I have to go to the photo lab," Devon said, getting up.

"Well?" Georgia prompted as Devon left the room.

"I don't want to say who it was," Nina said.

Georgia's eyes went wide.

"Why not?"

Because if Georgia knew, somehow, that information would spread. She just had that effect. Rumors lived in her blood cells. She was the universal Patient Zero of AHH, spreading information through her touch and her very breath.

"I can't," Nina said.

Nina could almost hear the file drawer in Georgia's mind opening, ready to receive the knowledge. She would find out somehow.

"What's with you and Tieboy?" Georgia asked. "With the secrets and the pictures?"

"Pictures?"

"Didn't you see it?" Georgia asked.

"See what?" Nina said warily. She wasn't in the mood for another surprise.

"The picture."

"What picture?"

"Come on."

Georgia waved Nina out into the hall, just a few steps down from the photography lab, where Devon was working. She pointed into a glass case.

"There," Georgia said.

There was a collection of pictures of body parts—an earful of studs, a bare foot, the back of a guy's neck, a hand. A hand with long fingers with several chunky rings on them and, farther up the wrist, the shadow of a white bracelet. It was Nina's hand.

Georgia was gaping at her wide-eyed, as if to say, "Well?" Nina pushed her along back in the direction of the office.

"He's taking pictures of you," Georgia said.

"Of my hand."

"Still."

"Boyfriend. Got one."

"In *Portland*. Tell me who's gay."

"Georgia . . ." Nina sighed. "I have to go to class. See you later."

▲   ▼   ▲

Doug and Jean were intensely interested in Mel today. All the mental vibes were directed onto her, not through her. Mel stared down at Doug's massive black cowboy boots with the white stitching and tried not to notice.

Maybe she was imagining it. She was very tired, and everything was a little foggy. She'd sat up half the night, wondering what Avery meant by "not gay" and looking at Web sites about bisexuality and sexual identity, trying to get some kind of understanding of what Avery was trying to say to her. She spent hours reading about femmes and butches and transgendered people, bouncing from page to page, topic to topic. In the end her mind was so muddled that she couldn't remember what it was she'd been trying to find out in the first place. What little sleep she got, she'd spent dreaming about those little bouncing icons people put next to their mood and current music selection in their blogs.

Parker was tapping a rhythm into the back of his head with a pen. Zimm was attempting to explain essay structure by drawing an upside-down triangle, a square, and a right-sided triangle on the board. Everything was fuzzing out. Mel reached up and unleashed her ponytail in preparation for making a hair shield to close her eyes behind.

"It's like a top," Zimm was saying as he pointed to the upside-down triangle. "The weight of the introduction rests on this one point, the topic sentence. The weight of the entire essay really rests there. You can put a lot on one point. Medieval scholars used to debate about how many angels could dance on the head of a pin."

Mel scrawled the picture into her notes and wrote, *Everything here. Angels.* She hadn't really been listening and didn't know what the *angels* part was supposed to mean. It sounded meaningful, though.

"Am I completely losing it, or was Vampire Douglas sniffing your head?" Parker asked the second they walked out of class.

"Sniffing my head?"

"It looked like he was leaning into you. I thought he was going to bite your skull."

As they walked down the hall, one of the guys she'd seen talking to Devon passed by. He looked at Mel and smiled. Parker noticed this as well. He didn't say anything about it, but he swung around and watched the guy as they walked in opposite directions.

They stopped at Mel's locker. It took her a moment to remember the combination. She shook her head, trying to get her mind back on track.

"Is there something really weird happening today?" Parker asked. "A full moon, perhaps?"

Instead of facing out toward the hall and giving a mumbled running commentary on the people who passed by like he normally did, Parker turned in and faced her. He didn't exactly box her in, but the exhaustion was hitting her again, and everything felt close.

"Is everything okay?" he asked.

"Huh?" Mel backed up a step.

"You seem a little out of it."

"I didn't get much sleep," she said.

She could tell he didn't believe her, but he didn't press the issue.

Avery was nic-fitting right now, in the middle of lunch. But the school rules prohibited anyone from leaving during the lunch period, so there was nowhere for her to go for a cigarette. She drummed her fingers on the table and ignored her tuna fish sandwich.

Gaz and Hareth, her lunch companions, were oblivious to this. At the moment they were preoccupied by the loss of Angry Maxwell's bass player, Margo. She had stormed out of Gaz's basement the night before, citing some specific issues with Hareth's rhyming style and the general "suckitude" of the band.

"If I'm rhyming," Hareth was saying, "I need a heavy beat under me, you know, to hold me up. We have to stay together, you know? Behind the rhyme. And if I'm rhyming . . ."

"It wasn't you," Gaz said as he sucked down a long swig of soda and rolled his upper lip toward his nose in thought.

"That's what I'm saying. I'm rhyming for all of us. And the beat has to stay with me. So if I move, the beat has to follow me. The beat's gotta be like *on my ass* the whole time. I need it that tight. And Go wanted her own beat, and you can't have that."

"It wasn't you," Gaz said again. "It was Go."

"You can give him a strong drumbeat," Avery said.

"I'm not the drummer anymore," Gaz said. "I've been playing lead guitar since Mike went to Mass Distraction."

"When did that happen?"

"About a week ago."

"What the hell are you going to do without a drummer?"

"Freelance," Hareth said knowingly.

Avery didn't even pretend she knew what this meant. Hareth had his own language.

"I found this keyboard in my garage," Gaz said. "I think it was Phil's. He played with us last year, and then he moved. Want to play it?"

Avery thought this over. It probably wouldn't hurt to join a group—even a really bad group like Angry Maxwell. Then again, she would probably end up beating Gaz and Hareth over the head with the keyboard. They were nice guys, but they weren't very technically proficient. "I'm getting a Kit Kat," she said, wanting to buy herself a few minutes to think this over.

She got up and walked to the back of the cafeteria, where the machines were. The school had blocked the use of the soda machines during the day in an attempt to make it look like they were part of the fight against obesity, but the candy and chips were, thankfully, still available. Avery dug around in her pocket for a few coins and dropped them into the machine.

And then she heard it. It was soft and indistinct, but she heard it.

"Dyke."

Avery froze. If she turned to see who'd spoken, she would implicate herself. Better not to associate herself with the term. Pretend like she didn't even know that it could be her that this person was talking about. She steadied her hand and hit the code for the Kit Kat. B2. The coil that held the Kit Kat started to rotate back to free the package.

". . . such a dyke."

Still just a little over a whisper. It was coming from behind her, from the direction of the soda machine.

The Kit Kat landed with a thud. As she bent down to reach for it, she turned her head just slightly to see who was talking. Two girls were leaning against the wall on the other side of the soda machine, deep in conversation about something. Avery only knew one of them. Her name was Alicia. She sat in front of Avery in geometry when they were sophomores. She had long, straw-colored hair that always reeked of really expensive-smelling hair care products.

As she passed them on her way back to her table, their conversation got just a tiny bit quieter, and there was a sliver of a pause during which Avery knew that they were both examining her reaction. She kept her gaze forward, as if she hadn't heard anything at all, and made sure not to increase her pace. She was instantly paranoid, sure that eyes were following her as she wove between the tables. *Everyone* knew.

Hareth was beating out a rhythm on the table when she returned.

"Mixing with this, mixing with that, Avery got a Kit . . . Kat." He stopped and turned to Gaz. "See?"

"Right," Gaz said. "You have to break there or else it makes no sense."

"Exactly."

Alicia and the other girl silently passed the table, never once turning back to glance at Avery. Once they got to their table, though, they bent their heads together again, and Alicia threw a quick look over her shoulder.

Now Avery's brain was moving quickly, filling with unformed thoughts. She looked down at herself. Jeans, a grungy vintage T-shirt for some plumbing company, heavy shoes, and a leather cuff bracelet. She could feel her cropped hair brushing against the back of her neck. The only makeup she had on was some dark liner around her eyes. Why didn't she just put on an I'm Not Gay, But My Girlfriend Is shirt and get it over with?

No one would call Mel a dyke. Mel wore pink shirts and cute little necklaces, and she had all of that long, orangey hair that was always whipped into some adorable arrangement. She hated Mel's cuteness at that moment. Hated that Mel had been so stubborn in the bookstore. Mel had nothing to worry about. Only Avery would be seen as the rough dyke who lusted after the cheerleaders and couldn't be trusted in the locker room after gym. Other girls would put their books up over their boobs when they passed her in the hall, and they'd stop fixing their makeup when she walked into the bathroom. They would see her as a predator trying to sneak a peek or cop a feel, even if she just bumped into them in the doorway or as she squeezed in between rows of desks.

"What do you think?" Gaz said, interrupting Avery's psychological meltdown.

"Oh . . . yeah."

She couldn't recall exactly what it was that Gaz had requested. Something about a keyboard. It didn't matter. Now she just wanted to be seen with some guys. She would need to stick close to these two.

"Right . . ." Gaz said, smiling.

Alicia and her friend turned away, but Avery knew she was going to be under observation from now on, like some kind of mutant organism trapped on a slide.

Halloween

October 29

TO: Steve

FROM: Nina

So, tomorrow night is one of the big events at AHH—the annual hayroll, which is run by the council, which basically means me. It's a hayride at one of the local farms. You know, get in the truck, ride around the woods, people in costumes go "boo."

Here's a little background so that you can feel totally in the know about My Life and the Stuff I Have to Do:

1. It's called the hayroll because people are supposed to try to lose their virginity on it, like it's supposed to be a hot farm sex fest. This is a total lie, because everyone's squished into the trucks together and there is no privacy at all. (Also, hay? Ouch.) This is an extra-big deal because if you leave our school a virgin, the bust of Alexander Hamilton in the front lobby is supposed to speak your name on graduation day.

2. The school actually seems to believe in this hayroll crap, because the teachers always make sure the reproductive system lessons come up in health class right beforehand.

3. Someone always throws up on one of the trucks—usually the one I'm on. Since I'm not taking the ride this year, it probably won't happen. Plus it's always crazy cold and I can't even wear two pairs of gloves this year because I have to count money and rip tickets.

Sorry. I usually sound a lot more enthusiastic. I think this is just one of those times when you feel extra far away because everyone's going to be talking hot farm sex all night. Also, if you're a couple at AHH, you have to go to the hayroll as a date, which means that Mel and Avery will be there together, probably talking h.f.s. too.

Okay. Here's something really weird. The more I try to just get used to the Mel and Avery thing, the more I keep . . . picturing them. It's not on purpose. I'm just trying to force the idea into my brain that they're a couple and it's all fine, then suddenly I've got an episode of "The L Word" going on in my head and I have to run downstairs and watch decorating shows until it washes away.

I may not live through this weekend. Remember, if I die, I love you, and you can have my Apple notebook and my label maker.

October 29
TO: Nina
FROM: Steve

This is one of those times I wish I was there (okay, which is always). I can handle hay. I am rugged and outdoorsy.

At my school it's Samhain time. Beltane is supposed to be the big sex holiday, but here every holiday is an excuse for sweet pagan love. I don't usually have to picture it because it all happens right in front of me. I'm that guy everyone feels comfortable around. It's like, "Steve won't mind if we have sex here on the coffee table. He's totally down with the Goddess." And it's not that I care, it's just that you're really far away, so I have to concentrate on things like how to get more people to reuse their plastic shopping bags and not my INCREDIBLY GORGEOUS AND AMAZING GIRLFRIEND ON THE OTHER SIDE OF THE COUNTRY.

See? All caps. That's how much this stresses me out sometimes.

Okay. Speaking of, I have a thing to go to tonight that my friend River is having, and it will totally be like what I just described. Great, huh?

I love you.

Plastic bags, plastic bags, plastic bags . . .

20

On the morning of the hayroll the *S* thief was definitely in the spirit. The sign in front of the school mysteriously changed from GET YOUR TICKETS TO ANNUAL HAYRIDE ON FRIDAY to the much simpler AL SES GET LAID. (Thus using his spare *S* but gaining a lot of new letters.)

Avery noticed this, not just because she liked to follow the exploits of the *S* thief, but also because she wasn't really in the mood for the hayroll at all. The last few weeks had been hard. Nothing had really happened except a few lingering looks now and then. Only a couple were unfriendly. Most were just curious or even kind of approving. Still, Avery didn't want to be observed, and the hayroll was all about public displays of coupledom, which was only going to make her feel more conspicuous about herself. Also, she knew that Mel was going to be on high alert for signs of romance, something Avery was feeling increasingly less comfortable supplying.

Fortunately, Mel had to work most of the night, but she was going to be getting off in just enough time for them to make the hayroll if she hurried. That would mean a talk about whether or not they should make it clear that they were going together. Avery just wasn't up for it.

When Avery went to Mel's locker after Spanish, a tiny, triangle-shaped note fell out. It read: *Hayroll 2nite, yes? —M.* Avery shoved it deep in her pocket. Then she went to lunch and asked Gaz to schedule a rehearsal for that night. Gaz never minded doing this because all rehearsal really meant was having Hareth and Avery come sit in his basement.

Even though Avery tried to keep a low profile for the rest of the day, Mel caught up with her in the hall between sixth and seventh. Mel was in a giddy mood. Her hair was loose and flowing, and she was almost walking on the tips of her toes.

"Do you want to pick me up right after work?" Mel asked.

"I have rehearsal," Avery said.

"Tonight?" Mel seemed to collapse a bit.

"Yeah. It just came up."

"Do you have to go?"

"I'm supposed to," Avery said. "I can't just skip."

Avery knew she should be feeling bad about this. She was basically lying. It was almost worse that she'd gone to the trouble of staging a cover story. Now Mel looked guilty for asking her to skip rehearsal because Mel was always supportive of Avery's music. If it was about music, Mel wouldn't argue.

Besides, what else was she supposed to do? Mel had hardly been taking the hint. Like now. Here she was giving Avery the sad eyes right in the middle of the hall.

"We can meet up after," Avery said quickly. "Okay?"

"Sure. Sounds good."

Mel wanted to say more. Avery could almost see her tiny muscles straining to keep herself in check, but she pretended not to notice this. She turned and went to class.

Frost was late, which was a first.

Most AP types normally sat and waited when teachers were running late because they were AP types, but the AP history students had the additional element of fear keeping them in their seats. They all seemed to understand that if anyone left the room for any reason, Frost would find them and head-butt them right in the middle of the hallway.

Nina took out her notebook and had started listing her current thirty SAT words when she noticed that Susan Yee was inching closer to her.

"Can I ask you something?" Susan said. She kept her voice very low.

"Sure."

"Are your friends gay?"

Nina glanced at Devon. He was deeply engrossed in cleaning off the viewfinder of his camera with his tie. As far as Nina knew, Devon and Susan weren't friends, so the chances were low that Susan had heard this from him.

Frost made her appearance just then. She stormed into the room with her usual subtlety.

"Books closed, my geniuses," she said. "Oral quiz."

Nina spent the rest of the period cultivating a slow-growing panic. If Susan Yee knew, things had gotten out of hand. The news had to be everywhere.

As Frost began to drill them, a strange line of thought entered Nina's head: Maybe people would assume she was gay as well. Not that there was anything wrong with it—there was definitely nothing wrong with it—but she *wasn't*. The fact that she didn't have a boyfriend whom she could bring in for show-and-tell didn't help matters. She was like those guys who always claim to have a girlfriend in Canada. Except she had a boyfriend in Oregon—she really, really did.

None of this was helped by the fact that Frost was throwing around questions like, "What was the outcome of *Marbury v. Madison*?" and, "What was the Nonintercourse Act a response to?" Nina got that second question, and, as suggestive as it sounded, she knew the answer was "public outcry over the Embargo Act of 1807." Except she was so jangled that when Frost turned to her Nina accidentally came out with "the Sedition and Alien Laws," because for some reason that phrase had been running through her head since she'd first heard of it two weeks before. It was so grievously wrong that Frost actually laughed out loud and marked off something next to Nina's name before she could correct herself.

When she got to the council office after class, the only person there was Jeff, sitting at a computer, his eyes glued to a countdown on his auction page.

"Eleven minutes," he explained to Nina as she came into the office. He repeatedly refreshed the screen. "Everything happens at the end."

Devon came in, sat down, and stared intently into the LCD screen of his camera and flipped through pictures.

Don't say anything, Nina told herself. *It'll only make it worse.*

"Thanks," she said, ignoring her own advice.

"For what?" he asked.

"You know what."

"I seriously have no idea what you're talking about," he said.

Jeff appeared to be engaged in his auction still, but Nina sensed that he was keeping one ear on the conversation that was taking place next to him.

"Never mind," she mumbled. "You ready for tonight?"

"You're going with Georgia to pick up the hayride food, right?" Devon asked, not looking up.

"Who's saying my name?" Georgia said, coming in and dropping her things dramatically on the table. "Speak it! Speak it!"

"We're getting the food, and we're meeting at the farm at seven," Nina said, trying to regain her council president composure.

"I love going to Moonstone," Georgia said. "It's our bakery."

(Georgia had a bakery that supplied her *house*. Even in the middle of this minor crisis, Nina felt a pang of jealousy.)

"The place is totally secret," Georgia went on. "It's not retail. Orders only. It's incredible. It's like in this woman's house, and she has this pet goat and all these ovens in her living room. You can't tell anyone about her, or my parents will kill you."

"I wasn't planning on it," Devon said.

Nina was sure he threw her a look.

"Wait." Jeff spun around. "Seven? I thought we had to be there at eight."

"It starts at eight," Georgia said. "But we *run* it, remember?"

"Oh, shit." Jeff scrambled in his bag for his cell. Georgia shook her head.

"Meet you boys at seven," she said, patting Jeff roughly on the head. "Nina and I have to go."

"What's going on with you and Tieboy?" Georgia asked as they walked down to the parking lot. The field hockey team was running circuits around the lot, making a weird and breathy *hup hup hup* sound. Seeing this kind of behavior made Nina glad that she hadn't decided to go the sports route.

"What are you talking about?"

"You guys were fighting."

It was weird the way Georgia picked up on things. It made Nina want to put on a tinfoil hat to keep her brain waves from being stolen.

"Is it because of your picture?" Georgia asked. "Is it because your love is forbidden?"

"It wasn't a fight. There is no love."

"Of course not," Georgia said. "But you guys will just have to huddle together for warmth outside tonight."

"What?"

"They're letting us set up the refreshments inside the farmhouse this year," Georgia said with a grin. "It'll be Jeff and me by the fire and the two of you out there."

Nina stopped in her tracks.

"Please tell me you're joking," she said.

"Tieboy and Nina at the hayroll. Story at eleven."

At eleven the last truck was making the circuit of the field. Nina and Devon were alone on the edge of the field with the trash barrels and the remains of the ticket stubs.

Even though they had been side by side for well over three hours, they'd exchanged only a few words—all concerning tickets, or change, or the money box. Nina just pasted on her best political smile and crunched down hard on her back molars, forcing herself not to speak. But she knew. All night as she punched her pumpkins, took the cash, loaded the trucks, she'd been breaking the thing down in her head.

The Avery and Mel thing was going to come out because of Devon. It only made sense. The fact that Devon knew before Georgia meant that he had to be the source. And the fact that Susan Yee knew by eighth period meant that Devon had spread whatever it was he knew. Scowling, smirking Tieboy had gotten into her friends' lives. Tieboy was going to go *down*. But not here. Not at the hayroll. Not when she had a job to do.

She still wished she knew how this had happened, what Mel and Avery had done. Not that it was their fault—they had a right to act however they wanted to. They could be as public as they wanted. But they weren't public. They'd made that very clear to Nina. So, they'd screwed up somehow. Screwed up in front of Devon.

From the direction of the parking lot, there was the sound of breaking glass.

"I'll go check it out," he said.

"No," Nina said, happy for the distraction. "I've got it."

She started off before he even had time to put down the money box.

There were very few cars left in the part of the field used for the parking lot. As she walked around looking for the source of the noise, Nina was surprised to notice Avery's old blue Volvo. Mel had told her that they weren't going to be able to come. Curious, Nina went over to the car.

It was definitely Avery's—and Avery was actually in it. There was the wine-colored leather coat and the long maroon scarf. Avery was turned away, and it took Nina a moment to realize that she was making out with someone. Her stomach took a familiar tumble, and she was about to back up and walk away when she realized that she could see the kissee's head over Avery's, which wasn't right. And the hair was light brown, not orange. And that was clearly a guy's arm.

Nina stood frozen to the spot. Avery, as if sensing her presence, turned and looked at her. The slow horror that spread across Avery's face told the rest of the story. Nina could see the guy clearly now. It was Gaz—some guy Avery hung out with in the music department.

Avery got out of the car. She kept her head down and didn't meet Nina's gaze.

"What the hell are you doing?" Nina whispered.

"Don't say anything, okay?"

Nina was unable to form words. Gaz climbed out of the other side of the car and stretched. He probably had no idea that there was even anything wrong.

"Please?" Avery said quietly. "It was just this . . . It won't matter. Seriously. It's not what you think."

"*Won't matter?*" Nina cocked her head. "Are you insane?"

Devon came up behind her, carrying the money box in his arms. "Everything okay?" he asked.

It took Nina a moment to realize that he was checking up on her. Devon was doing something nice, and Avery was cheating on Mel with a guy.

Was she on crack?

Devon looked at Avery and Gaz. The sight seemed to puzzle him as well. In fact, Gaz was the only person there who didn't seem utterly thrown by the situation.

"I'm going to go back," Nina said.

Avery gave her a desperate look.

"Talk to you tomorrow?" she asked.

"Yeah," Nina said absently. "Tomorrow."

Devon followed Nina back to the gate. They tramped over the crisp leaves, not speaking for a moment.

"That was kind of weird," Devon finally said. "I thought Avery and Mel were dating."

"The truck's coming back," Nina said dully.

They watched its slow approach from the woods. It was followed at some distance by various ghouls and zombies who were obviously sick of standing out in the cold and wanted to go home.

Even though she hadn't said anything, she felt like she'd done Devon an injustice. This wasn't Devon's fault. It was Avery's. *Avery* . . .

What had Avery done? What was she doing? *What the hell was going on?*

"Look," Nina said, "I'm sorry. About earlier. I thought . . ."

"I know what you thought. I didn't tell anyone. I was with three other people. We all saw them. I didn't say anything, except to you."

He was telling her the truth. She could hear it in his voice. She could also hear his tie flapping in the wind. Why Devon, of all people? Why did he have to be involved in this? The one person who really threw her off stride.

"Can you do me a favor?" she asked, not looking over at him.

"What?"

"Don't say anything about this either?"

"Wasn't going to."

They tramped their way back to their empty ticket table at the edge of the field.

"So . . ." This wasn't a greeting so, or an "I told you so" so. This was a "what happened back there?" so.

"I don't know," Nina said, poking a finger into one of her Leia buns, as if trying to find the button for her brain. The button that would turn on the section that could figure this out. Because things just got bad. Very bad.

"That kind of puts you in a suckass position," he said, eyeing the truck and the army of the undead that were almost to them now.

Well, he was right about that. She looked down and buried her feet under a blanket of leaves. She hated being out on nights like this. Hated the wind. Hated the black outline of the trees on the horizon—they looked like skeletal hands reaching up out of the ground, clawing for the sky, for air. There was silence now. She had to say something to Devon, but she didn't feel like discussing this anymore. There was nothing she could say.

"When did you take that picture of my hand?" she asked instead.

"AP. A few weeks ago, right before class."

"I didn't even notice."

"No flash."

"Oh."

It was no surprise she didn't notice. It was *good* not to notice. Her life would be easier if she noticed a lot less.

They let the matter of both Avery and the photograph drop, since the shivering, costumed horde was upon them now. She plastered on a smile. That was her costume.

"Okay!" she said cheerfully. "We'll regroup inside the farmhouse. There's hot chocolate and cider for everyone. Come on!"

21

Mel found herself staring blankly at her reflection in the lid of the ice bin. She was all wavy and her chest was covered in big round spots.

There was a promotion going on at P. J. Mortimer's: The Great Guinness Experiment. There was Guinness in everything. Guinness burgers, Guinness baby back ribs, Guinness mixed in with fudge and put on top of ice cream.

Management was going overboard with the Guinness buttons. They'd ordered a huge carton of them, some with just the logo, some with old pictures of pelicans. The new rule was they had to wear at least six of these on their front and eight on their back. Mel's suspenders were overloaded; they sagged and kept slipping off her shoulders, making it impossible to move her arms freely. She tried pinning the buttons right through the suspenders and straight through her shirt, but that didn't work either. The buttons were cheap and poorly made, with too-long pins. They pricked her chest and her collarbone. No matter what the slogan said, Guinness was not good for Mel.

Weeknights were usually sluggish, but tonight was particularly bad, hardly even worth the trip in. She was killing time in the pantry marrying ketchup bottles while her one table was eating. When she first got the job, she thought that was a funny term—marrying ketchup. It was a lot less funny when she had to scrape the disgusting black residue from under the caps and the tops of the bottles. The whole thing was a little nasty, even though she knew it was probably fine to dump ketchup from one bottle to another.

She felt *alone*. She'd felt alone all day. It only got worse when she messed up with the note and then got all weird about Avery's rehearsal. Why did she do these things, things she knew perfectly well would make Avery stress out?

Parker came in from the dish room with a large bin of freshly washed silverware. He fished a piece of lettuce from the pool of rinse water that the silverware was drifting in and grimaced.

"So worth missing the hayroll for," he said. "Want to take a break?"

"Sure," Mel said.

Outside, Mel walked along the parking lot dividers like they were balance beams. Parker walked alongside her.

"Can we talk for a minute?" he asked.

"Okay. About what?"

Parker went back over to the service door, opened it, and looked inside. Then he closed it again and walked over to the Dumpster and leaned against it.

"I heard something," he said, gazing down at his shoes.

Mel stopped her balancing and put her toe on the ground to steady herself.

"What?"

But it was already clear from the way Parker was chomping at his lower lip. She braced herself—actually tensed her legs as if preparing to be hit by a wave.

"Are you gay?" he asked.

He was leaning forward just a little, his hands burrowed deep into his pockets.

"Who told you that?" she asked.

"A guy in my Spanish class."

That was bizarre. *Some guy* in Parker's Spanish class knew about her. Maybe everybody knew now.

"I usually wouldn't believe something like that," he said. "But I guess I've been curious."

Mel teetered a little and stepped down off the divider.

"You can tell me," he said. "I'm all hooray for gay. It's not a problem. I just wanted to know, from you."

She looked up at him. He had a strangely expectant expression on his face, and he was pushing back his hair more than normal.

"It's true," she said softly.

There was something about saying this out loud that made it seem more real, more official, like paperwork might be required and perhaps even a notary.

"Oh," he said.

The wind whistled under the Dumpster lid, rattling it, banging the top like a drum. They both stared at it.

"You're the first person I've ever really said it to on purpose like that," Mel added.

Parker mused this one over for a second.

"This is going to sound wrong," he said with a touch of hesitation. "You don't . . . look gay. I know gay doesn't look like anything—but sometimes you can tell, right? With some people you can definitely tell."

They stared at each other.

"This is weird to you," she said, "isn't it?"

"It's not the gay part. Well, it is, but . . ."

He stepped on some flattened lettuce and ground it in with his heel.

"I had a huge crush on you," he blurted quickly. "Can I tell you that now, or is this a bad idea? We're being honest here. So I'm being honest. I'm insanely jealous of Avery, but I guess I'll get over it."

He gave a little laugh, and Mel looked down at her puffy blue coat, concentrating hard on the square islands of downy filling. She sat down on the divider, and after a moment he joined her.

"You know about Avery too?" she asked.

"Yeah," Parker said. "It was all part of the story. That's true too, right?"

Mel nodded.

"I thought Avery could be," he said. "I guessed that."

"She's freaked out about something," Mel said. "I get that she doesn't want to be seen with me around school, but it's more than that now. I wish I knew what."

"So why don't you ask her?"

"You can't do that with Avery."

"Why not?"

"Because you can't get in Avery's face with things." Mel sighed.

They sat in silence for a minute, listening to the song of the Dumpster again. It banged harder now. The sound was almost reassuring to Mel. She liked its loudness.

"Are you really okay with it?" she finally asked. "Nothing's changed between us, has it? I mean, if I wasn't gay . . ."

"You don't have to go there," he interrupted. "At least you've got a really good reason for not wanting to go out with me, you know? I can't really take offense if the problem is that I'm too masculine. I'm too much man!"

He flexed and then winced and grabbed his shoulder. Mel tried to laugh, but the sound that came out was more like a croak. All of her emotions were close to the surface. Parker's face fell.

"Hey," he said. "Hey, come on. Friends, right?"

"Right."

Parker hesitated for a moment, then quickly threw his arms around her. Mel got the feeling that he was working something out of himself by gripping her so firmly. That was fine with her. It felt good to be here. She rested her face against his wool coat. They stayed there like that for a moment, then Parker flinched slightly and reached under his coat and adjusted his suspenders.

"These suck," he said. "I didn't really want acupuncture, you know?"

He pulled off a pin and slam-dunked it into the Dumpster

with a yell. He jumped up, grabbed onto the edge, and continued screaming at the garbage, giving his very definite opinion of the Guinness promotion.

"If only the public knew what really goes on here," he said, sliding down and wiping his hands on his coat. "Family fun, my ass."

Mel managed a smile.

"Come on," he said, reaching down a hand to help Mel off the divider. "Let's go inside. I'm sure we're missing out on something fun."

22

Avery woke to the sound of something slamming into the bottom of her bedroom door. To her trained ear, it sounded like a Tonka pickup truck, thrown the length of the hallway as part of her brothers' "Is it really indestructible?" game. She then heard her mother yelling that they had better stop throwing that truck around or they would never see high school. A minute later Eric opened her door.

"Do you have batteries?" he asked hurriedly. Her brothers knew all about the Billy Bass thing, but they weren't foolish enough to search through Avery's things to look for the battery stash.

"What did I tell you about knocking?" she said, brushing her hair from her eyes.

"Do you?"

She didn't feel like arguing with her brother about batteries. She had a full-scale disaster on her hands.

"Here," she said, reaching over and opening a drawer in her bedside stand. She reached around and found the batteries and rolled them across her floor.

So now she was wide awake, which kind of sucked. She'd

been hoping to sleep a little longer. Until she was thirty would have been nice.

She hadn't meant for this to happen. The kiss with Gaz hadn't been planned. Hareth had bailed on rehearsal, so they'd decided to go over to the hayride. In the car Gaz made a joke about the whole hayroll thing, and much to Avery's surprise, he started flirting with her. And she liked it.

She'd only wanted to test it out, just to see how it made her feel. The way she saw it, her whole relationship with Mel was one big experiment, so the rules didn't always apply. She wasn't cheating—she was checking her homosexuality quotient.

It had been . . . different from what she'd experienced with Mel. Something had definitely stirred in her that didn't seem to happen while she was kissing Mel. But there was a lot missing, too. Being with Mel was warm and cozy and . . . complete. Being with Gaz was fun, but in the end she was just messing around with some guy in a car. Overall, kind of disappointing. Maybe a four out of ten.

Which kind of meant that she was right back where she started with the whole issue. And, as much as she questioned her *lesbianity,* there was definitely lots of evidence to support the idea.

One: She'd dated a girl for almost four months. She referred to this girl as her girlfriend. Not in public, but certainly in her own head and to the girl herself.

Two: She'd done things with aforementioned girlfriend that went well beyond kissing, things that might still be illegal in some of the more backward states.

Three: Mel beat Gaz's scores in all aspects of the event.

Ladies and gentlemen of the jury, verdict?

Gay. Gay as the day is long.

Except that she wasn't. Despite all the evidence, she was not gay. She knew it. Because gay women don't have sudden, overwhelming, and (she had to admit it now) *constant* urges to make out with guys.

Did they?

And now she had Nina to deal with. Not only had Nina caught her and looked at her with a dislike that Avery had never seen before—if Nina decided that she couldn't keep this a secret, everything was going to go *boom*.

The suckitude level, as Margo would say, was very high.

When Avery arrived, Nina was sitting in front of her computer with a physics book open beside her. She was fully dressed in jeans and the Little Miss Felon T-shirt Avery had given her for her birthday last year. Avery wondered if this gesture had some meaning—if she had worn the shirt to deliver a message. Just the fact that Nina was awake, showered (her hair was still damp), dressed, and *doing physics* at ten on a Saturday morning added to Avery's current low opinion of herself. If her brothers hadn't woken her, she'd still be in bed, drooling on herself and dreaming that she was grocery shopping with Jack Black.

"Can I talk to you?" Avery asked.

"I guess."

She sat down on Nina's plump cream-colored comforter. (Nina made her bed, too. She even tucked her pillows under the comforter and then pressed in the edge so that they were in a perfect little envelope, just like they did in ads for white sales.)

"You're mad," she said.

Nina didn't answer. She looked down at her long nail beds and massaged a cuticle.

"I'm really confused, Neen."

"About what?"

"About me."

"Oh, that's not *too* vague," Nina said.

Avery sighed. Before, when they only used to talk about guys, it had been easy to pour out details. Now she was loaded down with shame—about her behavior, her mysterious sexuality, that she wasn't showered and doing physics problems.

"I'm not sure if I'm gay, or straight, or bi, or what," she said.

"Maybe you should have thought that one through before you started dating Mel."

"It's not that simple."

"Why not?"

"I definitely like Mel. I like . . . the things that go along with dating. I mean, I have those feelings. But I think it might just be Mel that I like. That way."

"You like guys too?" Nina asked.

Avery felt her skin flushing. Something about that question made her feel like . . . a glutton. Like she wanted *everyone*. Guys, girls, dogs, cats, populations of whole cities.

"I was sitting with Gaz, and I realized I kind of like him,"

Avery tried to explain. "I felt something. I wanted to see why. I wanted to see what happened. I needed to check."

"So?" Nina asked. "What did you find out?"

"It was okay."

"What does that mean?" Nina asked.

"I have no clue," Avery said.

"Does Mel feel . . . like that? Confused?"

"No," Avery said, pulling up the little silver chain she wore around her neck and chewing on it. "I don't think so. Mel's pretty sure about herself."

"That's she's a lesbian."

"Yeah."

Nina tucked her legs up on the chair and rested her face on her knees. It looked like she was folding in on herself, creating a little temple where she could ask the gods for advice on this perplexing matter.

"If she finds out, she's going to get really upset," Avery said.

"No kidding," Nina mumbled.

While Nina thought, Avery got up and paced around the room, looking at Nina's pristine desk, with her little silver Apple notebook sitting perfectly in the center and the row of books lined up along the wall in order of height. Nina's bureau was completely stocked with makeup and lotions, yet wasn't overcrowded. Avery knew that none of the lipsticks had gotten all over the silver-twisty part or had their tips broken off by accident in the cap. Her perfumes and lotions were used to a respectable halfway point. Unlike Avery, Nina didn't keep piles of empty bottles because she was convinced that if she held them upside down or scooped her finger inside, she might be able to draw out just one more drop of shampoo or cream or whatever it was.

"I don't want to mess things up between you," Nina said, finally lifting her face from her knees.

Avery didn't know if she should say "thanks" or just "oh" or "okay." She nodded instead.

"It can't happen again," Nina said sternly. "It can't."

Avery resented the parental tone Nina was taking, but she couldn't really argue.

"I know," Avery said. "I promise."

Avery started across the room to give Nina the hug that always came at this point, but Nina turned away and looked at her book, scrunching up her forehead as if the whole time she'd really just been doing some complex problem in her head about what happens to a bicycle moving along at the speed of light.

Avery stopped and put her hands in her pockets.

"Thanks," she said before walking out the door.

23

The moment Nina had been dreading finally came on Monday morning, when Mel peeked shyly around the council office door. Nina had been hiding in there, stuffing holiday dance envelopes. The letters didn't need to go out for weeks, but Nina was briskly working down the assembly line she'd made for herself, trying to seem as busy as possible. Anything to stall for time.

"Have you got a second?" Mel asked.

"Um . . . sure," Nina replied with a slight nervous twitch.

"Need help?"

"No. I'm good."

Mel sat down at the table and picked one of the reservation cards out of the stack and stared at it. She poked at the snowflakes on the card with her finger, going from flake to flake like a little child with a picture book.

"Has Avery seemed . . . upset to you?" she asked.

This was it. The beginning of the lie. Every second Nina kept quiet would just make the lie bigger.

"Upset?" she said.

"She hasn't said anything to you about me?"

Between friends, not speaking was the same thing as lying.

Talking, not talking. It made no difference. She was screwed.

"Maybe I shouldn't get involved in this stuff." Nina asked. "I can't really take sides, you know?"

Jeff came in, gave a quick hello, then dropped himself at the computer and started checking his sales, bringing an end to their conversation.

"I better get to homeroom," Mel said, backing up.

Nina followed her to the door and grabbed Mel by the shoulder before she could walk away.

"Don't worry," she said. "I think it's just that she's getting used to the idea that people know."

"But did she say something?" Mel asked. There was a real urgency in her eyes.

Lies, lies, lies, lies . . .

"No," Nina said. "She hasn't said anything."

"Really?" Mel perked up a bit.

"Really."

"Okay," Mel said.

Nina went back into the office and sank down at the table. Georgia came in a minute later and threw down a container of small, dry-looking bran muffins. Nina gazed at them and realized that she had absolutely no appetite.

Third-period music theory wasn't a class Avery could really zone in since there were only four people in it, but it was hard to keep her mind on appropriate uses of the nondominant seventh chord when she could see Gaz out in the hallway, reading something off a music department notice board. He shouldn't have been there. He was supposed to be somewhere on the other side of the building. This had to mean he wanted to *talk,* which wasn't really like Gaz.

She'd just managed to get through the talk with Nina. She'd done her shift on Sunday then gone to see Mel. She'd played it well, but in her head, nothing was right. Mel was so tiny. Mel was so *squeaky.* Mel sat in her lap like some kind of overgrown orange kitten. Mel wanted to make out and would not let Avery watch *The Royal Tenenbaums,* because Mel did not understand the movie and anyway you're *supposed* to make out instead of actually watching movies. You're supposed to want to. But Avery didn't want to. She wanted to watch Owen Wilson go insane and crash his car into the building. Owen Wilson reminded her of Gaz. They were both blond guys, after all, with that same strange blank delivery. Nonchalant.

And they were *guys.* She had guys on the brain. She'd eyed up every single one of her male customers at work. She'd even looked at Bob.

She went through it again in her head. The car. The cold. Gaz's pale face, his thin, wide lips. He had muscles in his upper arms. She'd never noticed that before Friday. He'd always seemed like a beanpole.

Truth be told, the kiss wasn't a four out of ten. It was more like a seven. She'd happily do it again. But that didn't matter. It couldn't matter. That was the problem with dating your best friend—you needed a *really* serious reason to stop. It was kind of a permanent situation. It was like she'd gotten *married* without realizing it.

Oh, now the panic was going. Now she had it good. She jammed her pen hard up the coil of her spiral notebook and wondered if the gesture meant something.

And Gaz was outside the door, and the bell was going to ring. And she'd just missed the entire homework assignment.

Great.

She wondered if anyone would think it was weird if she just jumped out of the window and started running across the soccer field, escaping. Other people had to have these impulses.

Escape attempts are only bad if they catch you.

Which they would, given her current luck.

And the bell. *Ding.* Round one.

"Hey," he said, as she came out of the room. He looked really good today. He was wearing a black button-down shirt made of some kind of satin or polyester or something. It was tapered, but it still hung loose against his thin frame. It made him look taller. (What was with this sudden height obsession?)

"S'up?" she said, casting an eye over the board, but not really reading anything.

"Nothing."

Maybe she was going to get away with this after all. . . .

"You have a second?" he asked.

Nope.

"Um . . . yeah. If you walk with me to chem."

Gaz didn't say anything at all for about half of the walk. He just moved along beside her. There was nothing really different about his walk, except that it seemed kind of . . . possessive. Like he was with her.

"I was thinking . . ." he said.

Admittedly, this was kind of a major announcement, coming from Gaz.

"Right," she said, swerving to avoid half the lacrosse team. A few of them threw her looks. Lacrosse. *Screw lacrosse.*

"I heard something," Gaz said.

"What?"

"About you and Mel."

This was it. Moment of truth.

"It's just . . ." How the hell did she explain this? "I can't do anything about the other night. I'm in the middle of this . . . thing."

"With Mel?"

"Yeah."

He got it. She didn't need to draw a picture.

"I think it's cool that you're open to stuff," he said.

"So we're cool?"

"We're cool."

And that was that. He didn't even seem surprised. He wasn't mad, or revolted. He didn't ask to watch. He was just Gaz, and things were easy with Gaz. But something swept over his expression. He wasn't completely happy with this. There was just enough hesitation. . . .

And then there was the part that was both exciting and terrifying to Avery as Gaz left her at the door of the chem lab—nothing had ever been as appealing to her as his faint look of disappointment.

Thanksgiving

November 22

TO: Nina

FROM: Steve

I'm pretty sure we shouldn't be living in our house right now. The ceiling in my mom's studio is sagging from all this water that's trapped on the roof, our one toilet won't stop flushing itself, and the corner of the wood floor in the living room turned black overnight and no one knows why. Plus this herbalist guy is staying with us. He keeps burning things and the place totally reeks.

All of this has driven our cat crazy and he has expressed his dismay by attacking my good biking shoes.

The weird thing is, no one notices any of this but me. When I point to the water coming through the ceiling or the stuff that's growing on the floor, my parents just shrug and say, "What?"

I guess when you grow up in a teepee, some things just don't get to you.

I'm starting my application for Stanford. By the time I'm done, it's going to be wet and clawed up and smelly. At least I'll stand out.

Sorry to complain.

November 22

TO: Steve

FROM: Nina

You can always complain to me! I love you, and it scares me that you are surrounded by mold and sagging ceilings and crazy cats. Come live here! My mom and I have cleaning parties for fun! (Sounds like a joke but is not. We buy Swiffers, cleanser, and ice cream and play music. We are v. sad but we like it.)

November 23
TO: Nina
FROM: Steve

You and I have very different lives. Want to hear sad? Know what I bought my parents for Christmas last year? A vacuum. They never had one before. No one used it but me. It doesn't work anymore because somehow my brother accidentally chopped the cord off.

November 23
TO: Steve
FROM: Nina

Yes, we're different but that's what makes us so perfect! Every good couple is kind of mismatched. Don't you watch TV? (Oh, wait. You probably don't.)

I love you even more. I will buy you a hand vac when we get to school as a room-warming gift.

24

"*Miss.*"

Avery wasn't going to turn around. She knew what those women at table 22 wanted to tell her, and it was not going to make her happy. These women were Daiquiri People—one of the worst types of customer around.

"Miss?"

First of all, as far as Avery was concerned, a daiquiri was not something a self-respecting adult should be seen drinking—especially not a Mortimer's daiquiri, which came with whipped cream and a green crazy straw. Therefore Avery could ignore them in good conscience.

"*Miss.*"

Well, she could ignore them for a while, anyway. And then she would have to turn around and have all of her worst fears about them confirmed. They were going to say that there was no booze in their drink. Daiquiri People always did. Avery chomped down hard on her lower lip, then faced the four women in the booth. They were all in their forties or so and wore cute little cardigans that seemed to be passed out to all school secretaries, along with hair-frosting kits and jingly bracelets.

"There's no alcohol in these drinks," said the woman closest to Avery.

This was one of the few occasions when Avery hated to be proven right.

While she knew perfectly well that there was alcohol in there (buried under some heavy layer of strawberry or banana goo), she would have to take the drink back to the bar to make them happy. Normally the bartenders would drip a few drops of rum down the straw. This was a great trick to get people to stop complaining because the first sip they took would be overpoweringly strong.

But there was no way that was happening tonight. These women didn't understand that getting a frozen drink made on a Friday was no small achievement in the first place. The bartenders always took care of their own customers first, and the last thing they liked to do was fire up the blenders, which were loud and horrible and drove people away from the bar. But Avery had badgered the bartender and gotten this table their four daiquiris. There was no way she'd be able to get him to come back over and doctor the crazy straws just to make these morons feel like grown-ups. Besides, she had a big order to put in right now, while there was no line at the computer.

"I saw them put it in," Avery said. "I promise. It's in there."

"I'm telling you it's not," the woman huffed.

"Maybe you should stir it a little."

"Just get us some new ones, okay, honey?" The woman shoved her glass in Avery's direction and turned back to her friends.

Big mistake. Avery was not in the mood for this. She adjusted a Guinness pin that was jabbing her in the rib cage and studied the glasses. This was one of those no-win situations her job put her in on a far too regular basis.

"I'm sure they're fine," she tried again. "I was there when he made them. If you stir it . . ."

"How many times do we need to ask you?" the woman said, turning back around in annoyance. "We had to wait for them long enough as it was. We're not paying for them unless we get new ones. I'm not falling for this. I know this is how you try to get people, okay?"

Now they were accusing her of being part of a *cover-up?* The Great Mortimer's Daiquiri Swindle? They had made it personal, and this was more than Avery could bear.

"Why would I lie to you?" Avery asked indignantly. "Does that even make sense?"

"Excuse me?"

"It's not my rum," Avery said. "Why would I try to cheat you?"

"I'd like to speak to a manager."

Avery heard an evil laugh in her mind. These were famous last words. Finding a manager on a Friday night was impossible.

"I'll go look for one," she said dryly. She walked away, leaving the glasses where they were. As she walked back to the pantry, she glanced to her left and right. No managers in sight. She had looked.

As she stood at the computer by the bar, punching in the other order, Avery sighed. There would be no tip on 22, which was a blow. They were probably going to bail on their food too. She should probably just cancel their order. She'd do it as soon as she got some ketchup from the pantry for one of her other tables.

When she passed by it a few minutes later, 22 was still occupied, which was somewhat annoying. She walked straight back to the pantry, where she found Bob waiting. Parker was there too, prepping a few plates. He glanced over at Avery nervously.

"It was a daiquiri thing," Avery said, before Bob could get in a word. "I told them to stir it."

"You're fired," he said.

"You've got to be kidding me."

"I've warned you. Do you want to finish your shift or cash out now?"

"But it's just a drink thing! You can't be serious."

Bob turned to Parker.

"Want two more tables?" he asked. "You can have 22 and 25."

Parker glanced at Avery. She flashed him a look that told him she didn't mind. And she really didn't. It had nothing to do with him.

"I'll meet you up front," Bob said to Avery. "Bring your stuff."

"See you in a minute," she said brightly.

"That sucks." Parker was hanging on to his suspenders and looking very uncomfortable.

"It's my lucky day," she said. "I'm out of here."

"Yeah," Parker said, trying to match Avery's strained enthusiasm. "I almost wish it was me."

Such a lie, but it was the kind of thing you were supposed to say in situations like this.

It was over in just a few minutes. Now she was in her car, looking at Mortimer's from the outside—the only way she would ever look at it again. There was a small pile of cash on the seat next to her. It didn't amount to much. Maybe ten or eleven dollars, if she was lucky.

She started the engine.

Fired.

Fired was cool.

Fired implied attitude. Fired was very rock and roll.

Fired was also broke, parents screaming, no money for her car, and no way of even thinking about going to New York City for school because her parents sure as hell weren't paying for Avery to hang out with purple-haired, clove-smoking artsy trustafarians when Geneseo and Old Westbury were more affordable and infinitely less *furrreaky*. . . . Not that Mortimer's made her enough money to pay for school, but it was some form of cash flow. Something she no longer had.

She turned up the volume on her car stereo to the point where the sound warped. She dug around in her bag and found a cigarette and then peeled out of the P. J. Mortimer's parking lot.

I'm such an asshole, she thought, fumbling for the cigarette lighter in the dashboard. *How dumb do you have to be to get fired from P. J. Mortimer's?* She must have had a job death wish, just like she did when she worked at the gas station convenience store the summer after sophomore year, when she used to scream, "Fire me!" into the surveillance camera (before she found out it was video only, and then she made a sign on a piece of sandwich wrapping paper). But this time she had succeeded, and now she was royally screwed. She might as well drive right into a wall.

Except that she would probably live and just be carless.

She instinctively turned down the sound once she got to Mel's street. Avery wasn't conscious of driving there on purpose. She gave her usual quick greeting to Mel's dad. He was nice, if maybe a little oblivious, and he never seemed to care what time Avery turned up at the door. He was an extremely single dad and didn't question the needs of girls to talk to other girls at all hours, which had proved very convenient for the last few months.

Mel was looking at something online when Avery came into her room without knocking.

"How did you get off early?"

"Bob fired me."

Avery fell back on the bed and a stuffed palm tree fell over on her face. She pushed it aside. Mel came over and sat next to her, looking concerned.

"What happened?"

"Bob just did what he's been wanting to do for a while." Avery groaned, covering up her eyes with the heels of her palms. "Can you put on some music or something?"

Mel hopped up and switched on the MP3 player on her computer. Normally they put on music to cover up any noise that they made in Mel's room—sometimes when they were talking, but usually when they were making out. Mel turned on Norah Jones, one of her favorites. She came back over and stretched out alongside Avery so that they were front to front. They kissed a little, but for some reason, all Avery could think of was Gaz. Gaz with his long legs and fingers and his lazy smile. He was as tall as two Mels. Avery imagined that she was lying next to him. Her head would tuck under his chin, and her feet would only hit his midcalf. She wanted to be the smaller person right now.

Avery closed her eyes and rolled onto her back.

"I kind of want to just lie here," she said. "Cool?"

"Oh. Okay." Mel pulled herself upright and played with Avery's hair instead.

The music made Avery sad. She envisioned the daiquiri women snickering as they were told that they had just gotten her fired. In Avery's mind, they hated her deeply and personally.

"Maybe I'll apply to school in New York too," Mel said suddenly, twisting Avery's hair into a corkscrew around her finger.

"For what?"

"I don't know. Maybe nursing. Or business. I don't know. Something."

"Sounds like a plan," Avery said absently.

"And maybe we could share a place." Mel sounded eager now. "I could even just go there and work for a while. Wouldn't that be cool, to have an apartment together?"

Avery remembered a joke she'd heard somewhere: What does a lesbian bring on a first date?

Answer: a U-Haul.

What if there was some truth in that? What if Mel wanted to get married and have a commitment ceremony and play Ani DiFranco and k.d. lang songs and have cats as bridesmaids? That would be great for Mel, but it just wasn't something Avery could picture. The thought scared her. A lot.

"Mel . . ." she barked while pulling herself up. "I just got fired, okay? Can you please stop?"

Mel widened her eyes in a "stop what?" look.

"I have to go." Avery made her way toward the door.

"Why?"

She didn't answer. She left Mel sitting there holding her stuffed palm tree with a hurt expression on her face.

Avery wasn't ready to go home yet. She drove around and smoked until she accidentally blew a smoldering ash into her own backseat and had to pull over and smack out the little orange flame that was burrowing through the pleather.

Then she drove to Gaz's.

Avery let herself in through the outside door into Gaz's basement. She never had to knock there either. Gaz was watching *Willy Wonka and the Chocolate Factory.* He was on the scene where Willy Wonka was about to take the group on the psychedelic boat ride.

"What's up?" Gaz said, pausing the movie. Avery pushed

aside a laundry basket, sat next to him on the couch, and put her head in her hands.

"Things are really complicated," she said.

He accepted this statement at face value and let her stare into the basket of his shirts and boxers in peace. Two more reasons to love Gaz—he never hassled anyone for explanations they didn't feel like giving, and he *literally* kept his dirty laundry in the open. He was a transparent guy.

"I got fired," she said as her eyes went blurry from staring at a red-and-blue-striped pair of boxers for too long.

"Oh, man. Sorry."

She drummed her fingers on her knee and looked at the frozen picture on the screen. Wonka looked particularly nuts, all wide eyes and flying curls under that big purple top hat. Wonka was kind of her god—the creator of dreams, the exposer of the fake. Everyone's favorite sadist. His look questioned her now and demanded that she tell the truth about herself. She couldn't lie to Willy Wonka.

"Do I seem gay to you?" she asked.

"I don't know," Gaz said. He didn't sound like he thought the question was odd. "I guess anyone could be."

"I'm not," Avery said firmly.

"Okay."

Avery leaned back very deliberately and inserted herself under Gaz's arm. It felt as good to be next to him as she'd hoped. He was lean and warm and for some reason he smelled like french fries.

It happened gradually over the course of the next few minutes, without Avery really thinking about it much. Gaz slid lower, she moved closer—and they just kind of oozed over the line between spacing out and preparing to kiss. When Gaz turned his face to Avery's, the deal already seemed done, and she was content. She closed her eyes.

And it was good.

Again she didn't feel that rush she'd experienced with Mel, or the deep sense of connection. But Gaz had *something* she needed right now. Maybe if she just did this long enough, she would like it just as much as she'd liked being with . . .

Mel's face kept popping into Avery's brain, and she tried very hard to push it away and replace it with Wonka's intense stare, which was still frozen on the screen. She understood now—she had to make everything stop. It wasn't that she didn't like Mel or even love Mel—she just couldn't *date* her. Something had happened between them that summer, something that had felt right and had maybe even *been* right. But it wasn't right anymore. It wasn't who Avery was; it wasn't what she really wanted. And now she needed to undo it all, turn things back to how they were before.

That was why she was here, rolling over onto Gaz's lap. Going from friend to friend, girl to boy, employment to unemployment—one crisis to another. She didn't want to think about how Mel would cry, or how Nina would react, or how she would pay for her car, or what she was doing with her life.

Right now she just had to undo. One thing at a time.

25

When Mel got to school the next morning, she discovered that all of the things that Avery normally stored in her locker were gone.

No note. No explanation. Just an empty hook and a whole bunch of extra space.

Mel scrambled through the contents, but nothing of Avery's was left—not the music folder, or the chemistry book with the broken spine, or the cigarettes that Mel was always afraid someone would notice. And then Mel saw the worst of it. Sitting in the middle of the top shelf was Avery's thumb ring.

There was a buzzing sound in her head. Mel took the ring and quickly shoved it onto her own thumb. It was too large, so she put it into her front pocket.

She skipped first period, which was only twenty minutes anyway since it was the start of the Thanksgiving holiday. She sat in the last stall of the bathroom instead, flicking the lid up and down on the little bin marked Feminine Disposal that was attached to the wall. The bin also had no bottom and no bag, so it could never be used for anything except for making noise and transmitting this slightly scary message that Mel couldn't help but take personally.

An hour later Mel was still in the bathroom. She figured she was definitely marked absent by now and so there was no need to go to her classes. Instead she decided to venture into the halls and try to find Avery and ask her what was going on. Unfortunately, with all the dodging and weaving that she had to do to avoid being seen by any of her teachers or by the security guy who paced the halls, Mel managed to miss Avery at every turn. When she actually did spot her between seventh and eighth periods, it was in such a public place that there was nothing Mel could say or do without causing a huge scene (which would just make things worse), so she slipped out to the parking lot to stand by Avery's car and wait.

Avery must have bypassed her own locker after eighth because she appeared just a moment after the bell rang. She didn't look very pleased that Mel was standing by the car, preparing for a confrontation. This wasn't going to be pretty.

"Hey," Avery said, making sure not to look Mel in the eye. She started shuffling through her bag.

"You took your stuff," Mel said.

"I just thought it would be better," Avery replied, keeping her attention completely on the contents of her bag.

"But you left your ring."

"I just need a few days, Mel." Avery's voice was low but still cracking.

"A few days for what?"

"To think."

"About?"

"Stuff. I have a lot of . . . stuff. I just need a few days."

"What about this weekend?"

"I don't know," Avery replied, finally pulling her keys out of the clutter. "I think we should just spend time on our own. You have to go to your mom's anyway."

"I'm just going there for Thanksgiving dinner."

Avery was talking like it was no big deal at all to cancel four days' worth of plans, including Saturday night, when Mel's dad was going to be gone and Avery was scheduled to stay over. They didn't just skip those nights. Mel *lived* for those.

"It's just one weekend, Mel."

Mel felt her knees start to give. She carefully lowered herself and sat down right there between the cars.

"Mel, I'm late."

"Where are you going?"

"I've got my lesson now. I'll call you later, okay?"

Avery got into her car. It was punctuation. This discussion was over. Mel wanted to do something dramatic—leap up and grab Avery, stand behind the car and block it in, scream at the top of her lungs—all awful things that would do no good. As it was, she was already sitting on the ground in the parking lot, and people were looking at her, probably thinking that she was a crazy lesbian. But all she wanted was her best friend, the girl she loved, to put her stuff back in her locker and say she'd spend the next few days with her.

Mel watched the school buses come into the lot and Avery's car disappear around the block. Everybody looked so happy to have the next few days off. To Mel those days were just holes—big, deep holes that she'd never be able to fill.

26

It was plain black, very stark. Shiny. Thin columns of white print. Photos of sumptuously curved violins. Austere rehearsal rooms with blond floors and blank walls. The occasional conductor springing up from the bottom of the page or the string quartet leaping in from the side. Everybody looking serious, competent, and calm. There was something about the way this brochure was designed that screamed: YOU WILL NEVER BE THIS GOOD. GIVE UP NOW, LOSER, WHILE RITE AID IS STILL HIRING.

It seemed like Avery had had this brochure and application in her possession since the beginning of time. In actuality, it took her two weeks to work up the courage to rip open the envelope it came in. It had taken her another week to read it. Now she was lying on her bed in her favorite pair of gray sweatpants, which were cut off at midcalf. Her collie, Bandit, sprawled next to her like a living body pillow. Her hair was unwashed and sticking up at weird angles, and all she'd eaten were three pieces of bread with mustard and a few handfuls of cold leftover turkey. The tryptophan hadn't knocked her out, but she was feeling very languid.

Now that Thanksgiving was over, she had no plans at all for days. If she wanted to, she could go to Mel's on Saturday and stay. But then there would be a lot of sad faces and clinging, and Mel would want to talk about their relationship.

God. She was turning into a guy. Avery turned back to the brochure. She knew perfectly well that there was no way she was going to slip into this shiny, serious-looking world. But Avery went on, skipping over the first few pages, which described how hard the school was and how brilliant all the students were, and went right for the important part—the application procedure for piano students. They required a CD or tape along with the completed application. Postmark date: December 15.

She pushed the brochure away from her. Bandit put his paw on it.

What the hell was she doing with her life? She was just sliding by in her classes. She'd been fired from Mortimer's. If she was very lucky, she might be able to squeeze into a state school, pick some kind of noncommittal major, graduate, and get some generic job that required sitting at a computer. She'd gain weight from all the sitting and have to start eating frozen diet meals or drinking low-carb shakes from a can.

She carefully removed the brochure from Bandit's grasp and opened it again to the admissions page. She read through the list of pieces acceptable for the recording. There were enough listed that she was happy to find that she owned at least four of them and played two of them passably. This gave her the courage to continue reading:

If you are selected to audition, you will be required to play the following from memory:

One selection from J. S. Bach's The Well-Tempered Clavier *or the* Goldberg Variations

One sonata by Mozart or Beethoven (excluding Beethoven op. 49)

One 19th-century composition (solo piano)

One 20th-century composition (solo piano)

Following the audition, applicants will sit for an hour-long entrance examination in basic music theory. Callbacks will be held the same day, and a callback list will be posted by 4 P.M. on the day of the audition. If an applicant's name does not appear on the list, the applicant should assume that he or she is no longer under consideration for a place in the class.

Gaz had a Tascam four-track recorder, and Hareth had an illegal copy of Pro Tools. Either way, she'd be able to get something on tape. She could persuade her music teacher at school and her piano teacher at home to write up some letters pretty quickly—they were always on her case about applying to music school. If she actually got up, got dressed, and got her ass in gear, she might be able to put this thing together.

Instead she rolled off her bed and went searching for leftover turkey.

As Avery came from her darkened bedroom, the glaring lights in the hallway almost sent her reeling. There was a strong odor of pine coming from a candle burning in the kitchen. Avery knew what this meant. Her mother always felt that the second the turkey had been put away, she was allowed to start rolling out for Christmas. As Avery made her way down the hall, she heard the *20 Classic Christmas Songs* album on and saw her mother roping off the kitchen doorway with gold drugstore tinsel.

"Crime scene?" Avery asked. "Did someone murder an elf in there?"

"I'm going to pin it up so it drapes. Just go under."

Avery leaned against the wall as Bing Crosby bu-bu-bu-booed his way through "Mele Kalikimaka," the Hawaiian Christmas song.

"Bing Crosby used to beat his kids with empty whiskey bottles," she said, rubbing her eyes hard with the heels of her hands, trying to get them to adjust.

"That's a nice piece of holiday trivia."

"It was an early attempt at recycling."

"Mmmmm."

Avery slid down the wall and sat on the floor. She didn't even feel like making the effort to limbo the tinsel.

"What are you and Mel up to this weekend?" her mother asked.

"Me and Mel?" Avery said, her voice arching.

"I never see Nina anymore."

"She's busy," Avery said quickly. "Student council."

"Nina always was a hard worker."

And what did *that* mean? Avery wondered. That she wasn't?

Well, okay. She was slumped on the floor like a rag. Maybe it wasn't so unfair.

"What's the point of Christmas in Hawaii?" Avery asked.

"They deserve the holiday too."

"Yeah, but it must be weird."

"Only if you're not from Hawaii," her mother said. "Everything's normal to somebody."

And now Mom is a Zen master, she thought. *Is the tinsel halfway up the door frame or halfway down?*

With effort Avery pulled herself up from her seat. She would call Gaz. That was at least a start. Better than sitting here, wondering if the phone was going to ring or if Mel was going to turn up. This was her fate now. Inertia and life on the run.

It would make a good band name, but it sucked as a way to live.

Christmas

December 2

TO: Steve

FROM: Nina

Ugh. Here we go. December is like insanity month on the council. I had three different meetings after school for the toy drive, the food drive, and the holiday dance committee. How are things post-Thanksgiving? Did you eat Tofurky?

Mel and Avery both kind of vanished off the face of the earth after the holiday. Mel called me once, but I didn't see them at all, which was bizarre. Nothing has felt right since I saw Avery with that guy at the hayroll. I love you, and we are so much closer to being at school. They will be mailing the early decision notices sometime in the next 15 days, which is kind of more than I can even think about. . . .

December 4

TO: Steve

FROM: Nina

I saw you online the other night and sent like 2,000 IMs. I guess you weren't actually at your computer and your mom or one of your fugitive houseguests or the FBI read them.

You're probably saving a river right now, but can you write to me so I know you're alive?

December 6

TO: Steve

FROM: Nina

Seriously. I am about to call a search party. And I can never get through on your phone!

v.v.v.v.v.v. anxious to hear from you. I am kind of worried that the ceiling has finally fallen in or the black stuff on the floor has swallowed you up.

your neurotic girlfriend

December 7
TO: Nina
FROM: Steve

Sorry . . . we had computer problems. And the phone thing. I know. I'm really, really sorry. No Tofurky. Nut roast. Tasty but not very good on the intestines.

Things are crazy here now too . . . let me know about Stanford.

27

Mel waited. She was sure that if she was calm and didn't bother Avery that Avery would see there was no problem. Mel interpreted waiting as not even speaking of the argument because she didn't want it to grow larger and more important than it already was. If it was ignored, maybe it would wither and die.

First the Thanksgiving holiday went by. The Podds were visited. Mel found out that Richie had broken his collarbone jumping off someone's gazebo. Jim bought some kind of fancy new stove and Mel was forced to admire it. Lyla expanded her list of acceptable foods to incorporate mashed butternut squash with margarine. These were the highlights—the rest was unforgivably dull.

She spent the next three nights sitting with her dad, watching cheesy, romantic movies. Weirdly, her father was a huge fan of them. He owned DVDs of *Notting Hill*, *When Harry Met Sally*, *Sleepless in Seattle*, and *Four Weddings and a Funeral*. These were his favorites. If his day was particularly long, he'd come home with two boxes of mac and cheese and pop one of those movies in and they would watch together. Underneath that rugged contractor's exterior beat the heart of a sixteen-year-old girl.

Mel wished she could tell him as they were three hours into a Humphrey Bogart fest on AMC that she really didn't want to watch *Casablanca*, because her own heart was about to explode. She couldn't bring herself to do it. She sat there with him on the couch, the tissues on her lap, praying that Ilsa didn't get on her plane and leave Rick. But she did. It figured. Mel cried. Her dad cried. They were the Crying Family.

When she returned to school, just as an added precaution, Mel took extra time in the morning to make sure she looked her best. She kept her hair down because she knew Avery loved it that way. She wore skirts and her favorite ribbon choker. She got new lip gloss. She tried some eye liner.

She was aware that people were looking at her more than usual. She was too preoccupied to care. When a cheerleader got out of line in the cafeteria right as Mel stepped behind her, when a table of guys grew eerily silent as she walked past, Mel ignored it. Getting noticed by Avery was the only thing that mattered.

All this effort was for nothing, though, since Avery managed to make herself invisible. Mel tried to end up in the right places so that Avery would be able to see her, but the most she ever got was a glimpse of Avery's wine-colored leather jacket disappearing into the parking lot.

A week passed, and the waiting got harder. Mel started about a hundred notes and e-mails—she spent every class composing them in her head and sometimes writing them down. She went to school. She came home. She dumped her stuff on her bedroom floor. Sleeping made the waiting easier, so she took naps. Her dad would wake her up for dinner and ask her if she was feeling sick. She listened to the same songs over and over until they were imprinted in her brain and flowed through her dreams. The only thing Mel's life was leading up to was a phone call or a note or a visit that never seemed to materialize.

Things started to fall to the wayside. The random handful of college applications sat on her desk, unexamined. Every time she opened one and tried to read it, she felt a weird kind of paralysis—she couldn't imagine leaving here, leaving everyone, and going off to live in one of these concrete towers or stark brick buildings with a bunch of strangers. She picked at her homework selectively. She spaced out in class, looking at all the girls and imagining what it would be like to kiss each one, wondering which ones would actually want to try.

None of them would be like Avery, though.

Throughout all of this, Nina was insanely busy. Every time Mel saw her, she was running to a class or a meeting or an event. Besides, she'd already asked not to be put in the middle, so Mel said nothing to her. Instead she confided in Parker—before English, at lunch, at work, on the phone, online—nervously asking him over and over if that was the day she should finally talk to Avery. He always said yes, and he was always good about it, although he looked a little frustrated after two solid weeks of being asked the same question.

It all came to a head one night at work, halfway through December, as Mel was sliding two Mortiburgers from under the heat lamps and thinking about the fact that she hadn't even started studying for her trig midterm, which was only two days away. The cook leaned out and peered at her through the opening, his face spookily illuminated by the heat lamp, causing it to glow red.

"So," he said, "where's your girlfriend?"

And that was that. The bottom dropped out for Mel. She couldn't be in the pantry anymore—or in the restaurant—or possibly *anywhere*. Mel abandoned the burgers and ran to the nasty employee bathroom, back in the storeroom, and barricaded herself inside.

The void had finally swallowed her up: she was alone and confused and sick of waiting and repulsed by everything.

She wasn't coming out.

After ten minutes or so, one of the assistant managers knocked on the door. Panicked, Mel faked some coughing and retching noises, which probably didn't fool anyone, but she still managed to get off for the rest of the night. Parker wasn't working, but he was supposed to come by at eleven to pick her up. But it wasn't Parker she needed.

She called Nina.

28

Nina had been sitting at her desk, looking through the twelve-page study outline for the AP history midterm, which was in two days. It had just occurred to her that she was in serious trouble since she'd had no time at all to even think about studying for it. She'd been busy with the council, as well as four other midterms and the fifteen-page paper that she'd just handed to Frost that afternoon. She almost told Mel she couldn't pick her up, but when she heard the panic in Mel's voice, she accepted her fate and headed for her car.

She was doomed anyway. Might as well go down helping a friend.

Mel was waiting for her on a bench outside of Mortimer's, huddled in her blue coat. She got up when she saw Nina pull into the lot and quietly let herself in.

"What's going on?" Nina said. "Are you sick?"

With that, Mel dissolved completely into tears. Nina quickly pulled into a parking space and wrapped Mel in a hug.

"What happened? Are you okay?"

"Shewu call mee," Mel gasped.

"What, honey?"

"*Shheeeeewuughghhcalllghmeee.*"

It took ten minutes of sobbing and hiccuping before Mel was able to relate the story clearly enough for Nina to understand.

"Why didn't you tell me?" Nina said when Mel was through. She reached into the well between the seats and pulled out a tiny pack of Kleenex. Mel worked her way through half the pack.

"Can I ask you something?" Nina said tentatively.

"Sure."

"How did you know?" Nina asked. "About being gay. What was it?"

Mel rubbed the tip of her nose and looked over in surprise. Nina realized that this was the first time she'd ever really *asked*. Some friend she'd been.

"I didn't really get it at first," Mel said. "I thought I just really liked certain people. And then I realized that I *really* liked certain people. And then I noticed they were all girls."

"You don't like guys at all?"

"I like them," Mel said. "I think they're nice. But I never *felt* anything. Not like what other girls seemed to feel."

"How long have you known?" Nina asked.

"A long time," she replied softly. "Years, probably."

Mel sniffed for a minute and made a little pyramid of the tissues.

"I don't want you to feel like I thought Avery was better than you or something," she continued. "I think you're beautiful and great. No offense. I swear."

"I never . . ."

"It's okay," Mel said. "But just so you know. You're wonderful—but it's not like that. In my mind, you're Nina."

"But Avery is Avery," Nina said. "How is it different?"

"You know how you can sometimes tell when a person might like you?" Mel explained. "There's just something about the way they look at you or the way they keep trying to talk to you? Probably like you and Steve."

"Yeah," Nina said, stiffening at the sound of his name. "It was like that."

"I just want to give her another day or two," Mel said, sniffing. "I think it's just hard for her to get used to the idea of people knowing."

The words wanted to jump free of Nina's mouth—*I saw Avery with Gaz.*

"Mel . . ." she said.

She clamped down her back teeth again. Mel slumped against Nina's side, and Nina stroked her hair.

As they sat there, Nina realized that this was the first time in a long while that she hadn't been on the sidelines watching. She knew something that Mel didn't. She was needed. She was involved. And she could, potentially, use what she knew to get Avery to talk to her. Avery owed her, after all.

She felt a sudden surge of enthusiasm. She sat Mel upright.

"I'll talk to her," Nina said.

"I don't think she wants to talk."

"She needs to talk, Mel. It might be easier for her to talk to me because I'm kind of uninvolved. I know how to *facilitate*. I spent all summer learning about facilitation."

"Really?" Mel asked.

"This is us. This is the three of us. We can fix this."

This was the first time in months that the "we" actually included Nina. Mel seemed to realize this too because her eyes lit up.

"We can?"

"Totally."

Over Mel's shoulder Nina saw a familiar red car come into the lot. It was The Roach.

"Parker's here," she said.

Mel opened up the window and waved to him, and he pulled up alongside and got out of his car. His hair was all over the place, and he was wearing a pair of rumpled jeans and a long wool coat. Also he had on glasses, which Nina had never seen him in before. She guessed that he'd gotten out of bed to come and get Mel. Nina unlocked the doors and he climbed into the back.

"Hey," he said curiously, looking between the two of them. "Party in the parking lot?"

"I had a moment," Mel said quietly. "I kind of ran away from work."

"Shit. You okay?"

"Now I am." Mel looked over at Nina shyly. "Park knows all about it. *All* about it."

Parker nodded and stifled a yawn.

"Things okay now?" he asked.

"Yeah," Mel said while wiping away a rogue tear and mustering a smile for Nina. "They're going to be fine."

29

Nina woke up the next morning feeling like the world had realigned itself a little. She was fueled by a new sense of purpose. A righteous cause.

She decided to skip her run and took the extra time to take a long, boiling shower that flushed her skin. She got a little overzealous with her cucumber-cilantro body wash and had a distinctly saladlike smell when she emerged.

Today she was going to work it. She pulled out her knee-high, caramel-colored boots with the platform heels. An excellent start. There was something about the way those heels clicked on the floor and the three inches of lift that changed the way she saw the world. Deep brown skirt, a little indulgence she'd gotten for herself a few weeks before. (All hail Mom's AmEx.) Formfitting, cream-colored cashmere sweater (from Nan). This was her battle gear. Tight and tall. That was the only way to play it.

She tracked Avery down at her locker first thing. Down in the basement, things were fairly desolate. It was the closest thing you could get to privacy at AHH.

"I need to talk to you," Nina said.

"About what?" Avery was shoving her books into her bag in a disorganized fashion.

"What's going on with you and Mel?"

"This is your business . . . how?"

"Because we're friends."

"Uh-huh." Avery seemed unimpressed. This wasn't actually the way Nina had envisioned this starting off.

"We're not friends?"

"You can't fix this one, Neen," Avery said matter-of-factly. "It has nothing to do with you."

"It has everything to do with me."

"Because?"

"You know why."

Avery pulled hard on the zipper of her backpack, catching paper in the teeth.

"Listen," Nina said, "after school we'll all go to my place and—"

"This isn't a student council project," Avery said coldly, ripping the tiny corner of paper from the zipper track. "You can't just call a meeting whenever *you* feel like it."

"This affected me too, you know," Nina said, her tone growing more tense.

"You always do that," Avery snapped. "You always have to stick yourself into things."

"You had me *lie* for you about you and Gaz. I never told her. That's not me sticking myself into it."

Avery couldn't say much to that one.

Nina tried to simmer things down with some common sense. "All I'm saying is that you should talk to her. She's freaking out because she doesn't understand what's going on."

Bang. Avery slammed her locker and walked around Nina toward the stairs. Nina followed close behind.

"And I know *you* might not either," Nina added.

"Deep. They teach you that at camp?"

There was serious cynicism in Avery's voice now that surprised Nina. Avery seemed to be making fun of her—not in a joking way either.

"Why are you being like this?" Nina said.

"I just want you to stay out of my business."

"Friends are into each other's business," Nina shot back.

Now they were at the top of the stairs, in front of the frosted glass door that led to the main hall. They both knew this conversation couldn't go past that door.

"Listen, Nina. It's over," Avery said sharply. "We're not dating anymore. Are you satisfied now that you're in the loop?"

"Are you going to tell her, or are you just going to run for cover?"

"Why don't you do it?" Avery asked. "You seem to like playing counselor."

"Oh, I love it."

"I think you do."

The bell rang. Nina rubbed under her eyes. They were burning. She was tired. She didn't know this Avery. She wanted to go home, back to bed.

"I have to go," she said. "I'm going to tell her if you don't."

"Do it, then," Avery said, looking down. "And leave me the hell alone."

"Fine." Nina went through the door and slipped into the chaos of the hallway. Everything seemed rough to her. It didn't feel like the normal morning rush of people bumping and rushing to class. The hall was full of vicious, foreign mobs.

Nina planted her thumbs in the corners of her eye to cork up anything that might have leaked out.

For the rest of the day Nina had a blistering headache. The loudness of her heels and their shuddering impact with the linoleum didn't help much. The dark came early. By two the overcast sky made it look like dusk. Frost's class was gloomier than usual, although she ignored Nina for most of it. Devon was her chosen target of the week. He'd made the mistake of asking what was going to be on the midterm exam. That kind of thing never went over big with Frost.

When Nina got home, her mother's secretary, Gina, came bursting through the communicating door between the living room and the office. She was pinching an envelope between her fingertips.

"Look what came!" she said, wielding an envelope. "Look!"

Sometimes it was a little weird having someone who always went through the mail.

Nina took hold of it. This wasn't some generic letter. The envelope was made of high-quality paper—heavy, with a velvety finish. There was an insignia alongside the return address. Stanford.

"I saw you pull up," Gina said. "Your mom's with a client, but she's so excited. We've had this for four hours. We were going to call you, but we figured we'd wait."

Nina weighed the envelope in her palm. She couldn't gauge what was in it.

"I think I'm going to take it upstairs. . . ."

Gina looked a little disappointed, but she nodded anyway.

"Come tell us," she said. "No matter what."

"Okay."

Nina wearily walked upstairs and sat at her desk. This was the last moment of not knowing her fate. She carefully tore the envelope open along the stamped side, keeping the seal intact. The first words told all.

On behalf of the admissions committee, I am pleased to inform you . . .

Her eyes skipped along the page.

. . . the enclosed forms, along with a $500 deposit . . . look forward to seeing you on campus this fall.

She shuffled through the papers, barely processing what she was seeing. Forms on blue and green paper. Some kind of postcard. She spread everything out on the desk and looked at it. Automatically she opened up a new e-mail and quickly sent a note:

Steve,

It came. I got in. Write to me.

Love, Neen

There wasn't excitement yet. More like a dull thrumming in her head. It had happened—it was all real. She closed her laptop and stared at her bed.

She just had to tell Mel.

Nina reached for her phone and numbly dialed Mel's number. As soon as Mel picked up, Nina realized she didn't know what to say first.

"Did you talk to her?" Mel asked.

Maybe she should ask Mel to come over. No. Mel would just get stuck in the middle of the celebration that was about to break out in the house. Nina couldn't just leave either. Her mom and Gina would want to take her to dinner.

There was no good way of doing this. *How did I get here?* she thought. *Why am I breaking up for Avery?*

"Neen?" Mel prodded.

"I talked to her," she said.

Be direct. Don't drag it out.

"She thinks it would be better if you guys . . . didn't date."

"What do you mean?" Mel's voice was frightened. Nina could hear her mom and Gina bustling downstairs now, waiting for news. Pretty soon they would come up and knock on the door and they wouldn't understand why Nina couldn't talk.

"It's probably a good thing," Nina added, hopelessly. "It's good to know. It'll be okay."

"You mean we broke up?"

"We'll go out," Nina said. Then, not wanting to be misunderstood, she quickly added, "You, me, Parker. It'll be just like before.

We can even put Parker in a dress and give him a cigarette." No response. She shouldn't have joked. She knew she wasn't funny.

Footsteps on the stairs. Nothing from Mel except some breathing. And Steve was lost somewhere in the wild. Nina heard herself talking, telling Mel over and over how it would be fine. In fact, that it would be great and Avery had been wrong— and they'd been wrong about Avery forever. It had *always* been just the two of them—Nina and Mel. She just talked and talked until Nina wasn't even sure what she was saying or if Mel was still on the phone. She talked until the knock on her door finally came, and she really did have to go. Mel never said a word, not even a good-bye before hanging up the phone.

Nina's mother poked in her head.

"Well?" she asked, her eyes glistening. "Are you in?"

"I'm in," Nina said, forcing a smile. It was true. She didn't elaborate on *what* she was in, though.

New Year's Eve

30

If Nina's life was a movie, Steve would have shown up on her doorstep as a surprise. He would have been waiting on the porch with snow in his hair and a goofy smile and he'd say something like, "Should I have called first?"

But okay. He lived in Oregon. She wasn't asking for miracles. But he should have at least *called.* On New Year's Eve an e-mail does not do it. Especially an e-mail like this:

> *Neen,*
>
> *Happy New Year! Hope you have fun tonight. Talk to you soon.*
>
> *Love, Steve*

What the hell was *that?* Her mom sent more heartfelt and gooey holiday notes to her old clients. Nina knew this for a fact. She usually stuffed and licked the envelopes.

Four notes in four weeks. That's what he had sent. At first she'd found it hard to get annoyed at him. How did you fault someone who was trying to save the world and who didn't have a cable modem or call waiting or a cell phone or anything from this *century?* Still, even the people she read about in English wrote to one another constantly. If you could send two letters a day two hundred years ago, Steve had *no excuse* for four short, impersonal notes in four weeks.

She looked over at her phone. It was resting on the lip of her carefully folded-over flannel snowflake sheets. This was not the time to have this nervous breakdown. She had something much more important to concentrate on tonight.

For the last two weeks Mel had barely left her house or changed out of her pajamas. She sat in her room, playing Norah Jones and Elliott Smith and reading breakup stories online. It had taken Nina three days to persuade Mel to come to this New Year's party, and even then she had to bring Parker in for backup. In an attempt to wear Mel down, he rambled on for two hours about how this party was going to be the social highlight of his year and that if Mel didn't go, his whole life would be ruined and he would end up a lonely middle-aged guy who spent all of his time playing EverQuest. She eventually, albeit reluctantly, came around and agreed to take a break from her monklike existence.

If Mel could briefly drag herself out of her mournful stupor, Nina surely felt she should. Of course, she would be kissless and bitter, but she would be there for Mel in her hour of need. It was just the distraction she needed.

"No one goes upstairs," Georgia greeted them at the door. "No sex on the beds. That was the only thing my parents said."

"I don't think that's going to be a problem," Nina replied.

Mel and Parker were standing behind Nina, taking in the

wonder that was Georgia's house. Nina had seen the B&B many times, but they had never been inside before. A ten-bedroom house in a prime location across from the racetrack, Georgia's humble little abode was packed floor to ceiling with antiques, and the walls were either covered in expensive-looking dark wood or heavy old-fashioned wallpaper. Every surface was adorned with greenery, fruit, or little sparkling lights. Nina was amazed that Georgia's parents had turned the place over to her for the night since they didn't take guests over the holiday. But then again, they had company over for a living. Somehow the house seemed to explain Georgia's whole personality.

"Beer's on the back porch. Booze is in the breakfast room. If you're too drunk to drive home, you can pass out on one of the rugs or couches in the sitting room. Try not to barf on anything. You can put your coats behind the front desk. Go drink."

In the breakfast room there was a huge cut glass punch bowl filled with blue liquid with little red Swedish fish floating all over the top. Parker took their coats, and Mel and Nina took their drinks to the living room and stationed themselves on one of the heavy Queen Anne sofas. The people who had already arrived were from no particular group. Every part of the AHH population was represented, proof of Georgia's popularity and influence.

For a few minutes they sat quietly, sipping their punch. After Nina finished hers, she had a brainstorm and turned to Mel. "We need to find you a new girl," she blurted.

"Um, not really."

Nina ignored this feeble protest.

"What about her?" Nina asked, nodding to a girl in the corner. "I think her name is Lisa. She's in my French class. Or Rebecca, that girl there. She's a sophomore rep."

"You can't just point out girls with short hair," Mel mumbled, her chin pinned to her chest.

"That's not what I'm doing!"

"Yes, it is."

"Okay," Nina admitted. "Maybe. But how else can you tell?"

"Tell what? Who's gay?"

"Yeah."

"I have no idea." Mel sighed.

"So she might be! Go talk to her!"

"You go talk to her."

"I don't want to hit on her!"

"Neither do I."

"Mel . . ." Nina set down her glass rather unsteadily. She took one of Mel's hands and clasped it between both of hers. "You have to move on. There are so many girls out there. . . ."

Mel shushed her.

"Sorry. Was I loud?" Just then Nina realized what a lightweight she was. Only one cup of punch in and she was already nursing a good buzz. "You know what I'm saying. You've got to do something. If you play that album one more time, Norah Jones is going to come to your house and take it from you."

"It makes me feel better."

"It's sad."

"That's why I like it."

Parker returned from the Land of the Coats and sat down with them. He looked at Mel and Nina curiously. "What'd I miss?"

"I'm counseling her," Nina slurred.

"I have to go to the bathroom," Mel said before scurrying off.

As she scanned the room, Nina saw that couples were starting to clump together, magnetized by the approaching New Year and the influence of Georgia's blue punch. Nina put the tail of her Swedish fish between her teeth and started pulling.

"I guess I shouldn't be trying to set her up," she said.

"No," Parker said. "It's a good idea. She needs to move on. She's obsessed."

"She's not *obsessed*," Nina heard herself snap. It wasn't fair to snap at Parker. He couldn't understand what it was like to be in the Triangle. It probably did look like obsession from the outside, but Nina knew the truth. It was withdrawal. It was horrible. "I can't even give her any good advice," Nina added quickly.

"Why not?"

"Because I have a boyfriend who I never see and never talk to who never writes to me." Oh, how Nina's brain was praising the sweet nectar of the blue punch.

"How does *that* work?" Parker asked, raising his eyebrows.

"It doesn't. It sucks."

"Break it down for me."

"I have a cell phone and he doesn't."

"He can't call you because he doesn't have a cell phone?"

"He lives in Oregon," she explained. "It's long distance."

Nina immediately felt a backlash of semidrunken guilt. She was complaining about Steve because he didn't have as much money as her family did. And that was evil.

"It's totally understandable," she added quickly. "When I call, it's free."

"Sounds shady, but I'll let that one slide." Parker took a long sip of his drink. "But why doesn't he write?"

She leaned back and sighed. *Don't say any more,* she told herself. But she'd started talking, and the Swedish fish from the blue punch seemed to be insisting that she go on and on. Also, Parker was such a good listener and funny as hell—all of a sudden it made perfect sense why Mel would confide in him so much.

Nina tried to ignore this weird whirring noise that had just entered her head and focus on what she was saying. "He used to write every day. Now he writes once every couple of days, and the notes are pretty short. He's just a really busy guy. But I'm busy too, and I write *every* day."

"Want my thoughts on this?"

"Tell me."

"Okay." Parker turned himself around so that he was facing Nina directly. "If I were this guy, and I had a totally devoted girlfriend who wrote to me every day and called me all the time, I would drive out here and live in my car."

"But he rides a bike."

"He's going to need a car for my plan. It doesn't have to be a really good car."

"How's he going to live?" Nina asked. "What would he eat?"

"He can drink water from the springs. We've got a hundred frigging springs around this town spurting up the healthiest water on the planet or something, and it's totally free. He can live on that. Live to be a hundred."

"Just water?"

"Okay, water, and discount bread that they sell at the end of the day at the bakery. And there are ducks all over the place."

"He's vegetarian."

"Oh God," Parker said with a sigh. He plucked the Swedish fish from his cup and wielded it to make his point. "Fine. You know what? He can eat his car. Piece by piece. It's been done before. There are guys in India who have eaten whole cars just to show that they can do it. It's one of those David Blaine kind of endurance things."

"If he eats his car, where's he going to live?"

Parker rolled his eyes. "It's going to take him a *while* to eat the car," he explained. "It'll probably take until spring, and by then it'll be warm. He won't need shelter anymore."

"This is your plan? Is that what you do for your girlfriend?"

"That is my hypothetical plan for my hypothetical girlfriend."

"Well, I practically have a hypothetical boyfriend, so . . ."

"So there you go."

There was a brightness to Parker's eyes—a huge booming enthusiasm that was catching.

"I like this plan," she said, while getting up and making her way back to the punch bowl. "I wish he thought like you."

"If he's not writing to you, he's insane," Parker said. "And who cares if he doesn't have a phone? He can *borrow* a phone. How hard is that?"

That was a good point. Nina had never thought of that before.

"This is just my opinion," Parker added.

Whatever was in the punch made Nina feel mellow. She dropped her head on Parker's shoulder. An actual male shoulder. That was something she hadn't experienced in a while. Something human to put her head against. It felt different. Steve had well-developed arms and shoulders. Parker's shoulders were thinner, and there was a more wiry energy coming through them.

"I should go find Mel," she said drowsily. "Avery really screwed her over, you know that? I never thought Ave would do something like that."

"I know. It must be hard. You guys were really good friends."

Nina didn't reply. It was too difficult to explain that "good friends" didn't quite cover it. Besides, thinking about Avery made her sad, and she didn't want to ruin the calmness that had just come over her. She pulled her head up. It was heavy. It felt like everything she had drunk had run right into her skull and was sloshing around.

"I'm going to check on her," she said. "Be right back."

Nina took a rambling walk around the first floor, then went out onto the porch, where all of the beer was being kept cool. She pulled her cell phone out of her bag and sat down on an antique-looking bench. Maybe Parker's theory would come true tonight. Maybe Steve had borrowed someone's phone and called her. Maybe he'd realized that not only was she going to be alone and kissless, but that he'd really violated the good-boyfriend code.

Nothing. No little envelope on the screen.

It was stupid of her to have checked. This only sent her mood crashing down again.

She heard the front door open from behind her and turned to see Devon coming out onto the porch. In honor of the holiday he was wearing a black jacket over his regular shirt and tie.

"What's up?" he asked, grabbing a beer.

"Just checking my messages." She dropped the cell phone back into her bag.

Devon cracked open his beer and leaned against one of the porch columns as if he planned on staying and talking for a while.

"How do you think you did on Frost's midterm?" he asked.

"I don't want to think about it."

"Me either."

"I don't care that much," Nina said. Then it dawned on her that she could make herself feel better by taking a short but well-deserved ego trip.

"I already applied to college. I did early decision and got in, so . . ."

"You got in? Where are you going?"

"Stanford."

"No shit," he said, nodding. "Impressive."

"Thanks." Yep, it worked.

"I just sent out a few," he said. "I was putting my portfolio together while I was getting ready for the AP exam, so I was kind of freaking out. I didn't sleep for like three days."

This was the most personal information she'd ever exchanged with Devon.

"What about your boyfriend?" he asked. "Where's he going?"

"My boyfriend?"

"That guy on the sofa."

"That's *Parker*," Nina said.

"He's not your boyfriend?"

"No."

"Oh. I thought he was."

A weird thought passed through Nina's mind—maybe Devon was trying to tell her something. Why else would he be asking about her boyfriend?

Although Nina was quite aware that she was a tad on the drunk side, Devon suddenly seemed *very* attractive to her. He was hiding behind those ties, behind that perpetually disappointed scowl, behind the camera lens. Underneath all of it might be a really great guy.

"Got your midnight kiss lined up?" she heard herself asking.

"I've got this," he said, holding up his beer. He peeled off his beer label, rolled it up, and pitched it into a snow-filled trough that was already crammed with empties. "What about you?"

Nina held up the Swedish fish from her cup. "I'd like you to meet Marvin. He's very special to me."

"Pretty sad." Devon snickered. He was smiling a lot, and Nina felt herself smiling back. Was it any big surprise that she was feeling this way? After all, she hadn't been able to kiss Steve since *August*. It wasn't unreasonable to want a little contact with the male species. And Steve kind of deserved it right now.

Suddenly Parker appeared at the door.

"I thought you got lost," he said. "It's almost time."

"It is?" Nina said. For a second she was almost disappointed that Parker had picked this moment to turn up. "I thought it was ten or something."

"No. It's like eight minutes away."

Parker looked from Nina to Devon and back again.

She pulled herself from the bench and went to the door. Devon took another swig of his beer and raised it up in a salute-like fashion.

As soon as she got inside, Nina realized two things. One: that kissing Devon Wakeman was probably one of the best ways a girl could bring in the new year. Two: that she'd just come alarmingly close to cheating on her boyfriend. But luckily Parker had saved her. Indeed, Parker had saved her whole relationship. Nina loved Parker. She gripped his arm hard to show her appreciation.

"You all right?" he asked, looking down at the nails that were digging into the sleeve of his black shirt.

"I'm okay," she whispered. "Thanks, Park."

"For what?"

"Nothing. Everything. You know what I mean."

He looked baffled, which was understandable.

"I found Mel," he said.

"Mel?" Nina asked. She'd forgotten that was how she'd ended up outside in the first place—she was supposed to be searching for her best friend. Oh, she *really* had to get an enormous glass of water or mug of coffee, and quick.

"She's fine. She's saving our spot on the sofa."

Parker, Parker, Parker . . . Nina felt her emotions swelling for him. It was like he had stepped in at the critical point in their lives, maybe even to take Avery's place.

"You're the best," she said, giving him a quick kiss on the cheek.

Parker froze and peered down at her. He touched the spot where her lips had been.

"Um . . . thanks."

He smiled, but Nina noticed that the bright look in his eye that she'd seen earlier was gone. She wondered about this, but then she saw Mel waiting for them on the sofa, pointing eagerly at the countdown on the television, and the thought drifted away.

31

The breakup with Avery had not taken Mel by surprise. In her heart, she'd known it was coming since the day in the bookstore with Devon—maybe even before that. It was in all of Avery's hesitation, in her refusals to even say she was bi. It was just a looming thing on the horizon that got bigger as it got closer. When Nina broke the news to Mel, it finally came right up to her face and blocked Avery out of her view. But it wasn't a shock. It just depressed her and made her days dark and long and kind of pointless.

Nina, however, was as determined as ever to keep Mel moving. She had a bit more free time on her hands now that she had gotten into Stanford, so she came to lunch the very first day back from winter break and announced to Mel and Parker that Lake Lonely had frozen. (This sounded symbolic to Mel: Lake Lonely had frozen, but in Lake Love the waters were warm! Yeah—as if.) Lake Lonely was just the smaller body of water next to Saratoga Lake, so it always froze a little sooner.

Nina had decided that they were going ice-skating whether Mel wanted to ice-skate or not. Parker didn't own skates but agreed to come along anyway. His reply seemed a bit staged, and Mel got the idea that Nina had cornered him earlier in the day.

Mel's dad was out working on someone's kitchen, and Mel would have much preferred to go home and sit and listen to music. But here she was anyway, out in the freezing cold, tying up her laces. It was four, but it was already almost dark.

There were only a few good access points to Lake Lonely. The most crowded one was off a public access point. There was another that stemmed from a path of a gated community. But there was one that Nina, Mel, and Avery had used for years. It was behind a lakeside restaurant, at the bottom of a slope. Many people didn't know about this one, and the restaurant didn't mind if they used one of their parking spaces during the dead time in the middle of the afternoon.

All members of the Triangle were good ice-skaters. They'd skated together since they were just toddlers in double blades. Nina was especially good. She'd even taken lessons for a while and could do little jumps and arabesques. She laced up quickly and hit the ice to check it over. Mel took her time, sharing a rock with Parker, who was staring at the ice in deep dissatisfaction.

"What's the matter?" Mel asked.

"Nothing."

Mel was in no mood to press the issue, but she kept her eye on Parker anyway.

"It just pisses me off," he finally said.

"What does?"

"I don't get it. I thought that was just something from TV."

"What?"

"That women like guys who are assholes."

"We don't," Mel said.

"How would you know?"

Mel continued her lacing. She knew what Parker meant, but it still stung.

"Sorry," he said. "You know what I mean. See? I'm an asshole, and you like me. It's just that Devon is a dick. He wears *ties*. . . ."

He lowered his voice on this last word, as if "ties" was the offensive part of that sentence.

"I don't get it," she said. "What about Devon?"

"I think she's . . . into him." He nodded to Nina.

"Nina? And Devon?" Mel laughed. "There's no way. Why would you even think that?"

"They were talking at the party."

"They always talk, but she can't stand him."

"She was standing him."

Mel examined Parker more closely now. He scrunched up his mouth and plunged his hand into a nearby pile of snow.

"Holy shit. You like her," she said suddenly. Parker didn't respond. He just dug his hand in deeper until the snow covered his wrist.

"You do." Mel could see it all over his face now. "Oh my God. You do."

"Go skate." he said, avoiding her eyes.

Mel had no idea what to say. In her opinion, Parker and Nina would be great together—except that Nina was taken by some guy Mel had never met, and Parker was kind of . . . hers. Not in a dating way. Just hers, though.

Mel got up and made her way onto the ice. She skated briskly back and forth along the edge, where the ice was thickest. As she passed by, she watched Parker watching Nina, who was out toward the middle. Every once in a while he would throw a look in Mel's direction that said, "I will fatally wound you if you say anything." They were all in their own worlds in the quiet of the snow. Mel listened to the soothing sound of the creaking ice under her skates and gazed at the trees, which were covered in whiteness.

It was good to be out—out and not talking. Mel could concentrate on skating hard until her legs ached. She skated back and forth for a good half hour until her breath was coming hard and she realized that this was the longest stretch she'd gone without thinking about Avery in weeks.

Mel was about to do another lap when she turned around just in time to see a small white object flying through the air in her direction. She tried to move away, but she wasn't fast enough. It caught her right in the chest. She started coughing. It was a snowball. Actually, an ice ball. And it really hurt. From across the ice she heard Nina yelp.

In the next moment, another one got Mel in the knee and almost knocked her over. She tried to get away, but the snowballs seemed to follow her. They rained down surprisingly hard. Someone had been stockpiling. She looked up. There were a few guys behind some trees, about midway down the slope, throwing as hard as they could. And they weren't about to stop anytime soon.

She hurried over to Nina, who was already scanning the hillside.

"Where are they?" Nina asked.

"I don't know," Mel said.

The next one clipped Nina's left ear and left her clutching at it.

"What the hell?" Nina screamed. "You don't aim for my *head*. Where's Parker?"

Parker was no longer on the rock.

Another one, hitting Nina's hip this time.

"Did he *run?*" Nina said. "Oh my God . . ."

Mel dodged one that would have gotten her eye.

"What are you *doing?*" Nina screamed up the hill. "You're going to *hurt* us!"

Nina looked around for something to throw—a twig, a rock—but there was nothing but exposed water to their far left and to the center of the lake. They were stuck. Mel was afraid. This wasn't exactly a joke or a friendly little snowball fight. In desperation, Nina started skating back to the edge, trying her best to dodge the rain of ice balls that was still coming down. Mel followed her quickly.

And then miraculously they heard Parker's voice calling from somewhere above them.

"Hey, assholes!" he shouted. "Up here!"

The torrent stopped. Mel could see Parker at the top of the hill, standing next to a gray sedan.

"Is this your car?" he yelled down.

Parker ducked behind the sedan, and a moment later it began drifting down the inclined road. There was a series of yells, and their three attackers started tearing back up toward the lot.

Nina and Mel quickly got off the ice. Mel dropped to the ground and yanked hard at her laces, cursing how tightly and carefully she had tied them. As soon as she had enough of an opening, she pulled her foot through, almost twisting her ankle in the process. She stepped quickly into her boots. They both climbed back up the path, grabbing at the trees and exposed roots to balance themselves.

Parker was waiting for them at the top of the hill. Without a word, they climbed into Nina's SUV. Nina threw it into gear and U-turned without even checking the road.

"What did you do?" she asked, trying to catch her breath.

"Just took off the emergency, put it in neutral. It goes on its own."

He was laughing rather spookily now, like he couldn't stop.

"Oh my God—they were psychos! You okay, Mel?"

Mel nodded. She pulled up the leg of her pants and saw a slightly green bruise blossoming on her knee.

She had a strong feeling that this all had something to do with her.

When they got to Nina's, Mel curled herself on the sofa under a blanket and watched Nina and Parker. Parker kept looking out the front windows as if he were expecting the guys to pull up at any second. Nina became an avenging nurse. She supplied them all with tea, cocoa, and hot cider. She tended to Mel with a warm water bottle *and* an ice pack.

"That was amazing what you did back there, Park," Nina said as she forcibly removed Mel's damp socks and replaced them with dry ones. "You get a medal. You're a hero, forever."

"Yeah, I don't know what we'd do without you," Mel agreed.

Parker didn't have a comeback for that one. Instead he just played with Mel's wet left sock, gazing at it in a kind of wonder.

32

Steve,

Okay.

First of all, major drama here. We were attacked by insane snowballers. But that story has got to wait. I have to tell you something else.

Something has been bothering me, and I have to tell you about it or I'm going to go nuts. I don't want to be that girlfriend who complains, but . . .

I know you're busy, and I know it's hard, but I really feel like we have to try to talk more. Actually talk on the phone. I love the sound of your voice, and I need more of it. We're both busy, and I just feel like we both have to try harder to make contact.

I was thinking that maybe I can get frequent-flyer miles from my dad for my birthday and come out to Portland or something. Or you could come here. It's in mid-March, so maybe for spring break? I definitely want to be there for the mold season. ☺

Anyway, can you please call me when you get this, and I'll call you right back?

Love,

Nina

The phone rang the next afternoon while Nina was halfheartedly working her way through a calculus problem. It was the Steve ring. She snatched it up.

"Hey!" she said. "I'll call you right back."

"You don't have to," he said. There was a strange tone in his voice.

"What's up?" she asked.

"Listen," he said, dragging the word along. And then he didn't say anything.

"Listening," Nina said.

"We have to talk."

"Okay."

"There's something . . ." He exhaled loudly.

"Something?"

"Something's come up. There's a . . . Something's happened."

"What?" Nina said worriedly. "Are you all right?"

"Yeah, it's . . ."

In that second Nina knew that this *thing* was about her—and it was something she wouldn't like. As evil as this made her feel, she was kind of hoping he was about to say something like, "My mom has cancer." Something outside of them.

"I know this is a bad time to be doing this," he said. "I know this makes me the biggest dick in the universe. . . ."

Nina reached out and touched the colorful edges of the Post-its that popped out of the side of a nearby stack of books. She took a deep breath, but she couldn't hold it.

Another loud exhale.

"I've kind of started seeing someone here," he said. "Her name is Diane. She's in Earth Share with me."

Dead air for a good thirty seconds. Nina concentrated on the Post-its. They looked like tails of little tropical fishes hiding themselves in a reef.

"She kind of reminds me of you," Steve said. He sounded a little desperate. "She kind of wears her hair the same way."

"Don't tell me this," Nina said.

"Okay."

He had to have something to add. He couldn't just be calling her to tell her *this*—as awful as *this* was.

"Steve . . ." she said, her voice trembling a little.

"I still care about you so much. It was just hard being so far apart, you know?"

He was calling to tell her this. Just this. She sank down to the floor and sat with her legs apart, like a dropped rag doll.

"I managed," she said.

Her voice was hard now. She couldn't disguise it even if she wanted to. She felt herself trembling and steadied herself by taking a deep breath from her abdomen.

"So what are we going to do?" she said. "What does this mean?"

"I guess . . . I guess we're breaking up."

The conversation ended shortly after that. Nina couldn't even remember what she said. It wasn't angry. It was vague, a baffled and hasty goodbye.

Immediately after hanging up, she knew she had to call him back. She had to pin him down and make him talk because he would see that this made no sense, that it couldn't be real. This Diane with the kind of similar hair was not who he wanted. This was just a phase, a little problem, and they could work it out.

His phone was busy. It was still busy five minutes later. And an hour after that.

Nina didn't sleep that night. She didn't even put on her pajamas. She sat on the floor and thought about the fact that nothing changes when the boyfriend who was never there suddenly *goes away*. It wasn't like she had to go out of her way to avoid him or distance herself to forget him. She had all the distance she'd ever need.

She opened up her windows and let the freezing air come into her warm room until she couldn't stop shivering. There was a dull pain in her head that she suspected would never leave her.

The next morning, her eyes red and puffy from the all-nighter, Nina got in her car and drove over to her hair salon on Broadway. They managed to find her an empty space in the schedule and took her right back. She yanked out the bands that held up her Princess Leias. Her hair sprang out on either side of her head in two slowly unfurling corkscrews.

"What are we doing here today?" the stylist asked, coming over and taking the curls in her hands.

"Cut it," Nina said. "Change everything."

33

Dating Gaz was pretty much the complete opposite of dating Mel—in more than just the obvious male versus female way. For someone who didn't like having long relationship talks, it should have been a dream come true. There were no heavy conversations about where their relationship was going. They rehearsed together, and if Avery felt like it, she stayed late and messed around with Gaz on the basement couch. They both kind of knew they were together, and that was enough.

Except . . . that it wasn't. She still wasn't feeling anything particularly strong for Gaz, outside of the physical attraction. That would have been okay, except that Gaz's easygoing manner was starting to get to her, especially when it came to the band.

Somehow since New Year's, Angry Maxwell had acquired three new members. Avery didn't really even know where they came from—they each just showed up one day. Two of them, Rob and Dan, were guitarists. The third was a girl named Lizzy who didn't actually play anything. She said that she was Wiccan and that she channeled pure energy. Her talent consisted of spinning around, making shrieking noises, and falling down. She frequently fell into the keyboard. She would have been kicked out immediately if Avery had anything to say about it, but Hareth liked her, so she remained. Rehearsals, which used to be pleasant wastes of time, now turned into irritating ones. There were endless debates about what kind of sound they were shooting for.

After a few days with her new bandmates, Avery made an important discovery: It's easy to form a band. You just get a bunch of people together and *voilà*: band. But the big step is to move out of the basement and into a place where people have actually paid you to play—not offered to pay you to stop. One was the golden number. Once you got one paying gig, you were professional.

Avery was going to get that paying gig. Someone had to do *something* useful.

On Saturday morning she went to Philadelphia Avenue. This was the central meeting place of all Saratoga musicians. It always reminded Avery of pictures of medieval European streets. It was narrow, with hanging signs and brightly colored restaurants and bars. There was a wooden notice board at the top of the street, which had all the names of the local businesses painted by hand in funky white print. Next to that, there was a notice board jammed full of flyers for gigs and guitar lessons and Pilates classes.

Checking through the ads, Avery saw that there were plenty of places to play open mike, but that didn't pay. In fact, most open mikes required the bands to fork over some cash to get in. There was only one thing to do—she would just go from bar to bar, asking around to see if anyone was willing to hire them.

She walked through most of downtown that day, hitting about twelve bars, before she finally got someone to say more than just "no." One pub owner, a man in his fifties with a sharp white goatee, let her talk a bit while he smoked and unloaded a crate of liquor and stocked the well.

"You guys have a tape?" he asked.

"No . . ." Avery said. A tape would have been useful.

"Who do you play?"

Who do you play was a way of saying, "We don't want to hear any of your original crap. If you play here, play something we know."

"A normal mix," Avery said. "What do other bands play here?"

"Our customers like pretty regular stuff. U2, Van Morrison, REM, Jimmy Buffett. Stuff like that."

Middle-aged beer music, Avery thought.

"We do a bunch of U2 and REM," she lied. "We just did a whole set of music like that at Skidmore last week."

"Yeah?" The guy didn't look wildly intrigued, but at least he was still talking. "No tape, huh?" he said. "Not much I can do without a tape."

Avery looked around, trying to figure out a way to keep the conversation going. Over in a corner of the stage was a piano. She hadn't exactly prepared for this contingency, but . . .

"How about I play you something?" she asked.

"Like what?"

The only thing she could think of at that moment was "Piano Man," by Billy Joel, which had to be number one on her list of

Songs to Be Stricken from the Musical Record. It was a song she despised so much that she knew it perfectly, note for note, just so that she could hate it *in detail.* She knew it in her head, anyway. She'd never tried to play it. But to get this gig, she was prepared to do the unthinkable.

She pointed to the piano.

"Can I show you?" she asked.

"Sure." The man shrugged. "Go ahead."

Avery had a fairly well developed ear. This was still a gamble, but she thought she could pull it off. After running through the song mentally for half a minute, she started to play. Her version was dead-on. It actually creeped her out. She had talents she really didn't want to know she had.

The man stopped her after a minute or so.

"You like Billy Joel?" he asked.

"Um . . . yeah."

"I don't," he replied. "But that was pretty good. I'll tell you what. . . ."

He turned around and pulled a calendar off the wall next to the cash register. He pinched his bottom lip and pulled it out, moving it from side to side as he flipped back and forth between two pages. Avery could see that his bottom teeth were deeply yellow. She looked at the pack of Marlboro Reds that sat on the counter and wondered about the ashy taste in her own mouth.

"I can use someone to fill some time on the fifteenth of February. I've got a forty-five-minute slot that's empty. You'll get a third of the door. That would probably be about fifty bucks or so."

"Definitely. We'll do it."

"What's your band's name?"

"Angry Maxwell."

She felt ridiculous identifying herself as part of "Angry Maxwell," yet she knew that all band names sounded asinine until the band got famous. At that point there was a magical transformation, and even the most ill-conceived names took on a veneer of cool.

"Angry . . . Maxwell . . ." He wrote it into a calendar square in pencil. "Contact name and number?"

Avery provided hers.

"Okay. So you'll go on from seven until quarter of eight. Get here about an hour ahead of time to set up. And no 'Piano Man,' all right?"

"No 'Piano Man,'" she said. "Promise."

Avery lit a cigarette and triumphantly walked back toward Broadway, already putting a song list together in her mind.

Just as she came to the Army and Navy, Nina stepped out of a store just a few doors down. It took Avery a moment to register that it was Nina because her hair, which had always either been up in the buns or pigtails, was free. Not just free—shorter. The strands were about four or five inches long, and they flew loose around her head like a lion's mane. It was *diva hair.*

They both stopped and looked at each other. It was the first time they'd really come face-to-face in almost four weeks. Avery hadn't counted the time until now. Four weeks. That was unbelievably strange, but it was right.

"Your hair," she sputtered. Not the brightest comment, but really all that needed to be said.

"I just cut it," Nina replied, without much enthusiasm.

"It's incredible," Avery said. "I wish I had hair that could do things like that."

"Thanks."

"How's life?"

"Good. Busy."

"You want to get a coffee or something?" Avery asked brightly. Suddenly, seeing Nina in front of her, she realized how much she missed her. Except it wasn't like she was realizing something new but finally naming some kind of nagging ache that had been bothering her for a long time.

"Sorry," Nina said quickly. "I have to go."

"Are you okay?"

"Fine," Nina said distractedly. She clearly wasn't okay. Her eyes were red, and she kept looking away. Avery had known that things were messed up—they hadn't even spent Christmas or New Year's together. Avery had been so deep in her own head that she hadn't known what to say to Nina. But now she wanted Nina to tell her what was going on. She wanted to sit down with her, to give her a hug, to do all of the normal things.

"Neen?" she said. "What's up?"

Nina hit a button on her key chain and turned off the alarm

of her car. She hesitated for a moment, as if she was going to explain, and then she just shook her head.

"I have to go," she said again. "I'll see you later."

As she watched Nina get in her car and drive off, Avery felt a terrible sinking feeling. It wiped out any happiness that getting the gig had provided. Somewhere in her head, she'd always thought that even though they'd fought, things couldn't really be big-time bad between her and Nina. But they were big-time bad. In fact, Avery realized, they might even be over.

That was so unthinkable that she had to sit down because her legs had begun to shake.

34

Friday night marked the start of something else new and horrible at P. J. Mortimer's: Irish nachos. They were just normal nachos, except the chips were green and the chili topping was made with (big surprise) Guinness, which made it a very deep brown. They were topped with a white jack cheese and an orange cheddar cheese to reflect the colors of the Irish flag. The result was so nauseating that Mel couldn't look down when she took them out to people's tables.

It was crowded, as most Friday nights were. Unfortunately, both the kitchen and the floor were understaffed because of a flu outbreak. There were no pauses to even talk to other people for a minute. She and Parker brushed past each other a dozen times or more, barely noticing the other's presence.

"I wish I got the flu," Mel grumbled as they met up for a moment in the pantry.

Parker nodded grimly. He was struggling with a large canister of pickles, which was almost entirely empty. He cringed as he plunged his arm into the pickle liquid and fished around for the last remaining spear. When he pulled it out, his arm was completely dripping with greenish juice.

"Tonight's one of those nights," he said. "It's only going to get worse. I can feel it."

About an hour later Parker was proven right.

As Mel was taking an order from a particularly large office party, there was a loud noise—a massive intake of breath. She turned around to see a strange sight. Parker appeared to be flying through the air, his tray whizzing in front of him like a Frisbee. Three Cokes hung in the air at once, side by side, before plunging down. The nacho baskets skidded across the floor. The hamburgers and buns escaped the scene by rolling under chairs and tables. People yelped as they were hit with soda and ice and food.

It was so catastrophic that it brought all of P. J. Mortimer's to a standstill.

When the last plate had stopped spinning and there was a suitable pause, applause broke out at some tables. Parker got up stiffly. He made a short bow to the people who were cheering, but he didn't smile. At first he bent down like he was going to start cleaning up, but he just grabbed his tray and walked slowly back toward the pantry.

When Mel got there, he was at the sink, peeling hot cheese and beans from his arms as he ran them under water.

"Are you burned?" Mel asked.

"No," he growled.

"What happened?"

"I got tripped."

He turned up the water for a moment, wiping down his arms

hard. Mel handed him a few paper towels. Bob appeared in the pantry doorway.

"What the hell happened?" he said.

"I got tripped."

"Shit, Parker . . ."

"I know. . . . I know. . . ."

Mel wondered if Bob was actually going to ask how Parker *was*. That would have been nice.

"You can't go out on the floor like that," he said instead.

"Yeah, no kidding."

"Someone's going to have to take your tables."

Parker leaned against the black-and-white tiles on the pantry walls as if the wind had been kicked out of him a second time.

"Just do your side work," Bob said. "Mel, take 25."

"Side work?" Parker said incredulously.

"It has to be done." Bob shrugged an apology that didn't seem very sincere. "Sorry."

"I can't close out my tables and get my tips, but I can sit back here and roll silverware," Parker said as Bob headed back out to the floor. "Great . . ."

He sank down onto an overturned pickle canister and pulled a few green nacho chips off his shirt. Mel stood there next to him, not sure how to help.

"Just do me a favor," he said.

"What?"

"Don't tell Nina this happened."

Mel had never seen Parker embarrassed or agitated before. His face was flushed a deep red, and he looked small and young. She wanted to wrap him in a huge hug, but that didn't seem like the right thing to do. Not to Parker, anyway. He would know that it was pity, and maybe pity wasn't good. She leaned against the wall near him and flicked a piece of food out of his thick hair.

"This is good," he said, trying to recover. "I can say I was in a fight. It was kind of a fight, right? Makes me look manly. Strong like bull."

Mel smiled weakly. She wished he didn't feel like he had to keep up a good face in front of her.

Maybe a *tiny* hug. No.

"Go on," he said, nodding at the pantry door. "It's fine. Go get the damage report, soldier."

When Mel went back out on the floor, she found that the whole restaurant was in a heightened state. The crash made people louder, had customers chatting to their neighbors at other tables. None of Mel's customers had been physically affected by the flying objects, so she helped some other waiters get their customers cleaned up. Bob was jogging from table to table, spooning out apologies and comps.

"Bring some seltzer here," he snapped at her as she passed him.

"Okay . . ."

Mel headed for the bar. As she did so, she passed the spot where Parker had fallen. The busboys were all over it, like a containment team. Right next to them was a table full of guys who were laughing hysterically. Mel felt her fury rising and made sure to keep her eyes averted.

"Hey," one of them called.

Mel turned, her Guinness pins clacking loudly together as she spun.

"I have a question," one of the guys said. He looked vaguely familiar.

"Okay."

"Do you have a liquor license?"

She stood there, baffled by the question (the answer was obviously yes since they had a bar there). Then she suddenly realized that two of them were from the day at the lake. Obviously these were the guys who tripped Parker. They were all leering at her.

"*Liq . . . uor* license," the guy said slowly, with a very deliberate pause in the middle of the word. "Don't you have one of those?"

Mel stared at him for a second, sounding out the syllables in her head. She shuddered as the meaning sank in. A deep feeling of disgust and shame spread all over her, making her body cold and turning her stomach. This was one of those times she needed to be Avery—she would kill these guys. It wouldn't matter to her that she was an employee here and that confronting these assholes might jeopardize her job. But she wasn't Avery; she was Mel. Mel never had the right thing to say, and she did care that she was a waitress. Never in her life had she felt so useless and small.

She turned around, forgetting about the seltzer, and went straight back to the pantry. The table broke into riotous laughter.

Parker was standing next to one of the huge plastic trash cans, still trying to clean himself off. She came up on the other side of it and looked at him.

"What?" he said.

Mel couldn't answer. She could only shiver in anger and embarrassment. Parker stopped what he was doing.

"Did they say something to you?" he asked.

"It doesn't matter."

"What did they say?"

She shook her head. She couldn't repeat it. It was vile. They had tried to make her disgusting. Parker stopped what he was doing for a minute and leaned over the trash.

"It's okay," he said. "You can't blame them for being inbred."

"I know."

Two of the bussers came in with dishpans full of the remnants of the accident. Mel moved aside so that they could get in. They threw Parker up-and-down glances as they dropped off their load onto the dirty dish cart. Mel looked down at the pile of broken food bits and trash.

The idea came to her instantly. It was unlike any impulse she'd ever had, but the circumstances fueled her. She grabbed a plate from the prep rack and slammed it down on the counter. Pulling over the dish cart, she managed to recover a few chunks of nacho that were still glued together by the cheese. Using a spoon, she scooped out some of the topping that was sitting in a puddle of brown liquid (most likely Coke).

"What are you doing?" Parker said, coming up behind her and watching over her shoulder.

"Get me those chips you just put in the trash," she said.

From a rack of dirty dishes she cobbled together portions of guacamole and sour cream. Parker added in the trash chips. Together they quickly did an artistic arrangement of the pile, and they managed to turn it into a very convincing order of Irish nachos.

"We need something else," she said. "Something really hideous."

"Hideous," Parker said, looking around. "That shouldn't be hard."

He picked up the dish cart and tilted it slightly, examining its contents.

"Here we go," he said, pouring some brownish liquid that had accumulated at the bottom onto the nachos. "Special sauce."

"Perfect," Mel said, smiling.

They nuked it for a few seconds to bring it back up to temperature. They decorated the edges of the plate with some shredded lettuce remnants that sat in the bottom of a bin in the corner, waiting to be disposed of.

When another server came into the pantry, Mel grabbed her by the sleeve and threw her a pathetic look.

"I'm stuck here for a minute," she said. "Can you do me a favor? Take this out to 27, that table full of guys? Tell them it's compliments of Mortimer's because of the accident."

They watched the Franken-nachos making their way out to the infamous table.

"You have responded to my brainwashing excellently," Parker said with a smirk. Then he looked at Mel with a sense of genuine pride. "I am deeply impressed."

Parker waited around for Mel to finish her shift since he was driving her home. After the nachos he felt much better about the whole thing and made up songs about silverware (a tune called "My Name Is Spoony McForkenknife" was her favorite) as he did his side work. They were both surprised to see Nina's car waiting in the parking lot when they came out.

"Can I tell her about the nachos?" Mel asked. "I swear I'll leave out the other part."

Before Parker could answer, Nina opened her car door and stepped out. The nachos were temporarily forgotten.

"Your hair," Mel said.

Nina reached up and grabbed at a handful of what remained of her locks, running it through her fist.

Parker seemed transfixed by Nina's new diva look. It took him a moment to remember that he was covered in food stains. He stuck his hands in his pockets and drew his coat tightly around himself in a sudden, batlike gesture.

"Hey," Nina said. She looked like she was trying to smile, but the smile quickly turned into a grimace. "Can I talk to you for a second?"

Nina's voice was breaking. Parker shot a glance in Mel's direction.

"What is it?" Mel asked.

Nina just shook her head and started crying. She turned and put her face against the car window. Mel hurried up behind her and took her by the shoulders.

"Tell me," she said.

Nina couldn't answer.

"Did you talk to him?" Mel asked quietly.

Nina nodded. Mel put her arms around her.

Parker stood a few feet away, watching it all, now and then stepping a foot closer or a foot back. Finally he backed up and retreated toward his car. Mel and Nina stayed there for quite a while as customers came and went.

Valentine's Day

35

The S thief had gone out of his way to mark Valentine's Day. Instead of HAVE A HEART: GIVE BLOOD FOR VALENTINE'S DAY DANCE THIS SATURDAY, the sign now read: RUN: MUTANTS INSIDE. The *M* was made of two inverted *V*s.

Parker nodded to it as he and Mel pulled into the parking lot.

"It's a work of genius," he said. "And it's accurate."

"Are you finally going to do something tonight?" Mel asked as Parker brought the Roach to an abrupt stop. The car coughed and sputtered a few times before shutting itself off. Mel was used to this from the many times Parker had driven her home and found the shuddering rhythm of the engine soothing now.

"Yes," he answered.

"You're going to ask Nina to dance?"

"No. Tonight is the night I cure cancer."

Mel looked at him sourly.

"That's something," he said. "You weren't specific enough."

"This whole Steve thing has been bad, really bad. And she hated doing this." Mel pointed at the outside of the gym in an accusatory fashion. "Getting ready for Valentine's Day has been the worst."

"That's because Valentine's Day sucks ass."

"She likes you, so tell her you like her. Make it suck less."

Parker shook his head.

"No one can do that," he said sagely. "Not even the president, or Gandalf, or anybody."

Nina was at a table by the gym door when they arrived, selling heart-shaped tickets. She was wearing a delicate white blouse with raised dots, a gracefully formfitting red skirt, and a pair of low, deep red heels. Her hair was artfully teased out, and she had a faint glimmer high on her cheekbones.

Even though she looked beautiful, Nina also had that slightly sickly air she'd had for weeks. Mel knew that even though she tried to keep up her chipper attitude, Nina hadn't been sleeping or eating much. Her face had thinned out, making hollows in her cheeks and under her eyes. That was probably what she was trying to hide with the glittery makeup.

"Hey," Nina said, seeing them come in. "You guys look great."

Mel looked down at herself. She was dressed in a fairly bland pink shirt and a brown corduroy skirt. Parker was wearing a pair of khakis that seemed unfamiliar and a little dressier and thinner than his normal pants. The shirt was definitely new—it was white with narrow blue stripes.

"Did you buy an outfit for this?" Mel asked as soon as they were out of Nina's earshot.

Parker let out a strange *hmmm* sound and surveyed the room, squinting a bit.

They took seats high up on the bleachers, in an unclaimed corner. A DJ was playing while the band set up. A group of manic sophomore girls were dancing close to the stage, but otherwise people were clinging to the sides of the room.

Parker stretched himself out over a few levels of the bleachers and examined his belt. He pulled on the edge of his shirt and asked, "Which way says 'jerkoff,' in or out?"

"I like it the way it is."

"It doesn't matter, does it?"

"Why don't you just ask her, Park?"

"Ask her . . . for a light? Ask her . . . a pointed question?"

"Fine," Mel said. "I'm going to the bathroom."

"No," he said, grabbing her arm. "I know what happens in girls' bathrooms. They're like black holes. You'll never come back."

"So figure out something to do." Mel stood up. "Mingle. Turn on your charm."

"Where's the switch?"

"Let Nina find the switch," Mel replied with a grin.

Parker licked his finger and marked an imaginary point in the air.

"You aren't supposed to make jokes like that," he told her, shaking his head. "*Bad lesbian.* No Indigo Girls for you."

"Who?"

"Oh God." Parker clutched his head. "Just go. Go before someone hears you."

▲   ▼   ▲

In the four years of its existence, a dozen or more people had passed through Angry Maxwell's ranks and gone on to form other bands—bands that sometimes got the gigs Angry Maxwell could have tried for, if Gaz and Hareth had ever gotten their shit together and found their way out of Gaz's basement.

Ex-guitarist Margo had teamed up with ex-guitarist Mike and ex-bassist Fran The Guy (there was a Fran The Girl at one point). They'd found a drummer, formed The Militant Nobodies, and landed the Valentine's Day dance gig in the same amount of time that it usually took Angry Maxwell to decide whether or not they were going to hit Taco Bell before or after practice. Gaz, who didn't seem troubled by the fact that his former bandmates were happily forming other bands and getting gigs, insisted on coming by to see them play.

Even though she knew Nina would be there, Avery had assumed that the dance would be big and dark enough that she wouldn't be noticed. She was actually kind of startled when she saw Nina at the front table. Nina looked at her, then at Gaz. She sold Avery her ticket in the perky, polite manner she reserved for people she didn't know that well.

This put Avery in a foul mood, which was only worsened by the fact that The Militant Nobodies actually turned out to be good. Margo, much to Avery's surprise, actually sang as well, in a Chrissie-Hynde-meets-Liz-Phair kind of voice. They only did covers, but they were well-chosen covers, played well enough to actually peel people off the walls and get them milling around in a rhythmic way.

"This is what we should be doing," Avery said as they paused between songs.

"What?"

"We could have played this."

"We're playing at that bar," Gaz said.

"We're allowed to have more than one gig. Most bands do." There was an edge in Avery's voice that she did nothing to hide. Sometimes her dissatisfaction with Gaz was *profound*. He could be nice to the point of being useless. Rather than start an argument, Avery just went to the bathroom.

It was strangely fitting that she ran into Mel almost immediately, right in the bathroom doorway. Mel stared at her, wide-eyed. She almost looked like she was going to run for cover and hide in one of the stalls. She looked pretty . . . total Mel. Her hair was down, and it tumbled over her shoulders in that ridiculously perfect and unintentional way.

"Hey," Avery said. She spoke in a soft voice. She didn't want to spook Mel.

"Hey."

Well, Mel didn't turn and run. That was a good start.

"What's going on?"

Mel looked around her, as if trying to account for her time in the bathroom. Then she shrugged. But she was still there, still in front of Avery. This was a good sign.

"You want to talk?" Avery asked.

"I guess," Mel said.

"We could sit down."

"Where?"

"We could find a place."

Mel shrugged again. A "yes" shrug.

Avery walked down the hall, away from the bathroom and the gym. She scouted out the classrooms, testing doorknobs until she found an unlocked one. She heard Mel walking just behind her, and tried not to dwell on the fact that she had no script for what was about to happen. Not a clue.

Avery sat on the teacher's desk. Mel took a seat. It was dim enough in the room that they could only see each other's outlines, not their expressions. This was fine with Avery. She knew she had a wild, stunned look in her eye.

"So," she said. "How's Mortimer's?"

"Okay."

End of phase one of the conversation. Long, painful pause.

"This is kind of weird, huh?" Avery began again.

"Kind of."

"I'm going to sit down there. Is that okay?"

"Sure."

Avery slipped down off the desk and took the seat next to Mel. Now she could see Mel's face. Her eyes were wide, and she was mindlessly pulling on a loose strand of string coming off the bottom of her shirt. Avery could smell the watermelon shampoo aroma coming off her hair. Just this little hint of Mel stirred up all kinds of memories of the summer—some romantic, some just of work. Dumb things that felt huge.

"You hate me?" she asked.

Mel looked at her hands. Avery felt her heart sink.

"It's okay," she said. "It's only fair."

"I don't."

"No?"

"You're my friend," Mel said. "I can't hate you."

Avery felt her eyes tearing up, which was rare. But she couldn't help it. She sniffed back hard, and the sound was unpleasant. "I was stupid," she said. "I was scared."

"Me too," Mel said. "Scared. Sometimes."

In that moment Avery had the idea. If Mel didn't hate her, and she said she didn't, they could get back together right now. Everybody had heard about the two of them anyway, and they were leaving school in three months, so who even cared anymore? Yeah, there were things missing with Mel, things she felt with Gaz that she didn't feel when she kissed Mel. But there was so much missing with *Gaz* too. More important things, like being understood, having someone who just seemed to pick up where you left off. Avery could have all of that back if she just did something *right now.*

"Maybe we should get back together," Avery said quickly.

Nothing from Mel for a moment.

"I think that's a bad idea," Mel finally said.

"Why?"

"Because you're not gay."

"I'm something."

"What are you, then?"

Avery didn't have an answer. She turned around and faced

the board. There was a homework assignment still on the corner: pages 50 to 100 of *The Scarlet Letter*. Avery would have laughed, but her throat was too dry.

"Maybe after a while it goes away," Avery said. "Maybe you forget what it was like."

"What what was like?"

"Kissing, all of that. Maybe we'll just forget what it was like."

"You think so?"

"No."

Avery felt Mel reach over and take her hand. She squeezed it hard, and Avery squeezed back. She could feel Mel's pulse. All they had to do was come a few inches closer.

Then Mel let go, gently extracted her hand, and got up and left the room.

When Mel finally found him, Parker didn't even mention that she'd been gone for over half an hour, which even for a trip to the girls' bathroom was a little excessive.

"I need you to do me a favor," he said. "I just called someone. Something's going down. . . ."

Parker stopped speaking and looked down into her face.

"Is something wrong?" he asked. "You're all deer-in-the-headlights."

"Everything's fine." Mel pushed a clump of hair over her right eye to partially mask herself. "What favor?"

"Did you want to stay here much longer?"

"Not really."

"Oh, good. Okay. Can you say you're feeling sick and ask

Nina if you can take her car home? Make it something all feminine and gory so you can say that you didn't want to ask me to
take you because you were embarrassed."

"Why?" she asked.

"I have something up my sleeve."

"What?"

"Big secret. You'll be happy, though. I'm finally doing something."

"With Nina?"

Parker started bouncing around and doing a karate chop
dance.

"Will you do it?" he asked.

"Sure," Mel said. "I've kind of had enough anyway."

36

A thin layer of snow had fallen and frozen solid while they were inside. Parker hacked at the coat of ice that had glazed over the windows of his Bug while Nina huddled in the front seat. It was freezing in the car, and she pined silently for the heated seats of her SUV.

Parker opened Nina's door and leaned in. He had an icy residue all over his sleeves.

"Don't put your purse on the floor," he said. "Or any stuff."

"Why?"

"There's a hole in the floor on that side. Things fall out."

Nina bent down and examined the floor by her feet and found the source of the wicked draft that was blowing up her skirt.

"She is no pretty, the Roach, but she run like deer," Parker said. "Like sick deer. Sick deer with limp."

He closed the door and went back to his scraping. Nina gathered all of her things tightly on her lap.

Parker seemed to be doing an excessively precise job, chiseling away at the ice as if he were sculpting a piece of artwork. He waved hello to Nina periodically and kept checking his watch.

Finally he seemed satisfied and got in the car. His hands were almost purple from the cold.

He drove around the school very slowly and then stopped halfway up the main drive in front of the building. Nina looked at him in confusion.

"Why are we stopping?" she asked.

Parker was staring at something in front of them with an exaggeratedly baffled expression. Nina followed his eyes. The mutants sign was down. Now the floodlights were focused on the words NINA ROX.

"Huh," he said. "I wonder how that happened."

For a moment Nina was genuinely confused. She wondered who this other Nina was. Then she got it.

"You're the *S* thief?" she asked in amazement.

"The what?"

"The guy," she said, pointing at the sign. "The *S* thief."

"Oh. *S* thief. Because we used to take the *S*. I get it. Good name."

"We?"

"There are four of us," he said. "We operate in secret, under a cloak of darkness."

He pulled up his coat and peered at her over the collar. Nina looked at her name basking in the light. Now the question was . . . why? The answer seemed to lie in Parker's silence.

"It's really nice," she said. "I mean, you'll have to take it down or I'll be in tons of trouble, but it's nice. . . ."

Nina started involuntarily pulling on her rings, yanking them up to her knuckles and twisting them hard, like she was trying to unscrew the tips of her fingers.

"Can I just say something?" he asked.

"Sure."

He reached out and took her hand, the one that was sore from all the ring twisting. He gently pushed her two rings back down into position and rubbed her knuckles between his fingers. This gesture surprised Nina, and it was so calming that she didn't even try to stop him.

"Could I kiss you?" he asked.

"Parker . . ."

"We have a lot in common. You breathe air. I breathe air. You're the gorgeous and super-talented head of student counsel. I look like I'm twelve and I'm part of a secret society that changes the letters in signs. Or *a* sign. You're going to Stanford. I might get into SUNY Purchase. I think it could work."

"Park . . ."

"Think of this as one of those free samples you get in the mail. You try it. You don't like it, you just throw it away."

"Stop!"

It was too much. Nina felt herself shaking. It wasn't just the cold, but the cold was amplifying it. She pressed her cheek hard against the cold window and stared down at the Roach's ancient, grimy dashboard. Parker's car had that pungent, closed-up smell that Avery's car had.

"Sorry," she said quietly.

When Parker didn't reply, she knew she had to say something.

She owed him some kind of explanation.

"I had a boyfriend who is this amazing guy," she said, balling her hands up tightly. "He really cares about stuff—he's a serious guy. I trusted him, completely. I wanted to do everything with him. I would have changed where I was going to school for him. Then he just dumped me. Nothing happened. We didn't fight. *I don't get it.*"

Nina was surprised to hear herself almost shouting these last words, but she went on anyway.

"Everything bad that happened this year has been because of dating. Mel and Avery. Me and Steve."

"I get that," he said quietly. "I've never dated anyone for more than a week or two. And then I'd see whoever it was in the hall. And if she kept walking, or if I kept walking, I knew it was over. Or we'd just IM or something. We'd be like, 'Um, hey. I don't want to see you anymore.' 'Cool.' Not the same thing. I shouldn't even compare."

"It's not like Steve did more than that," Nina said bitterly. "I finally told him he had to call me. So he did. And that's when he did it. Over the phone. It was so bad. . . ."

Bad hardly described it. She remembered standing in front of her desk, hearing for the first time about the girl with the similar hair—the hair that wasn't so similar anymore. Hearing Steve, who she thought would do anything to be with her, getting rid of her. The void that seemed to open up in the floor by her desk. The fact that her future seemed like nothing at that second. That the path she'd been following her whole life was just rubbed out. The fear . . .

She didn't describe any of that, but she felt in the silence like

Parker could see those thoughts, like she was somehow project-
ing them onto the windshield. She heard him take a few deep
breaths, as if preparing to say something, then he would just
stop. He was out of jokes for the moment. He put his arm out
instead and pried Nina from the window and steered her into
his shoulder. She rested there for a moment. It felt right. Parker
had come to mean a lot to her. She didn't have Avery, and she
didn't quite have Mel. But Parker had proven himself over and
over again. And now there was the sign, right in front of them—
NINA ROX. For once this whole year, it was nice to have someone
there. Someone who actually paid attention to her.

"Valentine's Day sucks," she mumbled into his coat.

"More than a little."

Nina pulled herself back up and rubbed her face vigorously
with both hands. Parker shivered a bit too. They were both shaking it off.

"You don't look twelve," she said.

He shrugged. He seemed to know that she was trying to
thank him.

"You want to go?" he said. He was talking quickly now. "Come
on. You have to be cold. We should go eat some fat, like a greasy
cheeseburger. Something hot and fatty. I want to open a place
called Hot and Fatty. I have all these good ideas for restaurants. I
want to open one for bulimics called The Fork and Bucket."

He turned the key in the ignition, but Nina reached over and
grabbed a handful of his coat sleeve.

"Wait."

The Roach coughed once and then gave up the effort of try-ing to start.

"She listens," he said quietly. "She likes you."

In the distance, they could hear a car with a high-end sub-woofer making its bassy, window-rattling way along the road on the other side of the school.

"I don't want a boyfriend," she said. "I don't want anything I can . . . lose. Know what I mean?"

Nina was only somewhat clear on the point herself, but a look of understanding spread over Parker's face. Suddenly, every-thing about Parker was appealing. His smooth chin that came down to a firm, definite point, those bright eyes that had fixed their narrow focus squarely on her.

"I'm not your boyfriend," he said. "In fact, who are you? How did you get in my car?"

"That's what I'm talking about," she said, really smiling for the first time in weeks.

This was all right. This was good. This wasn't permanent. This was something she could do right now, and it would all be okay. This was Parker helping her forget Steve.

She unhooked her seat belt and practically fell on him, press-ing her lips into his, slipping her hands into the warm space between his coat and his chest. She was laughing—she was mak-ing up for a lot of lost time. And Parker grasped her tight, happy to participate in the effort.

37

Despite the disaster on the last attempt, Operation Drag Mel Out of the House was still in full swing. Through the intercouncil network, Nina got an e-mail about a gay and lesbian Post-Valentine's Discount Dance, which was being held at a school in Half Moon, about twenty minutes away. She hadn't so much as asked Mel as kidnapped her, going so far as to get Parker to switch shifts without her permission to make sure she was free.

So now, a week after the encounter with Avery, Mel found herself in Nina's SUV, parked outside a strange school. Nina was busily fixing her lip gloss in the driver's side mirror.

"Okay," Nina said, putting the gloss back into a neatly packed makeup bag. "If we go in together, people will think we're a couple. Which is no good. So, how do we play this?"

"We go home."

"The e-mail said that tons of people showed up for the last one."

"Uh-huh."

"What's the matter?" Nina asked.

"I just don't like crowds . . . of strangers."

"Ugh . . . let's go."

At first when they got their tickets and stood inside the gym, it didn't really look different from any other dance Mel had ever been to. The usual smattering of people on the floor, bunched up near the speakers, dancing. The spectators' gallery on the edges. The small groups of people who stood around talking, who might as well have been at Starbucks or sitting on the benches in front of the flagpole on Broadway, since they were seemingly unaware that there was any dancing going on around them. Mel got the distinct impression that everyone here knew everyone else. New people probably stuck out.

"Come on," Nina said, easing Mel into the darkness of the gym. She was putting on a good show, but Mel could tell from the way she was using her big smile and broad, stewardesslike gestures that she was nervous.

"I'm going to the bathroom," Nina said.

"I'm coming with you."

"No. Stay here."

"*Neen . . .*"

"I'll be right back."

Mel was left next to the refreshment table. She took a mint Milano cookie and nervously nibbled away at it with her front teeth. She looked around again, this time concentrating on the girls. At least here it was okay for her to do that.

Short hair was predominant, and it came in every style—spiked, slicked, buzzed, swept back. There were a few girls with mid-length hair, some with wild curls. There were two firecracker redheads, one girl with short electric blue hair, another whose short black dreadlocks had a green tint.

There was one girl who was just as petite as Mel, but she had just the lightest covering of peach fuzz on her head. She wore a black mesh top and enormous black pants that hung low around her hips and dragged along the ground, covering her feet and collecting dust. The girl was walking around the perimeter of the room, hands deep in her pockets, with a graceful, even gait, which looked kind of odd because Mel couldn't see her feet or legs moving much under the huge pants. She floated, in a way, with her chin tucked down and her eyes straight ahead. She occasionally nodded to people along the side of the room.

As she came around in her direction, Mel could see the glint of crossed pieces of what looked like duct tape on her pant legs and the sparkle of an earful of small silver rings. She turned her head just slightly and caught Mel looking at her. She had the quick, appraising glance of someone who was used to being stared at a lot and had long stopped caring about the fact. It wasn't an unfriendly look—it seemed completely indifferent. Still, Mel felt a rush of embarrassment and put her head down, focusing on the refreshment table.

She noticed that as she had been standing there, she had eaten at least half of the mint Milanos. This only increased her anxiety.

Mel raised her eyes just enough to see the girl continue all the way to the far end of the room. She sat up on the edge of the stage next to the DJ, a girl in a fuzzy, canary yellow sweater. Mel

was so busy watching her that it took her a while to notice that
a girl with short blond hair was approaching the table. She wore
a Wonder Woman T-shirt, a fairly nondescript pair of loose
khakis, and those Danish clogs that chefs and doctors wear. Her
stride was so determined that for a moment Mel was sure she
was coming over to yell at her for eating all of the cookies.
Instead she reached into a bowl of SweeTarts and took out two
packs.

"Hey," the girl said.

"Hi."

"What are you doing over here?"

"Nothing," Mel said, feeling the heavy weight of at least half a
bag of Pepperidge Farm's best in her stomach.

"I'm Kathy."

"I'm Mel."

"Was that your girlfriend with you?" Kathy asked, ripping
open a pack and tossing a SweeTart into her mouth.

Okay, so Mel had been watched.

"No," Mel said. "She's my friend. She kind of dragged me
here."

The girl appeared to glean a wealth of information from this
simple statement. She nodded knowingly.

"Where do you go to school?" she asked.

"Alexander Hamilton."

"What year are you?"

"Senior."

"I'm a junior."

"At Hamilton?"

"No," Kathy said. "Here."

"Oh, that's cool."

"You want to dance or something?"

Actually, Mel wanted to stay right where she was, with the cookies, in safety. But instead she accepted the invitation and walked onto the dance floor.

Nina, who had been hiding in the bathroom, trying to think up every conceivable thing she could do with her hair and the limited amount of makeup she had in her purse, finally emerged. Mel was not where she had left her. She took a quick look around and spotted her dancing with another girl.

She sat down to wait on the bleachers and took her phone out. She went through old messages, played a memory game, checked her settings. When she looked up, Mel was still with the blond girl. The girl was talking, and Mel was slowly backing up toward the edge of the floor. Nina was about to go over and join them when a very young guy neatly dressed in a shirt, tie, and jacket sat down in front of her. Nina was struck by this adorable freshman boy who had gotten so dressed up for a dance. But when he turned around, Nina realized that she was looking at a girl, probably her age.

"Hi," the girl said.

"Hi," Nina said. She felt like she should round out her statement somehow, so she added, "I like your tie."

She did like the tie, actually. It was a dusty rose, cut through with diagonal stripes of blue. It was nice to know that in other schools people other than Devon Wakeman were free to wear ties.

"Are you here with . . . somebody?" the girl asked.

"My friend," Nina said. "We just came together. As friends."

At that exact moment the music made the critical shift from dance to slow. They both turned and looked around, as if the music could be seen.

"Want to dance?"

"Dance?" Nina repeated.

The girl looked down at her tie. Nina tightened her grip on her phone, hoping to squeeze a ring out of it. Across the room Mel seemed to be doing well for herself. Nina watched her heading back out to the dance floor with the tall blond girl.

"Oh," Nina said. *"Dance."*

She said it as if she hadn't understood the word at first. It would seem a little weird if she sat in the corner playing with her phone all night. Besides, if she refused, would that seem rude? Homophobic?

It was just a *dance,* anyway.

"Um . . . sure," Nina said, tucking her phone into her pocket.

Tie Girl rose, and Nina followed.

The girl was about three inches shorter than Nina. She held herself stiffly, obviously trying to respect personal boundaries. She was also a rocker, shifting from foot to foot mechanically, like a slow-moving windup toy.

"What's your name?" the girl asked in a quiet voice.

Nina wondered for a moment if she should just make something up. There weren't many Ninas in the greater Saratoga area, so if this girl told anyone that she danced with a tall girl with coffee-colored skin and a disco 'fro named Nina, chances were that someone was going to know exactly who she was.

But then again, she wasn't going to lie.

"Nina."

"I'm Alex."

That was the extent of their conversation. It was amazing to Nina how long one song could last while she danced with someone in total silence. Nina gently tried to steer Alex a little closer to Mel and her blond girl. Mel leaned over the girl's shoulder and gave Nina a look of total amazement.

When the dance was over, Mel quickly came over and joined Nina, and Alex stepped away shyly and headed for the refreshment table.

"What were you doing?" Mel asked.

"Dancing."

"I mean, why?"

"She asked," Nina said. "I didn't know what to do."

Mel peered over Nina's shoulder to the tie girl.

"She's so cute."

"She's nice," Nina said. "Her name is Alex."

Mel's focus was steady now. Tie Girl definitely interested her.

"Who's that girl you were with?"

"Her name is Kathy. She kind of talks . . . a lot."

"Ask Alex next time," Nina said. "She's nice, and I don't think she's here with anyone."

Rather than rejecting Nina's idea, Mel looked hopeful. Then she glanced over at Kathy and bit her lip.

"What do I do?" she said. "I feel kind of . . . responsible now. For her. I think she wants to stay with me."

"I'll free you up."

"How?"

A good question—with only one answer.

"I'll ask her to dance."

"Are you serious?"

"I'm completely serious," Nina said. "I just danced a second ago."

Kathy was talking to two other girls in the corner. She was going to have to interrupt a conversation and then ask another girl to dance.

It's for Mel, Nina told herself. *You can do this.*

When the music was right, of course. Or whenever Kathy looked like she was going to approach Mel again. Whichever came first.

Nina reached up and touched her hair. She looked down at her black miniskirt and the pearl gray sleeveless sweater she had on. She had tried to strike a balance between party wear and casual, but she'd ended up dressing like a paralegal. This outfit was way out of place.

Nina felt like she knew what guys were interested in, but it occurred to her that she had no idea what girls were looking for in other girls. There was the very real chance that Kathy might take one look at her and say, "No thanks."

What if she got *shot down?*

"Are you okay?" Mel asked.

"Great."

The music slowed.

"Okay," Nina said. "This is us."

She walked right up to Kathy, who had turned to look around the room, probably for Mel.

"Hey," she said brightly. "Would you like to dance?"

Kathy seemed surprised by this. She did, in fact, look Nina up and down and take in the officewear.

"Okay," she said.

It wasn't, Nina noticed, said with a lot of enthusiasm. It was a pleasant but lukewarm "Okay."

Kathy and Nina were about the same height. Kathy wasn't a great dancer either, but she wasn't nearly as timid. She pummeled Nina with questions about where she went to school and who she knew. By the end of the song Nina had the strange feeling that she'd just been interviewed for something. An inclusion into the local gay and lesbian alliance, possibly. Maybe even a job.

Nina glanced over her shoulder and saw that Mel and Alex were dancing. Their scheme had worked.

When the song was over, Nina hurried out through the lobby and stood outside in the frosty night air. Her brain was reeling. This situation was no longer hypothetical. She had just danced with two girls, who probably thought she was gay—and for good reason. Showing up at a gay dance. Dancing when asked. Asking other girls to dance. These signals were pretty unambiguous.

That was it. She was going to sit in the car, scrunch down low in the seat, and play with her phone for the rest of the night.

"She's from Albany," Mel said, rushing out and joining Nina. "Oh my God. Am I all red?"

"A little," Nina said, managing a smile. It had been a long time since she had seen Mel this excited.

"Are you okay?"

"Fine."

"Thanks," Mel said. "For doing this. I know it has to be weird."

"It's not weird," Nina said, smiling even more broadly to cover the hugeness of the lie. "It's just dancing. It's cool."

"We don't have to stay. . . ."

"Did you get her number yet?"

"Oh God." Mel looked thunderstruck. "I can't. That's too weird."

"So ask for her e-mail address."

Mel thought this one over.

"It feels weird," Mel finally said. "I feel like I'm cheating on her or something. I know that's crazy."

"It *is* crazy. No crazy talk. Avery's not here. But Alex is."

"I saw her on Valentine's Day. We talked."

"Who? Avery?"

"Yeah."

"What did she say?"

"Not a lot," Mel said.

Nina leaned against the door and sighed.

"That's good, I guess."

They both fell quiet. Mel kept staring at the shapes her breath was forming.

"Okay." Nina stood up straight and adjusted her skirt. "We're standing outside in the freezing cold talking about things that suck when you could be *inside* talking to Alex, your hot new girl."

"She's not my girl."

"Not yet," Nina said, giving Mel a gentle push. "But I have a good feeling."

Saint Patrick's Day

38

Nina slipped out from under her heavy down comforter and pulled up her blinds. The sun had decided to come out after days of flurries and overcast skies. It reflected off the thin coat of snow on the ground, making everything intensely light and radiant.

It looked like an eighteenth birthday. Kind of gleaming.

Things had gotten better for both her and Mel in the last few weeks. Mel had been e-mailing and IM-ing Alex for almost a month. They hadn't actually managed to set up a date yet, but it seemed like that was the way things were headed. Mel had her own timetable, and at least Avery was coming up in conversation less and less. They were both getting used to that fact.

Parker had been Nina's major development. He had kept his promise to the letter—he was a perfect not-boyfriend. When she was busy, he made himself scarce. He didn't bog her down with text messages and notes. At school or in front of Mel he didn't even hint at the fact that there was anything going on between them. But there was. He was always there, waiting at the other end of the phone or online. She'd get in touch and he'd appear, and they'd go for coffee. Sometimes they'd just take Nina's SUV (the Roach had personality, but there was no getting used to that hole in the floor in the winter) and just park in the lot behind the Visitors' Center. But each time felt like a separate event. It wasn't building to anything. It was just the arrangement they had worked out, and it was good.

Tonight, he wanted to take her out. That was fair enough. It was her birthday, and it was a beautiful day.

She switched on her computer and ran down the list of e-mails that had come in. It was a love shower this morning. Birthday e-mail. There were about five e-greeting receipts waiting for her, two messages from Rob, a string of thirteen notes from Parker. But what caught Nina's eye was a note in the middle.

Carson88. Steve. The subject line simply said "Hi."

Hi.

Very casual. *Hi. Remember me?*

Nina sat for a solid ten minutes before double clicking on the note.

Dear Neen,

Happy birthday, first of all.

I know it's weird that I'm writing and that you may not want to hear from me, so I'm going to tell you why.

Diane and I broke up. It happened two weeks ago. She's a good person, but I honestly was thinking about you the whole time and even talking about you a lot.

So I've been sitting here for two weeks, going nuts, trying to figure out what to say that wouldn't make me seem like some kind of ASS because I'm really, really nervous even writing this now.

I guess I should mention that I got into Stanford too. So you're going to see me even if you don't want to, and if you don't want to, I'll totally hide in the hills and stay clear. But I'm really, really sorry for what I did. I think I went insane. It was raining here all the time (big surprise) and some kind of pernicious (SAT word) mold completely took over our bathroom. My dad's been out of work (lots of lentils) and everything was just kind of grim and sucked. I was just kind of depressed, I guess, and I felt like I was never going to see you again. Last summer was the best time of my life. I got lucky. I met you. I felt so weird when we both had to go home. I figured it would be easier to pretend like you weren't even there and see someone else. Does that make sense?

I sound so lame.

I miss you and I'm sorry and I'll do anything I can, but please, I am telling the complete truth.

I hope my writing doesn't make you sick or anything. I don't want to ruin your birthday. I just want to say that I'm sorry and that I'm here anytime you feel like talking about this, if you ever do. I want to keep writing, but I should probably stop.

—Stickboy

Nina curled her arms over her stomach. The feelings came back all once, in a surprise attack. There were the scary ones that she'd had to beat down when he wasn't writing and after they split up. There were the warm ones—the ones that caused her whole body to shake when she heard his voice.

She couldn't think. There was something so real about what he was saying, but she kept picturing him with the girl with the similar hair, imagining all the things they'd been able to do together. So many things she'd never know about.

Nina went over and climbed back into her bed. She wondered if she could stay there all day. She'd never faked being sick before. But a birthday was a way too obvious time to start. Besides, she didn't want to be stuck alone with that e-mail all day. She'd definitely lose her mind.

When she came into school, Nina saw the balloon tied to her locker from halfway down the hall. As she got closer, she saw that the locker door had also been covered in streamers and had a HAPPY BIRTHDAY sign attached to it. These were all things she expected, and she was grateful, but she didn't want them today. She wasn't ready for today anymore. She needed her birthday to be postponed at least a week. She hurried to her locker, hoping to avoid any major contact. If she could just get to the council office and sit for a few minutes, she would probably be fine.

A small crowd screamed a greeting when she walked into the room.

Georgia had decorated the student council office in streamers. There was an extra-large pile of muffins on the table. These weren't just the nasty raisin-bran ones that she usually brought in. Today Georgia had obviously stolen the good ones as well—the lemon poppy seeds, the glazed orange, the chocolate cheesecakes. The underclassmen reps had stuffed her box full of cards and small gifts: a Glinda the Good Witch magnet, two carnations, one pink rose, a mini–Chinese food carton full of candy. She duly sat at the table and opened all of these, thanking each person with a hug.

As she was carrying her armload of gifts back down the hall, she was caught again, this time by Mel, who was running up to her with a huge smile on her face.

"Hey!" Mel said. "We've been looking for you!"

The "we" included Parker, who stood behind Mel, waiting his turn.

"I got ambushed in the office," Nina said.

Parker was smiling broadly. For a moment, it looked like he was going to lean over and kiss her.

"I need her for a second," Mel said. "I'll bring her right back."

She pulled Nina down to the bathroom and then checked it over to see if anyone was there.

"Okay," she said. "Special news. I'm telling my dad tonight."

"*Telling* him, telling him?"

Mel nodded.

"Oh my God." Nina tried hard to curb her feelings for a moment to show some enthusiasm. The best she could come up with was a wet smile. "Are you sure?"

"Yeah." Mel nodded. "It's time."

"Why now? I mean, I'm glad, but . . ."

"After I went to the dance, I felt really good. And Avery wasn't. . . . Avery was different. Avery didn't want to talk about it. All those people there—they were just being *normal* about it. It made me feel normal. Does that make sense?"

"Completely."

"Alex came out when she was fourteen. She said she thought her mom was going to freak, but she was really good about it. She's had girls over for dinner and everything. I don't think my mom would be okay with that, because, well, you know my mom. But my dad might. I think my dad would, right?"

Mel was speaking breathily and pacing the bathroom, touching all the pink tiles above the sink with her index finger as if they were huge buttons—all systems go.

"You're dad's great."

"I know. And I had to pick a date, so I figured why not your birthday? Mine's not until May and I don't want to wait that long, because then it's prom, and that's a whole different thing I have to explain anyway. They even have a prom! In Albany! And I have it all figured out. I'm making my dad's favorite dinner, this chicken thing, and then I'll tell him right afterward. I'm telling him everything. Even the parts about Avery, because he'll figure that out anyway."

This was the most Mel had ever said in one go. She was barely even taking breaths. But Nina's brain was still stuck on one note. *Steve is back. He didn't mean it. Similar Hair is outta here. Steve is sitting in the rain, thinking about me. Steve was sad. Steve cheated on me and gave up. Steve misses me.*

Would he like her new hair? She reached up and touched the springy tips—her new nervous habit.

Screw him. He would be lucky to *see* her hair again.

"It's all working out, Neen," Mel said, coming close. "It seemed so bad before, but it's working out."

The door opened, and Mel quickly backed up.

"It's great," Nina said, stepping forward and grabbing Mel's hand very deliberately. (So what if the soccer girls standing on the other side of the room were watching? Whatever. They could go bend it like Beckham and shut up.) "It's the best birthday present."

She wanted to tell Mel everything—explain to her that the reason that her eyes were misting over had more to do with Steve than anything else. Forget Steve. This was Mel's shining moment. . . .

"It's great," she said again. "Everything's great."

39

When she got home from school, Nina spent half an hour sitting in front of her computer, not writing a reply to Steve. This was pretty much in keeping with her entire day, which she'd spent composing e-mails in her head that she knew she wasn't going to be sending to Steve.

In one second she put her fingers on the keys, intending to pour her heart out and tell him that she understood and that they weren't really starting again since as far as she was concerned nothing had ever really changed—her love was true and constant and she knew it would all be all right in the end. Then she'd curl up her fingers, and the next time she went to type, she planned to write a stunning description of Parker's many fine attributes, concentrating on his single-minded devotion to her happiness. (All phrased in the most apologetic terms possible. Rub his nose in her goodness. Make the boy *suffer* a bit.)

In the end, all she did was bring up a blank note and open and close it a few times. She wasted the entire afternoon that way, and before she knew it, it was dark. Parker would be on his way soon.

"It's all ready," he said as she climbed into the Roach an hour later.

"What is?"

"You'll see."

He turned left and headed back toward school. Nina was surprised when he turned into one of the back lots and parked.

"We're going back to school?" she said. "Is there another sign?"

"Ask no questions!"

Parker led her around to one of the doors near the gym. Even from the parking lot, she could hear a chorus unevenly singing a bright show tune. She'd forgotten that rehearsals for the spring musical had just started. She listened as the group worked through a line or two and then stopped and restarted, getting only a bit further each time, chopping their way through the score with rough, loud strokes.

It was eerily dark in the hall outside the gym. Nina had been in school plenty of times after hours, but that was always for official reasons, and she rarely strayed much farther than the council office. Parker took her back along the hallway with all of the trophy cases. He stopped in front of the double doors of the main lecture hall, where they showed movies and had smaller, single-class assemblies. He produced a key from his pocket and unlocked the door.

"How'd you get that?" Nina asked.

"I know one of the AV guys."

"They give AV guys keys?" Nina asked, feeling a little jealous. "I'm the president of the council and I don't even get a key to the council office."

"It's one of those secret power positions," Parker explained, holding the door open for her.

The auditorium was even darker than the hallway. Nina heard Parker somewhere in the shadows, and a moment later the room was partially illuminated. He came over and took her hand and led her down to the center aisle. In the middle there was a small pail of snow chilling several sodas and a pint of ice cream. Stretched between the armrests of one of the seats was a cloth-covered piece of cardboard, which had several large boxes of candy, a bag of multicolored gourmet chips, and a small bouquet of flowers.

"Movie is your choice," Parker said. He opened up a back-pack, which was there on the floor, to reveal a stack of brand-new DVDs, still in the shrink-wrap.

"Where did you get all of those?"

"Ah, the power of credit cards and returns," he said. "Just pick which one you want to see."

Nina shuffled through the pile. Parker was leaning over, watching her reaction to everything, and her reaction was defi-nitely becoming stranger and more strained.

"Doesn't have to be a movie," he said. "We could always debate current events."

"No, it's great, it's just . . ."

"Just what?"

"I have this problem," she said.

"Oh." He leaned back and stroked an imaginary beard. "Problems. I'm good with those. Lay one on me."

"Steve wrote to me today."

Evidently this was not what Parker was expecting to hear.

"Because it's your birthday?"

"Well, yeah. But . . . there was more."

"More what?"

"He wants to get back together. He broke up with the other girl."

"That's great." Parker sat back and stared at the blank screen.

"Park . . ."

"Of course, this is the guy who didn't even think to write to you for like two months."

"There was a reason."

"I guess there was. What, did he have a *really* slow Internet connection?"

"He's not a bad guy," Nina said. "Actually, you're both really great people."

This was supposed to be a compliment, but from the look on Parker's face, Nina got the idea that he didn't see the great honor in being compared to Steve.

"He dated some other girl. He never wrote. He never called. How great a guy can he be?"

"I think," Nina said diplomatically, "that it was just hard being apart. I know it was for me. And we're going to the same school in the fall."

"So it'll be more *convenient?*"

"Look," Nina said, "we're not dating, remember? I'm not even sure what to do about him, anyway. I'm just *telling you.*"

Parker didn't answer. He grabbed the bag of chips and began squeezing it between the tips of his fingers, crushing the contents little by little. That's when it really hit her. This was not a casual thing to Parker. He'd been playing along the whole time, pretending like it was casual, because he knew that was what she wanted. Now the truth was in his face. His scowl. The fact that he wouldn't look at her.

"Can we just talk this out?" she said cautiously.

"Talk it out? What's there to talk out? Your asshole ex is back." He slumped petulantly in his seat.

This was too much. It would be all right for her to call Steve an asshole, but not Parker. Now he was sulking, but Nina was sure there was something even bigger lurking underneath. Something really painful.

"I'm going to go," she said quickly, reaching for her coat. She looked around at the many things he'd brought for her, unsure what to do with them. Taking them would seem greedy. Leaving them behind would be insulting. She compromised and grabbed the flowers. There was nothing he could do with them, at least. The rest—the food, the movies—he could keep all of that.

Her sudden movement startled him, and he stood up.

"No," he said. "It's fine."

"I'm going, Park."

"Let's just watch the movie. It's all good."

She was already out of the aisle.

"Whatever." His voice cracked a little. "He's just going to do it again. I guess that's what you want. Some dickhead who doesn't even . . ."

"Just shut up, will you?" Nina was angry now. "You don't know him. You have no idea what he's like."

"I could guess. Birks? Light on the showers? Does he use one of those crystals instead of deodorant? Oh, and cheats on you. Forgot cheats on you. You're right. I can see the appeal."

"He's done more than you ever have. Sorry he doesn't spend all his time screwing around online and messing with signs. What's your big contribution? You don't do *anything*."

She didn't mean to say it. It just came out. Steve had to be defended. And it was true, after all. Steve fought for things. Steve suffered. Steve bought vacuums and helped people and got scholarships and was mature. Parker was just a guy with a bag of DVDs and some ice cream, standing in the middle of the auditorium, looking like a kid who just lost his soccer ball.

More than that. Looking very hurt.

"I drove," he mumbled.

"I'll walk."

"Neen . . ."

But Nina was already out the door.

Nina took a strange route home, weaving from street to street and cutting through parking lots so that the chances of Parker driving by and seeing her were minimized. She was so absorbed in her evasive tactics that she was halfway home before she remembered that she had an important phone call to make.

Mel's dad picked up the phone and seemed surprisingly happy to hear Nina's voice.

"So, I heard the big news," he said. It took Nina a moment to remember that there were other traumas going on tonight and Mel's had a much greater explosive potential.

"Oh," Nina said cautiously. "That's good. That's really good."

"I wasn't really surprised, though."

"No?"

"I always had a feeling."

"Really?"

"Always."

Nina was floored. Mr. Forrest was the *coolest dad ever* and way more perceptive than she'd ever been. He'd always been a nice guy, but who knew the depth of his awareness and openness until now? At least one good thing had come out of today.

"I'm really happy to hear that," Nina said, feeling her eyes tearing up a little again. "I wish Mel had told you sooner."

"Well, I know now, and I think it's great."

"I knew you'd be fine with it," Nina fibbed a bit. "And you know, there are lots of groups for parents in case you wanted to talk to some other people."

"Groups? For parents?"

"Support groups and pride groups—I love my gay teenager, that kind of thing. Maybe you can go with Avery's parents."

The pause that followed was just slightly too long.

"What did you say?" he asked.

Wrong tone. Definitely the wrong tone.

"Is Mel there?" she asked quickly.

"Hold on. . . ." Again his voice was too deep.

Nina swallowed her panic. Maybe everything was fine. Maybe she hadn't just made the life-altering mistake she thought she had.

Mel sounded slightly guilty when she got on the phone and said hi.

"Just say yes or no," Nina said quickly. "Did you tell your dad?"

"Um . . ."

"Say yes or no!"

"No."

"Oh my God."

"But I will," Mel insisted. "I was going to, and then I just bailed. But I will. Definitely this week. Don't be mad. . . ."

"Is your dad still there?" Nina asked frantically. "Like, *right* there?"

"Yeah."

"Move away," Nina said, her panic growing. "Go in the other room."

Nina could hear her walking along the hall by her staircase.

"I moved," Mel said.

"What big news did your dad hear?"

"What?"

"He said he heard the big news."

"About you and Stanford," Mel replied after a moment. "I guess you probably haven't spoken to him since you got in."

Everything was spinning down, down, down. . . .

"Okay," she said slowly, "I think I just did something."

"What?"

"I think I just outed you."

Silence on Mel's end.

"It sounded like you told him," Nina added quickly. "It seemed like he knew."

Still nothing.

"Mel?"

"I think I'd better go," Mel said.

When Mel had hung up, Nina touched the buttons on her phone, tapping out Steve's number without actually pushing hard enough to dial.

Mel set the phone down on her dresser. She could still hear the television coming from downstairs, which seemed like a good sign. Actually, she was ready to interpret anything as a good sign. She decided to spend the rest of the night in her room. If necessary, she would spend the rest of the *week* in her room.

Within about five minutes she heard a creak in the hall. The soft knock followed, and her dad cracked open the door to her room. He stood there in his white undershirt and jeans, looking lost. He didn't offer up any small talk—no *hi*'s or *what are you up to*'s.

The phone started ringing. Neither of them moved for it.

"Nina said something on the phone just now," he said.

He looked at all of her little decorative boxes and picture frames that sat on her bureau. He saw the shadow box collage that she had made of the Triangle when she was thirteen.

Something about it seemed to disturb him. He shook his head and turned back to her.

"Do you want to tell me anything?" he asked.

Mel had hoped that when this moment came, she would declare herself proudly. But instead heaving sobs just came up, even though she wasn't ashamed or sad. She clawed her fingers into her pillow and tried to speak.

He didn't come any closer. He lingered where he was in the pocket of shadow between the hallway light and the muted glow of Mel's blue-shaded bedside lamp.

"I'll have to talk to your mom . . ." he mumbled.

"Okay." Mel was still gulping back tears.

She wanted him to say something else. Anything would have been fine. He appeared to be searching for the words but then gave up on the effort, wished her a good night, and quietly closed the door.

40

When they were nine years old, Mel and Avery got in trouble. It was all because of Nina's chicken pox.

That was their first separation from Nina—she was quarantined in her house for two weeks. Since neither Mel nor Avery had had chicken pox by that point, they didn't quite understand what was happening to her. She was covered in red spots. She had a bad fever. She was sick enough to have earned an all-milk-shake-and-Jell-O diet. That had to be serious.

They were just old enough to be allowed to stay in the house alone by themselves, and one afternoon Mel's mom went out for an hour. They took advantage of the time by looking through everything that was normally off-limits, like the contents of the top kitchen cabinets. It was there that Avery found the cake mix, and it was her idea to make a cake for Nina. Mel agreed, of course.

By the time Mel's mom returned, the kitchen was tropically hot and there were two burned cake pieces in badly sizzled tins. There was smoke, spill, and general disaster. Mel's mom did not take it well.

What Avery remembered most clearly was that there was

something unbearably awful and embarrassing about getting yelled at by someone else's parent. Avery could still remember standing there in Mel's kitchen, tears streaming down her face, staring resolutely at the remnants of the cake mix box and the still-unopened container of frosting.

Soon after that, Mel's mom went off to live with Jim Podd, and a little while later she had another baby girl. Avery wondered at the time if the events were connected—if Mel's mom was so mad about the whole cake thing that she'd actually gone off and started a whole new family, complete with a new kid.

Nine years later and here they were again. The lesson seemed to be: when Nina went away for any extended period, shit hit the fan. The corollary was that Mel's mom seemingly had the ability to call them both on the carpet. Nothing really ever changed in her life—things just got bigger, longer, and increasingly complicated.

Avery could see the confusion on her parents' faces when they told her that Mrs. Podd had called and asked that they all meet at Mel's house to discuss "something very important." Avery pled ignorance, then got in her car and drove around the neighborhood in circles, chain-smoking all the while, until she was out of time.

When they arrived at the house, Mel's mom answered the door—something that hadn't happened in years. Mel was sitting in the living room, chin resting on her chest. After exchanging a few puzzled pleasantries, Avery's parents asked why they were there.

"I thought it would be best if we all sat down and discussed this together," Mel's mother said. She hadn't actually looked at Avery up until this point. She did now.

"What are we discussing?" Avery's mom asked.

"A situation. Something that's just come to our attention."

"What kind of situation?" Avery's dad asked.

Mel's mom fixed her blouse for a good two minutes while her dad looked down at the floor.

"Avery and Melanie have been . . ."

Mel's mom stopped and looked at the heavy green winter curtains, which didn't quite match the slightly different green of the rug. The clash genuinely seemed to disturb her.

"Have been what?" Avery's mother asked.

"More than friends."

She seemed to hate these words even more than the curtains. She didn't say them in any kind of evil, Cruella De Vil voice, but Avery could feel her disgust.

"Is this true?" Avery's mother asked.

"We're not dating," Avery said in a low voice. That was true, at least.

"Then why did Nina say that we would all want to join a group for parents of gay teenagers?" Mel's mother asked.

Avery had no idea when or why Nina would have said that. It didn't even matter now.

"Look," Avery's mom said slowly. "We know these are two good girls. And if they're gay—"

"I'm not gay," Avery cut in.

"They have to be comfortable admitting that to us."

"But I'm not."

"Because they are still our daughters." Mrs. Dekker patted Avery's shoulder. Avery rolled her eyes to the ceiling in despair.

"If that's how you want to raise Avery, fine," Mel's mother said. "But I don't want this for Mel. When she's older, she'll regret all the things she could have had—a husband, kids. She'll see that people treat her differently, and she won't like it."

"I think if our daughters are discovering their sexuality, we should at least listen to what they have to say."

"Discovering their . . ." Mel's mother huffed. "I don't think you're dealing with reality here."

"I'm not discovering *anything*," Avery said.

"She's really not," Mel added.

"She's not?" Avery's mom said. "You're not?"

She almost seemed disappointed—nearly as disappointed as Avery was that her resolutely normal mother was all too ready to accept her as a lesbian. No fuss, no look of shock or dismay. It was *profoundly irritating.*

"Then what is this about?" Avery's mother asked.

Again everyone turned to Mel, but Mel was staring into the cover of the *TV Guide* as if it held great meaning. Mel held the key to this whole discussion now. It was up to her how it was going to go.

"Nina made a mistake," Mel said. "Avery's not gay. I am."

The silence that greeted this announcement was the kind of silence that usually thrilled Avery—it was that loaded half-note pause before the devastating final chord, the time between the squeal of the tires and the sound of the impact. It wasn't pleasant now.

"But you've dated boys before," Mel's mom said.

Mel shrugged.

"How could you date boys if you're gay?"

"I didn't really date any."

"Yes, you *did*," her mother said, a little more urgently. "There were a few."

"For a few days. I never really dated them."

"This is not as simple as you think," Mel's mother spat. "Don't you understand that what you do is a reflection on us?"

"I can't help what I am."

"You are *my* little girl."

"I'm still a girl." Mel said it very quietly.

With Avery in the clear, the Dekkers were just bystanders now, watching another family's trauma unfold in front of them. Mr. Dekker swung his arms wide, as if he was trying to get a group hug going. Nobody paid much attention to this, so he put them down again.

"I just don't understand," Mel's dad said. He spoke quietly. He seemed so genuinely sad that no one spoke for a moment.

"It's okay, Dad," Mel said. She looked up at her father now, trying to reassure him.

"It's not okay." This brought Mel's mother out of her short silence. "I'm not going to support this kind of lifestyle. Neither is your father, and neither is Jim. Don't expect us to pay for your college or for your living expenses. If this is how you're going to be, then you'd better be prepared for some reality, little girl."

"Just stop," her father said. "You've said enough. Be quiet."

"I will *not* be quiet. Mel is my daughter as well. . . ."

"I don't like your threats."

"It's not a threat. It's a fact. After she's eighteen, we're under no legal obligation to provide anything. Let her find her own place to live. Let her try to find a job. Let her see what the world is really like."

This direct assault on Mel stirred something in Avery, especially after Mel had just spared her. After what Avery had done, the logical thing for Mel would have been to take Avery down with her. But Mel didn't do that. Because they were friends.

Avery felt a heat in her chest. Words were rising in her throat.

"You can't be serious," she said. "What's reality, dumping your family and ignoring problems that are right under your nose?"

"Avery!" her mother snapped.

"Brendan is a hacker," Avery continued. "You talk about it like it's a major accomplishment. Richie needs medication, like, now. And you're worried about Mel being *gay?*"

"That's enough, Avery," her mother said firmly.

"It's true," Avery said. "Brendan hacks into sites and takes people's personal information. He is a criminal. They know it. They talk about it—how he's going to get some job with a company that hires hackers to help their security. He has a *padlock* on his door."

"Okay, Avery . . ." Her mother was serious now. "You're finished."

"This is not about Brendan," Mel's mother said coldly.

"Are you saying being a criminal is better than being *gay*?" Avery turned back to Mel's mom. "Are you really that dumb?"

This was a terrifying yet oddly liberating experience. Avery had never had a true smackdown with an adult before (well, at least one who wasn't a customer), and the adrenaline was rushing through her system. But before she could push this any further, Mel stood up and politely excused herself. There was something strange about the way she was walking—it was a slow, straight gait, like she was making her way through shallow water with something balanced on her head.

Without waiting for permission, Avery bolted from the sofa.

Outside, the night sky was a light pink—a bright warning of snow. Mel was sitting in the middle of the lawn, gazing up at it. Avery walked over and stood by her.

"It shouldn't snow in March," Avery said. "It just seems wrong."

Mel just kept looking at the sky. Avery took a seat next to Mel on the ground.

"Why did you let me off the hook like that?" Avery asked.

Mel turned to Avery and gave her a quizzical look.

"I just told the truth," she said.

"We did date, though."

"I know."

"So you could have told them."

"What for?" Mel shook her head. "You shouldn't have to deal with it."

"Why not? You have to."

"Because for me it's permanent. Besides, you said a lot of stuff I've always wanted to say. You stuck up for me too. You totally went after my mom."

"Yeah." Avery nodded. "That was actually kind of fun."

Mel smiled a little.

"I'll bet there's a really interesting conversation going on in there," Avery said.

"Go listen."

"That's okay."

Instead they stared up at the sky. It seemed to hang low and close. It reminded Avery of when they used to make forts out of blankets or sheets.

"Tell me something good," Mel said. Her voice had a dreamy lilt to it. "What's going on with your music stuff?"

"I have an audition Sunday morning at nine. I'm taking the bus down to New York on Saturday."

Mel turned and looked at Avery.

"That's great. What do you have to do?"

"Play a bunch of pieces. I have some kind of written test afterward at noon. Then I have to sit around until four to see if they want me to play again."

"You'll be awesome," Mel said. "You're the best."

"I wish you could be there. I'm kind of freaked out."

Mel smiled. Her pale skin was bright pink in the cold. Avery heard the door open, and soon her mom appeared outside. She came over to them and squatted down in front of Mel, then put her hands on Mel's knees. "If you need a place to go," she said, "you just come over. Anytime. You don't even have to call."

"Thanks," Mel said. Her voice was thick.

"Are you going to be okay?" Avery asked.

"I think so."

"Call me if you need anything."

"I will."

Avery's mom stood and took Avery lightly by the arm. Even though she didn't want to leave Mel, she knew it was time—this discussion, in some form or another, had been on its way for years. Mel was going to square off with her mom, and she had to do that on her own. Avery watched her, even as she backed up to the car and as they pulled away. She also noticed something else. Mel didn't seem that small anymore.

Mel sat on the lawn for a while after Avery and her family left, listening to her parents fighting inside the house. Strangely, this noise comforted her. It reminded her of being little. Some of her earliest memories were of hearing arguments in other rooms. She just thought it was the noise families made, no more significant than the mumblings from the TV or the grinding of the garbage disposal. It was only after her mother left and the house became fight-free that Mel realized how much she missed the sound.

Her mother came out after a while.

"Come inside," she said.

"No."

"I'm not playing around with this, Mel. Come back inside."

"You don't live here," Mel said, a few loose tears dribbling down her face. "You can't make me."

"Are you angry at me, Mel?" she asked, her voice low. "Is that what this is about?"

"Why do you think this is about you?"

"Fine. Talk to your father."

Her mother got into her car and left. When she was down the street, Mel got up and went inside. Her father was still in the living room.

"You look cold," he said.

"I am."

She sat down next to him on the sofa. He wrapped her in the fleece throw they kept over the back of the couch and rubbed her arms to get her warm.

"I'm sorry," Mel said.

It probably sounded like she was apologizing for being gay. That wasn't it. She was apologizing for her mother and for making something in his life that he took for granted suddenly foreign.

"Your mom did have a point," he said. "It's going to make things hard."

"Faking the rest of my life would be harder."

He considered this.

"I know that this makes no sense to you," she said. "But it doesn't have to change anything between us."

"Mel, you know I'm going to love you no matter what, right?" her father said, pulling her close for an embrace.

Mel couldn't have felt more grateful.

"What about Mom?" she said, tears coming to her eyes.

"Don't worry about her. She's just mad that this is one situation she can't control."

"I think she hates me," Mel cried. And this really seemed true.

"No, she doesn't. She's just . . . Don't worry about her."

Mel's father kept her in his arms real tight, and they sat like that together for a long time.

41

Saint Patrick's Day weekend at P. J. Mortimer's was greeted with the kind of frenzy that only accompanied things like flash floods. Special staff meetings were held and memos were distributed making it clear that this was a Very Big Deal and that all of Saratoga was going to descend on Mortimer's to get their jig on. It was all hands on deck; *no one* could call in sick. More green food was introduced—spinach pasta, split pea soup, mint ice cream. They had even tried putting some green dye in the onion blossom batter, but this just made the onions look moldy and mossy. Even really drunk people wouldn't eat them when the batch of testers was offered free at the bar.

On Saturday night Parker stood in the corner during the shift meeting. His brow was furrowed, and he put all of his concentration into drawing little zigzags on the frosted window.

In the middle of her family trauma Mel had heard what had happened between Parker and Nina but hadn't really been able to say or do anything about it in the last two days.

Parker took his order pad from his pocket and opened it

and clapped it shut several times. He refused to look Mel in the eye.

As it turned out, there was a good crowd and a decent hour-long wait, but there definitely wasn't enough business to justify the fact that they had one server for every two tables. This just overcrowded the pantry, and everyone kept bumping into one another in the doorway. Throughout the shift Mel tried to catch Parker's eye, but he kept his focus turned away. She finally ended up standing next to him as she waited for the bartender to give her a tray full of Paddy's Frozen Peppermint Patties and Parker was dully waiting for a few Guinnesses.

"My dad found out," she said quietly. "About me."

This, at least, caught his attention.

"Whoa. How'd that happen?" he asked.

"Pretty much the same way you did." No point in mentioning Nina's role in all of this.

Parker's eyes flicked back and forth between the sets of bar taps before settling on Mel.

"Are you okay?" he asked.

"It was kind of hard. My dad told my mom. My mom told Avery's parents. They all had a big meeting, tried to do an intervention on us."

"Jesus. When did all of this happen?"

"He found out on Thursday."

"Thursday?" Parker laughed. "Well, that was a banner night for both of us."

"It's probably better this way."

"Are they mad?"

"My mom called yesterday and told me she made me an appointment to go to a psychologist," Mel said. "But my dad has been good. I don't think he really understands it, but he's not going to throw me out or anything."

They leaned against the edge of the bar and looked down into the tiny pools of beer and icy slush that were all over the rubber mat that covered the servers' pickup area. Parker flicked a beer cap with his finger, and it flew behind the bar and bounced off a bottle.

"I screwed up," he said. "Bad."

"Oh, Park." Mel wished her friends weren't going through all this.

"And then, because that wasn't enough," he went on, "I got a credit card and bought a metric shitload of DVDs so that she could pick the one she wanted to watch. I was going to return the rest. But the credit card company noticed that the first purchase seemed weird, and fraud protection flagged my card and put a hold on it. So now I might not be able to return them on time, and I'll have to pay four hundred bucks. Which is just perfect, don't you think?"

The birthday jig alarm went off. Julie, Avery's replacement on the keyboard (not that she was anywhere nearly as good as Avery), took her position, and the army of servers descended on the unsuspecting victim. Parker and Mel looked at each other and then quietly stepped away from the bar and slipped through the glut of servers who came forward to stomp around the doomed birthday person's table. They went right to the pantry and out the service door.

Once outside, they stood coatless in the cold, peering at the massive pile of cartons that preparations for the holiday had generated. They meditated on the garbage and their respective problems for a while; then Mel's mind drifted back to Avery. She was so relieved that Avery wasn't "a problem" anymore. Now Avery felt like Avery, her best friend. She'd said that she was nervous about her audition and that she'd wished Mel could be there. If things were how they used to be, Mel probably would have been. In fact, all three members of the Triangle would probably have made a trip of it.

She looked up at Parker suddenly.

"Avery went to New York today," Mel said. "She has her big audition in the morning."

"Hooray." Parker said flatly.

"I want to go, and I want you to come with me."

"To her audition? What, do you want to sabotage it or something?"

"I'd like to cheer her on."

"What page of the script are you on?" Parker asked. "I think I just walked into a very special episode of *Seventh Heaven*."

"I'm serious," Mel said.

"Well, in Reality Land, where I live, I work tomorrow."

"Call in."

"I would, but I can't, now that I have this massive credit card bill to pay. Also, Nina hates me now. Also, Avery's the one who broke up with you, so why are you chasing her to New York to support her? Also, also, also." He started picking Guinness pins from his suspenders and throwing them angrily across the lot, timing each of his *also*'s with the hollow ping as they hit the Dumpster.

"Avery said she wanted me there."

"She *dumped* you."

"She's still Avery."

"Avery, the girl who decided to make somebody else give you the news that you two were over. You were crying for like two months. Do you and Nina like to date people who don't call you? Is that like a big turn-on or something? Why didn't someone tell me that's all I had to do?"

"She's been my friend my whole life. She stuck up for me the other night. We stuck up for each other."

"Okay." He sighed. "I give. There was sticking. You want to do the rah-rahs for Avery, fine. But why would I go?"

"Because you're our friend. Because you like Nina."

"Who probably never wants to see me again."

"Look," Mel said firmly. "Do you want to figure it out, or do you just want to complain about it forever? Come with me. Talk to her."

Parker ran his hand through his hair, then paced over to the Dumpster, retrieved his pins from the ground, and reattached them to his suspenders. Mel could see his lips moving. He was mumbling to himself, trying to figure out what to do. After a few moments of this, he came back over.

"If you can find a way to convince her to spend hours with

me in the car, I'll go," he said. "But she won't. I'm telling you, she won't."

"If I promise you I can do it, will you take off and come with us?"

"If you can do that, then I'll do anything you want, because that means you have magical powers."

"Be at my house at eight-thirty. Park down the street."

He crossed his arms over his chest and leaned against the door.

"Now you're scaring me," he said, finally smiling in the way he usually did. "You're getting all tough and mastermindy."

"I know," Mel said, flushing with pride. "I think I'm a butch."

"I always think that when I see your sparkly T-shirts."

"It's not the clothes," Mel said, moving him away from the door to go back inside. "It's the attitude."

42

Why am I doing this? Nina thought as she pulled into Mel's driveway at nine on Sunday morning.

Of course she knew why she was doing this. She had just outed Mel and potentially ruined her life, so if Mel wanted to go to New York to reunite with the girl who dumped her, then Nina was going to drive her. She was going to do whatever Mel wanted her to do for the rest of her life because what she'd done was the kind of thing you can't really make up for with a chai and an e-card.

But it was still a really, really bad idea. One, because as much as she missed Avery—and she did miss Avery—Avery had done a lot of really wrong things. And two, it was about to snow. Seriously snow. The forecast was calling for about a foot, and the only way she'd been able to go out at all was by telling her mom that she was spending the day at school and attending a completely fictitious faculty-student curriculum panel, promising that she'd walk home if the roads were bad. She foresaw some serious stopping and sliding and cleaning off of windows. They'd probably only make it an hour down the highway.

Mel came out, bundled in her heavy green winter coat and green-and-white mittens and hat. She had a duffel bag slung over her tiny shoulder. And behind her was Parker. Mel got into the car as if nothing strange was going on at all. Parker climbed into the back without a word.

"Okay," Mel said cheerfully. "So, I've packed stuff for the trip. Maps and directions, snacks, some CDs. I even made a thermos of hot chocolate. See?"

She held up a silver workman's thermos like it was a trophy.

"Can I talk to you for a minute?" Nina asked. "Outside, please?"

They got out of the car and walked to the end of the driveway.

"Why is Parker here?" Nina asked.

"I thought it would be good to have a guy along," Mel said innocently. "If we have to push or if we have trouble parking or something."

"God, Mel." Nina let out an exasperated sigh.

"If I get one favor, *ever*, I'm asking for it now."

Nina could have easily pointed out that many people would consider driving four hours through a blizzard to be a favor, but again, she was in no position to argue.

"Okay," Nina said, throwing up her hands. "If we're going to do this, let's do it all the way."

Since she was never famous for her conversational ability, Mel was at a loss to fill the deafening silence that filled the car as they drove. She tried a few times to get something going, but Nina was intent on her driving, and Parker refused to say a word. So Mel spent most of the time looking out at the heavy snow sky and the bleak view of bare trees and road. About an hour in, the snow began to fall. The first few minutes brought flurries, but these soon became wet, heavy flakes, blanking out the horizon.

Nina tried to keep going, but it was almost impossible for her to see, even with the windshield wipers at full blast. The snow blanketed the other windows, making the inside of the car dark and close and even more quiet. Nina was becoming visibly upset at the worsening conditions. She shifted down and went even slower, but other cars were losing grip and fishtailing. A rest stop finally came into sight. She eased the car off the road and drove into the parking lot, which was already full of people who seemed to have the same idea. Parker opened his door.

"Anybody want anything?" he asked unenthusiastically.

Both Mel and Nina shook their heads. Parker got out and headed into the service plaza. Mel turned to Nina, who stretched her arms out and held them stiff against the steering wheel.

"Neen," Mel said, "maybe just try to . . ."

"He doesn't want to talk."

They watched Parker hastily making his way into the plaza. She couldn't really disagree with Nina on that one. He wasn't even trying.

"I need to stretch," Nina said.

Nina opened her door and got out, leaving Mel sitting in the car alone. Mel watched Nina wrap her arms around herself tightly and walk up the sidewalk. The snow caught in the tips of her hair, giving it a strange white frosting.

This plan was horrible, Mel realized. This was why Nina had always been the planner. Throwing two people together in a car, forcing them to drive to New York together wasn't fun—it was stressful. And now she was going to get them all stranded or killed.

Nothing to do now but wait it out a bit. Hopefully Avery would still be in New York by the time they got there. Of course, they'd probably miss her completely, and since she didn't have a cell phone, they'd never be able to find her. This whole trip would be a huge exercise in pointlessness.

Sighing, she decided to go inside and at least make another attempt with Parker. Or maybe she would just hide in the bathroom and try not to cause any more problems. That was probably the wiser move. She opened her door and stepped out into a good inch of sticky snow. Nina turned and started to run over to her.

"Mel . . ." she cried.

Mel shut the door and hurried toward her, hoping that she'd changed her mind, that she was going to try to talk to Parker again. But Nina just looked horrified and stared at her car.

It took Mel a moment to realize that she probably should have turned off the car and removed the keys from the ignition before she'd gotten out.

43

At nine on Sunday morning, Avery walked up the wide stone steps of the Albertson Music Building on Eighth Street. She hadn't been sure what to wear, so she'd ended up putting on standard art student gear: black pants, black turtleneck. These were actually her P. J. Mortimer's pants she was wearing. Though she'd washed them since then, they still retained the faintest odor of hamburger, ketchup, and industrial cleanser.

Once inside, she was given a folder of admissions information and brochures by a student guide and sent upstairs to wait for her audition. She sat on the floor with her coffee and reviewed her music, even though there was no point. It had to be in her head and in her hands by now. She'd played each song hundreds of times. Looking at the notation only confused the issue.

She put the music back in her bag and stared at the wall. There was a bulletin board there, overflowing with posters for chamber music recitals, summer institutes, choir performances, and music festivals. A soprano was doing her scales somewhere down the hall, and Avery listened in amazement as she nailed a high A with perfect clarity and roundness, then easily ran back down the scale.

Across from her, a girl in a long black skirt with a shock of blond hair wrapped in a red scarf was sitting with her eyes closed and smiling to herself. She swayed back and forth and beat out a complicated rhythm on the floor with a flat hand.

Some of us don't need stereos, Avery thought. Truthfully, Avery could be like that too: Sometimes she could hear music that clearly in her own mind. But she disliked public displays that made it clear that she heard fully audible noises—and occasionally voices—inside her head.

When she came to the end of her song, the girl opened her eyes and smiled at Avery.

"Here for piano?" she asked.

Avery nodded.

"What are you playing?"

"Chopin's Etude Opus 10, number 1, and William Bolcom's *Graceful Ghost Rag*, plus the Bach and Beethoven."

"I'm doing Stravinsky's *Four Studies* and the Rondo in B Minor by Clara Schumann," the girl offered.

Avery didn't know those pieces, but they just sounded better than hers. The girl was wearing a flowing peasant blouse made of linen. It seemed more artsy than Avery's generic poseur black turtleneck.

The soprano hit a high B with equal ease.

"She's good, huh?" the girl said, nodding toward the end of

the hall the sound originated from. "She was doing a little bit of Susanna from *Figaro* right before you came in. I think she was just kind of screwing around, but still, it sounded really nice."

Avery vaguely recognized that this was a reference to *The Marriage of Figaro,* which was an opera. And that was where her knowledge of that subject ended.

"I heard the theory exam is really easy," the girl went on. "Basic stuff, like how to convert a natural minor scale to a harmonic minor and a melodic minor. Scale degrees. The difference between the leading tone and the tonic. A few transpositions. Stuff like that."

It all echoed in Avery's head. This was stuff she knew. But it wasn't the kind of stuff she poured out to total strangers in hallways. And why was this girl even here? It sounded like she already had her music degree. Maybe she did. Maybe she was a plant, sent here by the school to freak out the auditioners.

One of the doors opened, and a young woman emerged. She and Scarf Girl exchanged looks, and Scarf Girl jumped up from her seat. From their high-pitched greetings, Avery gathered that they knew each other.

"Avery Dekker?" Another student guide was peering from a doorway down the hall. Avery nodded and was waved back.

"Your turn," Scarf Girl said, turning from her friend. "Good luck."

"Right . . ." Avery quickly gathered her things. "Maybe I'll see you."

Avery was ushered into a long, spare room with a hardwood

floor and a wall of floor-to-ceiling windows. Pigeons sat along the sills outside, puffing themselves up to protect them from the cold and the snow.

At one side of the room was a grand piano. Not a baby grand—a grand, easily eight feet long and stark, shellacked black. There was a padded bench with a knob on the side to raise or lower it. On the other side three people, two men and one woman, breezily chatted with one another and sipped coffee. The two men were similar in appearance—clipped salt-and-pepper beards and V-necked sweaters. The woman had a great pile of wiry gray hair wound on top of her head and a black angora shawl wrapped dramatically around her shoulders. They didn't seem to notice that Avery was there. After a moment one of the men turned and looked at Avery with a polite smile.

Avery had a strange impulse to ask if they were ready to order.

"Miss Dekker." He spoke very softly.

Avery nodded.

He shuffled a pile of folders in front of him and drew one from the stack.

"We're going to have you start with the Bach," the man said, opening the folder. "What will you be playing?"

"Fugue number 19, from the first book of *The Well-Tempered Clavier.*"

"Fine." He waved toward the piano and shuffled through her file. "Whenever you're ready."

After a moment, when the man gave her another little wave

to encourage her, Avery walked over to the piano and sat down, taking a minute to adjust her bench. Whoever had played before her was tall. She had to raise the seat and move it closer to the piano. She set her fingertips lightly on the keys. There was a wobble building in her wrists that was trickling down to her fingers.

Just start, she told herself. *Don't think.*

She hit the first notes of her piece. The Bach was mechanical and demanding but she knew it cold. She'd played it hundreds of times. This wasn't going to be a problem. She ran through it automatically—a little hurriedly, and right around the fourth measure her fingers fumbled. Avery retracted her hands from the keys in horror.

In the deadly pause that followed, Avery almost wanted to laugh.

"Take a moment," the man said, his voice unperturbed. Bored, even. It was as if he was just going through the motions now, saying what he needed to say to get Avery through her piece and out the door.

Avery pulled her hands from the keys and gave them a sharp, snapping shake. She tried to imagine the nervous energy flying from the tips of her fingers in bolts and settling harmlessly into the floorboards. It didn't quite work. Her hands began to tense, freezing into stiff claws with nasty, short nails on the ends. She settled her fingers back on the keys. They felt cool and a little foreign. This wasn't her piano. The old piano she had at home had keys that plunked down easily and issued a tinny, almost toy piano sound. This piano responded athletically—the keys sprang back. It would all be fine if she was at home, playing on the instrument she knew, with Bandit at her feet and her brothers running behind her.

One of her examiners loudly turned a page on his pad of paper. She started again, exactly at the spot where she had fumbled.

She didn't play cleanly for the first minute. She was landing the notes, but her timing was off. Everything went a bit fuzzy, and she realized as she went on that she could barely remember how she had just played. Her brain could retain only about five seconds of performance, and then it was gone. She could only go forward, deeper into music that she could see now in her mind's eye—but the notes would change on the score in her head, and she didn't know if her fingers or brain knew best. She could only play and play and play. For all she knew, she was digging her own grave with every note, every mangled measure, every flattened crescendo.

And then she was done. She realized she'd come to the end of the last piece. She looked over at the three people at the table. They seemed deeply disinterested, and in fact seemed to notice that she was finished long after she did. They smiled three blank, polite smiles at her.

"Thank you, Miss Dekker," the man said. "You can go wait downstairs."

He gave Avery another small nod to let her know that she could go. The woman shoved more orange into her mouth and adjusted the arrangement of her great pile of hair.

Avery went back out into the hallway. She could hear the

overhead lights humming. Scarf Girl and her friend were still there. She could hear the friend offering last-minute words of encouragement and advice. Scarf Girl hadn't gone. Scarf Girl hadn't messed up. Scarf Girl's chances seemed pretty good at the moment.

She hated Scarf Girl.

"How'd it go?" Scarf Girl asked.

"Great," Avery lied, lurching past her to get to the elevator.

Once downstairs, Avery sat numbly in the cold corner of the lobby. She had two hours to kill. Around her, other auditioners were waiting. Most were cramming for the theory exam. A few were analyzing their performances over the phone, citing specific technical achievements. Avery could barely remember the names of the pieces she'd played. Her mind had blotted out the entire episode, probably as a means of self-preservation.

She reached into her bag and pulled out the crib sheet she'd prepared for herself, but studying seemed useless. Instead, she watched the students coming in and out with their instrument cases, all looking purposeful and blasé. This place was their life. Physically, they didn't fit any particular type. Some dressed a little more fabulously than most. A heavy knit white poncho wrap with long fringe. Skinny jeans and massive and furry wooly mammoth boots. Some were inconspicuous in their sweatshirts, wet hats, and scarves. Some obviously just rolled out of bed; some preened themselves carefully, cultivating the fabulousness they seemed to know they carried inside. Because that was the thing—all these people had *it*. It was the *it* that got them in, the *it* that made them able to perceive and perform music far better than mere mortals. They were superior beings. The universe yielded her secrets to them and perfume ran through their veins. That was what *it* was like when you had it.

As she sat there, becoming dimly aware that she was resting in a small puddle of melted snow, Avery was pretty sure she didn't have *it*. She wasn't sure if she had anything. She couldn't quite remember why she'd come.

44

The SUV made surprisingly little noise. The snow blanketed it, muffling the engine. Mel and Nina tried all the doors multiple times, in the hopes that something would suddenly give.

"I'm so sorry," Mel said, close to tears. "I'm so sorry."

"It's okay," Nina said, her expression dark as she tried to look down into the window well of her car. "I should have taken out the keys."

"Don't you have one of those remote locks?"

"It's on the key chain." Nina sighed.

Parker came over with a steaming cup in his hand and surveyed the scene.

"What are you guys doing?" he asked.

"We're locked out," Nina said.

"The engine's on," he said, stopping in his tracks.

"Noticed that. Thanks, though."

Parker came over and peered into the window on the opposite side.

"Isn't there a way of opening this?" Nina said, looking desperate. "Like with a clothes hanger?"

"I don't think so. Not with this kind of lock. You need a slim-jim."

Mel walked over, swept a spot clear on a bench, and sat down. The back of her jeans soaked through almost instantly. Her coat was still in the car, so she was shivering, but she didn't really care.

"Triple A," Nina said, digging into her purse for her wallet and phone. "I'll call them and they'll come out and open the door."

It took Nina about ten minutes to get through. Parker sat next to Mel on the bench. He offered her his drink, but she waved it away.

"I'd say it's going pretty well," he said.

When Nina hung up the phone, she turned to find Parker sitting alone.

"Where's Mel?"

"She went thataway." He pointed to the building. "Really fast."

Nina leaned up against her purring car.

"They said they have a lot of calls from people stuck on the road. It'll take them anywhere from an hour to three hours to get here."

"Well, it's nice weather to sit around in and wait."

"We're going to miss her," Nina said. "We're going to get to New York too late, if we ever get there. We know what building she's in, and that's about it."

"It's only New York. How hard will it be to find her?"

"I have to stay here to wait for the truck," she said. "You can go inside if you want."

Parker didn't move. He just poured some of the hot liquid from his cup and watched it dissolve a hole in the snow.

"So, why are you here?" Nina asked.

"Why are any of us here?"

Nina just stared.

"Because Mel asked," he said.

"Did you know I was coming?"

"Mel mentioned it. Why are *you* here? I thought you hated Avery."

"I don't *hate* her," Nina said. She looked up into the falling snow. This always made her lose her perspective and gave her a sense of rising and falling at the same time.

"But you don't like her."

"I don't like what she did," Nina said. "It's complicated. This whole thing is actually ridiculous."

"So what did you end up doing with . . . ?"

Parker spoke with an ill-concealed anxiety. Nina didn't feel like answering his question, but she was kind of stuck. Literally. Stuck in the snow, with her car, with him. It wasn't like things could get much worse.

"I haven't really figured all that out yet," she said. "Why don't you go wait with Mel? I think she's a little upset about the thing with the door."

"Right." Parker hopped up. He was smiling, though it wasn't a happy smile—more like the smile of someone who's been proven right about something.

The truck arrived a half hour later, and the door was popped open in about ten seconds. This bothered Nina somewhat. She felt like it should have taken a little more time and effort. She'd spent more time opening jars.

The sky was now a feverish pink, and the snow showed no signs of stopping. Nina put the car into four-wheel drive and made her way along slowly. It took two more hours to get into the city. Traffic around New York was snarled and insane, and they spent almost an hour at a standstill waiting to get on the George Washington Bridge. It was too nerve-racking even to get excited about going to the city. Not that they could see the city, anyway. The sky was full of white drifts that obscured the view. It just felt like they were in a snow globe.

Once they made it over and got into the city proper, Mel became too agitated to follow the map, and Parker had to take over. He also had to crisis-counsel Nina as she experienced multiple panic attacks as yellow cabs skidded by her, coming within inches of her car. They managed to get onto the FDR Drive and basically slide down the side of Manhattan on packed snow, going way too fast in an attempt to keep up with the traffic.

"Are we in the nothing-left-to-live-for lane?" Parker asked.

They swung off somewhere in the twenties and managed to make their way down Second Avenue to an area that Mel vaguely recognized from studying the school's Web site.

"Parking lot!" Mel cried. "Parking lot!"

Nina made a sharp left and turned into an underground garage. As they made their way out to the street, the snow was shooting down the narrow paths between the buildings and going right into their faces.

"So, where is this place?" Nina asked. She had only been to the city a handful of times with her parents, and she had never gotten much farther than Macy's or the Empire State Building. This part of New York was completely strange to her. It was a tangle of stores, academic buildings, and delis. It was hard to look up and see how high any of the buildings were, but Nina could tell that they weren't huge skyscrapers.

Parker was scanning the street.

"Turn right at the Starbucks, walk past the Starbucks, and keep going until you reach the third Starbucks on your left." He shook his head. "Maybe they grow them here."

"Eighth Street," Mel said, brushing snow off her printout. The ink on the map smeared over the page. "Eighth and Greene. It's near a park. Where are we?"

"Lafayette," Nina said, squinting at a sign. "Which way do we go?"

"Um . . ." Mel rotated helplessly. "Maybe we ask someone?"

"Let's walk until we see what number street we're on," Parker said. "We can at least get to Eighth."

They walked along as people were out with shovels and salt, trying to do battle with the elements and losing.

"Great Jones Street," Nina said as they reached the next corner. "That's not a number. I'm going to ask someone."

It took one or two tries, but Nina managed to flag down a woman who told her that the school was just a few blocks over.

"Okay," she said, checking her watch. "We have ten minutes. Let's go."

45

Avery watched the snow beat into the glass doors of the lobby. Every time the doors would open, an artic gale would rush through the room. It would hit the security guard head-on and she would shiver dramatically and say, "Mm-mm-mm," in a disapproving tone. To Avery, it seemed like a comment on her entire life. *Mm-mm-mm, Dekker. You blew it. Game over. Thanks for playing.*

She'd considered walking out before the theory exam, but she couldn't pick herself up and get out the door. So when the exam room was opened, she shuffled along with the others. The test itself was nothing. She breezed through it. (It was easy to take a test when she felt like she had nothing to lose.) She'd planted herself in the corner of the lobby again, stuck her earphones in her ears, and tried to blot the world out. But that stupid "Mm-mm-mm" had penetrated. She'd been listening to that "Mm-mm-mm" for over an hour.

Scarf Girl and Friend of Scarf Girl were there too—they'd been hip to hip the whole day. Avery had managed to gather that they'd gone to some music camp together for several years when they were kids. She vaguely wondered if they were dating, or if it had ever crossed their minds to just kiss, to hold on to each other in this cold lobby and just make out like maniacs to get through this agonizing wait.

But then, not everyone was like Avery. Not everyone gave in to their whims and destroyed their friendships in the process. Some people actually had a grip. Some people could keep their friends, and those people didn't have to sit by themselves in a puddle in the freezing cold, waiting for the what was potentially the biggest piece of news (probably bad) they'd get in their lives.

Even the music Avery was listening to was depressing her. She connected songs to events and people and times and places, and every line drawn from every song seemed to connect to Mel or Nina. She yanked out the earphones and listened to the girl next to her jabbering into her phone. She was having a particularly soap-opera conversation—the kind of overly loud one that was clearly meant to be heard by everyone around her. Lots of *I know!*'s and *Shut up!*'s and even one *For serious? For totally serious, serious?*

When the girl said, "Oh . . . my . . . God!" nothing really registered until Avery noticed that almost everyone had jumped up and was rushing the hallway on the far left, forming a confused tangle.

This could only mean one thing.

Avery stood up slowly. She made no effort to get to the front of the throng. She hung on the edges until a spot was clear, which took some time. Finally, she saw a lonely list stuck to a door. It contained only one small column. Remarkably small.

Some people around her were gushing, and some were on the verge of tears.

Avery stepped a bit closer and ran her eyes down the page. She ran down again.

Her name was not there.

This time, she did laugh. Everything swam a bit. She turned around and almost walked straight into a guy who had come up behind her.

"Sorry," she mumbled.

To Avery's amazement, the guy responded by tweaking her on the top of her earlobe.

"What the f—"

"Tagged her," he said.

She looked up into Parker's grinning face.

"I tagged you," he said. "On the ear. Like they do with animals. In the jungle. Get it? Jokes are funnier when you explain them, huh? I was going to pretend to hit you with a knockout dart, but that's a two-person joke. You'd have had to fall down, and you wouldn't have known to. So I went with the tag. I think it went over pretty well. Stop me anytime."

Avery was still just staring up at his smooth chin, trying to figure out why and how Parker had come to be in front of her at one of the worst moments in her life, rambling about jokes and tags and darts. In the next moment, Mel squeezed into the frame, sliding between Parker and Scarf Girl. Either she was very excited or she lost her balance, because she threw herself forward and grabbed on to the lapels of Avery's coat for support.

"Hi," she said. "We got a little lost. . . ."

There was snow in Mel's hair. There was snow on Parker's shoulders. Avery began to put it together. Obviously, they'd just run in. Mel had heard what she was saying the other night, and she'd recruited Parker to come to New York with her. And for nothing. It was all for nothing. Avery couldn't bring herself to speak, so she went back over to her corner and slid down the wall. Parker and Mel followed and stood looking over her.

"Were you guys in the area?" she finally said.

"It was just a fun day for a drive," Parker replied. "We heard twelve inches of snow, and we said *road trip*. So, what's happening here? Anything going on?"

He turned and looked around at the crowd. Mel kept looking at Avery, then she sank down and sat by Avery's outstretched legs.

"They put up the list," Avery said simply. "I'm not on it. I blew it. It's over."

She tried to sound cavalier, but it didn't really work. Parker looked away, and Mel reached out and held on to Avery's arm.

"Oh," she said. "Ave, I'm sorry."

"I'm going to . . ." Parker jerked his head toward the door. Mel seemed to understand what this meant and nodded. He walked off toward the door and disappeared back out into the snow.

"You came a long way for nothing," Avery mumbled.

"Not nothing. We came to see you."

"Well, here I am."

Avery didn't want to stay in this place. She didn't want to stick around long enough to get a clear memory of it that she could recall later. She pulled herself from the ground. Mel silently fell in beside her as they walked to the door. Scarf Girl stopped Avery halfway there.

"Why are you leaving?" she asked.

"I didn't make it," Avery said in a low voice.

"How do you know?"

"I'm not on the list."

"They haven't posted the list."

"Yes, they have," Avery said, looking at her in disbelief. She turned and pointed to the crowd of people behind her, all push-ing in close to the door. "What do you think they're reading?"

"The woodwind list. Woodwinds are posted on room 403. Piano is going up on room 410. There."

Scarf Girl pointed to a door on the other side of the hall that was completely list-free.

"I missed that memo," Avery said weakly.

"Good thing I caught you."

Avery turned and her shoe made a loud squawk against the floor. Her movement put her face to face with Mel, and she caught herself just before she leaned over and kissed Mel on the bridge of her nose. It was just automatic—an old habit from the summer, and something that really couldn't be more inappropriate.

"I guess I wait," she said.

The draft blew through the room again, and Avery heard another "Mm-mm-mm." At the same moment, the crowd began shifting around again, and there was more noise coming from the area by the doors. Avery turned wearily and saw a woman hanging up another piece of paper on a door on the other side of the hall.

"It feels like it should be something more dramatic," she said, her stomach taking a sudden tumble. "They should engrave it on stone tablets or something."

"Come on," Mel said, taking her hand.

"Can't. You look," Avery said.

Mel nodded eagerly and pressed into the crowd.

"Hey. You in the corner."

This was Parker's voice. When she looked up, he was back again, brushing fresh snow from his sleeves. Next to him was Nina, her huge crown of hair tipped in snow.

"I was looking for the building," Nina said quietly. "They all look alike. Especially in the snow."

"Yeah," Avery said, numbly. "They do."

They looked at one another, sizing one another up. Nina. Mel. They'd both come. In fact, Mel was pushing through the lump of people.

"She made it," she was gushing. "She made it."

"I'm on there?" Avery asked.

"She made it!"

"I made the first round," Avery corrected, still trying to process what she was seeing. "It means I have to go back and play again."

There was already a line for the elevator, a little frenzy that had sprung up in the air. Avery clutched at the fingers of each of her hands, as if checking to make sure they were still attached, still flexible, still able to play. Nina. Mel. Too much information . . .

People were cramming onto the elevator.

"You'll still be here when I get back, right?" she asked quickly.

Nina hesitated a moment.

"We'll be here," she said.

Avery backed slowly toward the elevator, keeping an eye on her friends, then looking for puddles on the ground.

"You coming?" a guy asked, holding his arm in the door for her. Avery slipped into the last available space on the elevator. She noticed, just as the door was closing in front of her, that Scarf Girl wasn't coming. She was standing with her friend. She had her hands over her face.

She was glad that Scarf Girl wasn't alone.

It had been an hour.

Mel couldn't keep still. She paced the perimeter of the room, touching the elevator buttons, running her fingers along the edge of the now-empty table where the greeters had been. She pressed her palm against the shiny folders.

Nina and Parker watched her. They watched the snow fall outside. They watched the custodians trying to keep the floor dry. This was not a hugely successful effort—there were dirty, footprint-shaped pools everywhere. There was very little to buffer the cold now that the lobby was almost empty. It seemed to reflect off the floor and the marble slabs on the walls; it leaked through the door and the long, high windows. They had to stay side by side simply to keep from shivering.

"Okay," Parker finally said. "I give."

"Huh?"

Parker shifted and pressed his palm into Nina's hair, flattening it back against her head.

"Your hair has been in my eye for the last five minutes."

"Why didn't you say something?"

"I don't know," he said, rubbing at his eye. "I didn't think of it until now."

Nina pulled her hat on to keep her creeping locks down. Mel started another circuit of the room—elevator buttons, table, folders. They all turned as the elevator door opened, but Avery wasn't among the people who got out. Mel started pacing again.

Why are we here? Nina asked herself. *Why does Mel care?*

As she watched Mel adjusting a line of pencils for the tenth time, Nina realized that she was equally as nervous. She was just holding the feeling tight in her stomach.

Okay, she thought. *And why do I care? After what Ave did, why do we both care?*

Because it was Avery.

Nina remembered the day that Avery had come to her and tried to explain that she was confused, that she didn't think she was gay. At the time, that had seemed ridiculous—not like something you could be in a gray area about. And then it dawned on her. Avery had just fallen for a friend, and then realized that she didn't really like her that way. It was actually kind of logical. It wasn't unlike what had happened with Parker. Nina had no doubt that Avery had really fallen for Mel—she let her feelings play out. Avery was big on honesty, always trying to get to the bottom of things.

It all began to unravel.

Now that Nina thought about it, if Avery hadn't been there, who even knew how long it would have taken Mel to come out. Maybe she never would have come out. With Mel, that was possible. Avery had helped draw her out. Maybe on some level, she knew that's what she had to do. And the result was that though Mel had suffered, she'd become stronger. She'd come out to her parents. She'd set up this whole trip. She'd forgiven Avery—more than forgiven her. Mel understood.

Parker had helped. This was undeniable. Parker had been there all along, holding Mel together. He'd helped Nina when she needed him. And now, without even thinking about it, she was leaning into his side, close enough to stab him in the eye with her hair.

"So, are we going to do the awkward thing or not?" she asked.

"Sounds so good when you put it like that."

"Park . . ."

Parker pulled his coat tight over his chest.

"Okay," he said. "Fine. I know I got weird. But it was only because I like you, okay? Like you a lot. Want to be the boyfriend, but you said no boyfriend."

"What if I want a boyfriend?" she asked.

Parker's eyes regained their bright spark, and then narrowed even narrower than usual.

"You're not talking about me, are you?" he said.

Nina looked down at her boots. She rubbed some rock salt off the toes.

"Can I just ask why?" Parker said. "I don't get it."

"Because he said he was sorry," Nina said. "And he meant it."

"Sorry?"

"Sometimes you have to let people say they're sorry," she said.

"I always do this," he said. "I like girls I can't have. It's like the number one thing I look for—total unavailability. I liked Mel, even though I was pretty sure she was gay. I liked you, and you had a super-serious boyfriend. I'm thinking that maybe next time I'll look for someone in who's in jail or a coma. One for the shrink, I guess."

"I really like you Park," she said. "I like you so much."

"Don't say, 'Let's be friends.' Just stop now while I still have some dignity."

"Don't do that!"

"What?"

"The 'don't say let's be friends' thing. I mean it, Park. You're really my friend. Don't blow me off like that."

"There are too many don'ts in this conversation," he moaned.

"I'm serious. We're friends. That's not a blow-off."

He didn't reply for a moment.

"My goal was to date all of you," he finally said, heaving a deep sigh. "Avery's next. I want to be the official boyfriend of the Bermudez Triangle."

"I dare you."

"Dare me something else."

"I dare you to make Mel stop OCDing around the room."

"You *dare* me?"

"That's what I said."

"Because what do I have to lose? I'm not trying to impress either of you anymore."

"Double dare," Nina said.

"Oh, no, you didn't. Done. Fine."

Parker glanced around, thinking for a moment. Then he stood up and made a loud whistling noise.

"Hey, Mel!" he said. "Check out this kung fu."

Parker broke into a strange dance in the middle of the lobby. It was kind of like bad martial arts combined with jerky hip-hop moves. He accompanied himself with some beat-box noises.

Mel stopped. Everyone stopped. For the first time, Nina could hear the faint sounds of music overhead, and a woman by the door shook her head and said, "Mm-mm-mm," under her breath. Nina pulled her hat low over her eyes and pushed herself deeper into the corner.

Parker went on, unconcerned by the silence. He bit down on his lower lip and let his hair flop freely. He switched from karate to disco, sliding through the lawnmower, the driving the bus, the swim. Then, to Nina's amazement, people started to clap, providing him with rhythm. It was a scattered clapping, which mostly came from people nervously clutching folders of music to their chests—but it grew stronger. It was as if the crowd had been waiting for someone to snap.

Music students passing through glanced over, unconcerned. Some nodded. Mel, of course, was transfixed. At the height of it all, as Parker was sinking down to his knees and popping up again, the elevator door opened and Avery stepped out, her face looking very waxy. She regarded Parker for a moment, shook her head, made her way over to the corner where Nina was. Mel hurried over, and Parker broke off mid-routine. He got a scattered round of applause. He bowed.

"I'm not even asking what that was," Avery said, as Parker joined them.

"Well?" Nina asked eagerly.

"I think it was good." Avery rubbed her hands together vigorously, as if trying to blow off the energy that still ran through them. "I didn't start screaming or puke or anything. They look for things like that."

She looked up at Parker.

"Okay," she said. "I'm asking. What was that?"

"What was what?" He blinked innocently.

"What happens now?" Mel asked.

"I guess I go home, unless Speakerboxxx here has another number to perform."

"Performances are at four o'clock and seven o'clock, daily," Parker said crisply.

"Uh huh." Avery gave her bag a light kick with her toe. "Time to go."

"Wait," Nina said.

"What?"

"Come on," Nina said, taking Avery's hand and pulling her up. "You too, Mel."

Parker looked over in confusion.

"It's a thing," Nina said. "We'll be right back."

They went into the hallway on the right, the one without the lists and the crowds.

"Okay," Nina said. "Let's do it."

"Come again?" Avery asked.

"Triangle off."

Avery rolled her eyes up to the ceiling, clearly in an internal struggle between her natural impulse to make a snarky comment and the desire to just give in. Because she knew what it meant—it meant something huge and emotional and un-Avery-like. She plunged her hands deep into the pockets of her leather coat, then pulled them right out again and presented them to Mel and Nina.

"I don't get you guys," she said quietly. "I did so much stuff. . . ."

"Forget it," Nina said, joining hands.

"I can't just forget it. I did it. I didn't mean to hurt you guys. I just started getting everything wrong."

"It's over," Nina said. "We're here."

Mel started to cry.

"See what you did?" Avery said.

"What *I* did?"

They were still standing in this position, when Nina realized that someone was standing at the end of the hall. She turned and saw a man with a short beard watching them.

"Miss Dekker," he said.

"Yeah, uh . . . ?" Avery said, quickly correcting to a "Yes?"

"I'm Doctor Howe. I'm in charge of all piano majors."

"Oh." This was all Avery could think to say in response to this. She slipped her hand from Nina's as surreptitiously as possible.

"We mail letters in late March. Good luck, Miss Dekker."

"Thank you," Avery said, her shoulders slumping.

The man opened the velcro strap on his umbrella and shook out its folds. Right before he walked away, he turned and looked at Avery one more time. His expression was unreadable, but the length of his gaze told Nina that he was registering information.

"Come on," Avery said. "I have to get out of here before my head explodes."

They returned to the lobby to find Parker deep in conversation with a girl with a red scarf tired around a head of choppy blond hair. He was demonstrating smaller, more conservative moves from his earlier routine. The girl's eyes were red and puffy, but she was looking at Parker with just a hint of a smile. The girl and Avery seemed to recognize each other. They each gave a small nod.

"How'd it go?" the girl asked.

"I just finished my callback," Avery said with a shrug, obviously trying to be low key. "Kind of sucked. Dr. Howe said hi to me. Told me when they mail the letters. That's it."

"He said that?"

"Yeah."

"I heard he won't talk to you unless you're in. He's supposed to be weird that way. He walked right past me."

"Oh." Avery raised her eyebrows, and Nina saw her sucking her stomach in as she drew a deep breath and held it. "Sorry."

"It's all part of the deal. You audition. You get some. You lose some."

"Right. Is your friend . . . ?"

"She's upstairs. She got called back for voice. Then she's got to go. Her family's waiting for her."

"What about you?" Avery asked.

"I live in Jersey. I'm just going to hop a train home. Good old New Jersey Transit."

The girl tried to broaden her smile. Even Nina could see this was hard on her, and she didn't know the first thing about auditions. What did she need to know, really? Rejection was rejection. This girl was handling it well, especially considering the fact that a whole group of strangers were standing around her, staring at her, asking her about it. *Tell us more about getting your dreams crushed. . . .*

"You should come with us," Parker suddenly said. "We can't go anywhere for a while. It's snowing. They have to plow. Then they have to put the salt down. These things take time. And we're obviously going to need fries, and Hard Rock shirts, and little models of the Empire State Building. You know. For the car."

He threw Nina a quick look, checking to see if this request was okay.

"Yeah," Avery said. "I haven't eaten in about a day and a half. And if I don't get some coffee, things are going to get ugly."

"It's okay," the girl said. But she didn't move away. She wanted the company.

Parker was still looking at her, waiting for some sign.

Nina was already well past the point where she could get away with the "meeting at school" story. They were stuck in New York in the snow. It would take hours and hours to get home. She was probably going to have to call her mom and come clean and take the consequences.

The consequences were nothing, though.

"Nope," Nina said, hooking arms with Mel and Avery, leaving Parker to escort their new companion. "It's been decided. We need help anyway, in case he decides to start dancing again. One of us to restrain each limb. That's how they do it in hospitals."

The Bermudez Triangle, and Parker, and the girl in the scarf all headed out into the blizzard together. The snow was coming down sideways, wet and heavy. Cars were sliding. It was wonderful.

"One of us for each limb," Avery whispered into Nina's ear. "I like it. Very smooth."

"I'm always smooth."

"Me too," Avery said.

The three of them slipped ahead, tightly holding on to one another for support on the slick sidewalk, and let Parker and the girl lag conveniently behind.

MAUREEN JOHNSON grew up in suburban Philadelphia. She received her MFA in Creative Writing at Columbia University. She is the author of *The Key to the Golden Firebird*.